MAN AFTER MIDNIGHT

MAN AFTER MIDNIGHT

DEVYN QUINN

APHRODISIA

KENSINGTON BOOKS

http://www.kensingtonbooks.com

APHRODISIA BOOKS are published by

Kensington Publishing Corp.
850 Third Avenue
New York, NY 10022

ISBN-13: 978-0-7582-2851-2
ISBN-10: 0-7582-2851-1

First Kensington Trade Paperback Printing: April 2009

10   9   8   7   6   5   4   3   2   1

Printed in the United States of America

To Vanessa Hawthorne, a very talented artist and author
in her own right.
Vanessa is my dearest friend who holds me up when
I am down, listens to my rants and raves and always manages
to assure me that all is right in the world when I think it's
all wrong.

Acknowledgments

Once again, I have to credit my incredible editor Hilary Sares for her support and encouragement during the writing of this book. Her patience and encouragement really helped pull my ass out of the fire! And to my absolutely smashing agent Roberta Brown for holding my hand and lending a friendly ear for me to yak in. I couldn't do what I do without either of these charming ladies, and I am grateful to have them on my side every day of the week!

1

Butterscotch.

The stranger watching her dance had hair the color of butterscotch, a rich warm shade that just begged for a woman to run her fingers through it.

Barely able to keep her grip on the stripper's pole, Dani Wallace swung around for another glimpse of the mesmerizing man who'd hired her for a private strip session. Her palms were so damp she barely managed to hold the slippery metal bar.

She rarely looked twice at the men who came to watch her dance. From the stage, the faces all blurred together, one barely standing out from another. Her job wasn't to gawk, but to entertain, to fulfill the fantasies of the customers paying to watch her pare down to bare skin. The rule to keep her distance from the patrons was one she'd never broken.

Yet.

Taking a deep breath, Dani hooked one leg around the pole and bent herself over backward. *There's a first time for everything.* This hunk of eye candy designed to delight the female senses was too enticing to pass up.

Even upside down the stranger looked fantastic. His fashionably mussed shag framed a high brow and finely chiseled cheekbones. Deep-set eyes, a straight nose and a mouth just made for kissing finished his face. Broad shouldered and narrow hipped, he had long legs that stretched out endlessly. His clothing was casual but chic—black jeans and boots, white shirt open at the neck and a black leather duster. His presence held a sense of command, as if those around him were automatically beholden to serve him, to please him.

Stretched out on the leather lounge bracketing one wall, he had her pinned down under a penetrating stare that never once deviated from her body. Such intense scrutiny would be frightening had he leered, but he didn't. He appreciated. Eyes locked only on her, his nostrils flared. Hands curled into fists, his body was as rigid as the cock straining against the front of his tight jeans—an impressive sight in itself.

Dani pulled herself up and shimmied down into a deep squat. The fine hairs on the back of her neck tingled with subtle awareness. Her nipples were hard little nubs, aching to feel the brush of his hands, the scrape of his teeth. The heat behind his intense gaze felt hotter than the surface of the sun.

The stranger had been showing up at *Faster Pussycats* for about a month, always alone, always standing at the rear of the club. He just watched her—never speaking to her, never approaching her. Tall, impeccably groomed and mannered, he was impossible to miss. Tonight was the first time he'd requested a private session, paying the nightclub's price of three thousand dollars to claim her for the entire evening.

He'd paid in full, in cash. A percentage of the money would be going into her pocket when the night was over. While money might have come easy in his world, she needed every penny she earned. Damn credit cards. The joy she took in plastic had put her over the limit.

Still . . .

Tonight didn't have to be entirely about the job. A little naughty fun would be nice for a change.

Dani sneaked a glance over one shoulder. His mere presence threatened to overwhelm, yet he hadn't said more than "please" and "thank you" to her. Through the last half hour he'd watched her gyrate through a medley of innuendo-laced dance beats, slowly taking off her costume until she wore nothing except a beaded G-string and a smile. Moisture seeped between her legs, exacerbated by the rub of the silky material against her sensitive clit.

Her tongue snaked out, tracing her lips. Her grip tightened on the pole, more slippery than ever beneath her sweaty hands. Inside the private VIP suites, the normal rules governing a dancer's actions ceased to exist. Anything could happen if a woman felt generous and the right man came along.

I've never slept with a client.

Common sense told her it was stupid to even consider the idea of having sex with a stranger. Her body had other ideas. Heavy awareness pulsed through her, an arousing accompaniment to the sensual music playing in the background. Put together in one very alluring package, this man was an enthralling enticement to any female. His bad-boy posture practically screamed temptation and trouble.

Dani swallowed the lump building in her throat, fighting to clear away the images unspooling across her mind's screen—images of her butterscotch stallion pinning her beneath his weight. She couldn't help wanting him. Attraction had smacked her upside the head like lightning striking the ground, unavoidable and with electrifying force. It was impossible not to imagine all the things she could do to his magnificent body. She hadn't had sex since breaking up with her boyfriend three months ago. Horny was her middle name, and she needed a little relief from the tension building up inside her. Her admirer seemed to be the perfect answer.

But would the risk be worth the physical gratification? Lust warred briefly with common sense as she imagined how great his lovemaking would be.

Lust won.

All tingling nerves and rising anticipation, Dani decided she had to have him. This man was too damn hot to pass up. She'd worry about the consequences later. She barely restrained herself from dancing over, unzipping his jeans and straddling his lap right then and there. No, she wouldn't go to him. She would make him come to her. Pleasure her.

Expertly balanced in a pair of six-inch stiletto heels, Dani rose to her full height and rotated around the pole. Smiling to herself, she kept perfect time with the heavy pulse of the sensual music, dancing until her entire body shimmered with a light mist of perspiration.

Heart hammering in her chest, she glanced at the stranger. As she suspected, he was thoroughly turned on by her blatant sexual display. He knew exactly what she was doing, as caught up in his moment of voyeurism as she was in her flagrant sexual exhibitionism, revealing every angle of her firm young body. In that moment she was his everything—his mistress of pleasure, the ball-breaking cock-tease, the bitch-goddess who would bring him to his knees to satisfy her own headstrong desire.

As the last song faded to silence, Dani leaned back against the pole, briefly cupping her full breasts before sliding her hands down her flat belly. Her fingers stopped just above the thin line of her G-string, the last piece of clothing she wore.

The hush around them was ravenous. Over the silence, she detected the sound of his heavy breathing. The odor of sweat laced with desire permeated the air between them, thick enough to cut with a knife.

"You like to watch." Her voice was husky, barely recognizable to her own ears. She kept her gaze on his face, watching his reaction to her blatant proposal. Desire coalesced into a hard knot deep inside her core. It was easy to imagine him naked, all rippling sinew and anxious anticipation.

He nodded, an intimate grin unfurling across his fine mouth. His gaze probed her as if seeking entry into the very depths of her mind. A connection, an instantaneous sexual charge, had definitely passed between them. "Very much."

Grinning wickedly, Dani passed the palm of one hand over her Venus mound, slowly sliding a single finger into the cleft between her thighs. "I know you want me."

He eyed her, clearly intrigued. His mouth slowly curved into a cynical smile. "Am I that obvious?"

Yes, he was. Transparent as a piece of Saran Wrap. "All men have only one thing on their minds." Dani tossed her head, giving her long ponytail a saucy flip. "Are you man enough to take what you want?"

His gaze drifted over every inch of her. Yeah, he was interested. Definitely. "Depends on what I would be getting."

Catching her lower lip between her teeth, Dani briefly cupped her breasts before tracing the pink areola with the tips of her fingers. "Whatever you want."

He arched one perfect brow. "Anything I crave?"

No time for second thoughts. It was too late to back down now. She'd extended the invitation. Whether or not he'd accept remained to be seen.

Dani nodded. "All access granted."

Abandoning his seat, the stranger stood and slipped off his expensive suede duster. He casually tossed it aside. "Desiring a woman is one thing." A few steps bridged the invisible boundary separating them. He deftly caught one of her hands, offering a courtly bow and a kiss. An electric shock traveled from his lips to her skin. "To take her is quite another."

Dani gulped against the involuntary reaction of muscles clenching deep in her core. "Oh, my . . ." Knees threatening total collapse; a shudder whisked down her spine. Good grief.

She'd never had a man kiss her hand, but his unexpected act of courtesy absolutely charmed. The only men she knew that kissed a woman's hand existed solely in the pages of romance novels.

The pressure on her hand tightened subtly. There was no obstruction between them but hesitation. His fully clad body was mere inches away from her all but bare one, taunting her with his nearness. "That you would grant me such a liberty is something I had hardly dared hope. Simply being allowed to admire you from afar is a privilege unparalleled, and quite an enjoyment within itself."

Gently freeing her hand, Dani shifted slightly to ease the press of the pole against her back.

"Am I being romanced or seduced, Butterscotch?"

The nickname seemed to please him. "Neither," he said softly. His fingertips grazed the curve of one bare shoulder, reigniting the buzz in her veins. "Let us say you are being persuaded, for I must admit my intent to be less than pure." His voice was deep but gentle, slightly tinged with an accent she couldn't immediately identify.

Their gazes locked. Lashes longer and thicker than any man had a right to have rimmed his eyes. Now that he was so close, she saw his irises were a fabulous shade of cobalt blue, thickly ringed at the edges with silver. No way in the world that color combination could be natural, but who cared. Combined with the rich shade of his hair, the look was stunning. Tiny lines around the corners of his eyes put him at a mature age, thirty at least. That made him old enough to know his own mind but young enough to go after what he wanted.

Dani gulped against the involuntary reaction of muscles clenching deep in her core. She skillfully slipped around the pole before he could repeat the caress. "Why me?" Despite her move, she was enjoying the game. Her willpower had already crumbled under the onslaught of temptation, but it wouldn't hurt to play out the tension. She didn't want to appear too eager, too easy. Her sidelong glance dared him to follow.

Laughing softly, her enchanting suitor circled in front of her with a smooth step of his own. He was so close that the smell of heated male skin permeated her senses. His presence seared, his inner primal nature threatening to overpower her sensuous cravings. She easily identified the mingling aromas of his cologne, a heady scent of musk mixed with sandalwood. It gave the impression of shadows, of things ancient and mysterious. Whatever the brand might be, it was thoroughly enticing. Just standing there, breathing him in was a turn-on.

He cupped her chin, scraping her bottom lip with his thumb, branding her. There was a tremble behind his touch, a longing barely contained. "More than beautiful, I find you to be a refreshing surprise, a woman who revels in her sexuality, embraces it," he answered in that enthralling way. "I wanted you since I first set my sight upon you."

Dani raked her tongue over paper-dry lips. "Is that so?"

A hint of shadows darkened his eyes, so immediate and so brief as to be barely detected. "Despite my contaminated intentions, I am, my lady, your most committed admirer."

Her knees threatened total collapse as a shudder whisked down Dani's spine. Something about him all of a sudden struck her as being eccentrically out of place, but she couldn't quite put her finger on it. His command of the English language was positively quaint. He was definitely a foreigner. At the moment it only served to make him that much more mysterious, and desirable.

"Flattery will get you everywhere." She tried to sound flippant, but her words came out strained. The oxygen in the room seemed to be seeping away, leaving her breathless.

The stranger leaned closer, erasing the distance between them. A gaze she could drown in locked and held hers. "I speak no flattery, only truth."

A forbidden thrill snarled its web around Dani's heart.

She couldn't believe what was happening, yet couldn't stop it. She didn't even know his name but didn't really care. Maybe she'd find out later, maybe not. It didn't matter who he was or where he'd come from. Their bodies were doing the communicating on an instinctive, more primitive level.

Bending closer, he brushed his mouth over hers. Her lips parted under the press of his tongue seeking entrance. Dani willingly opened to him, letting him in for deep exploration. The hot, sweet taste of him enhanced the wild, savage need he unleashed inside her.

Their kiss broke with the pressure of his warm palm settling on one bare breast. Exploring fingers grazed the bead-hard tip, rolling it between thumb and forefinger, gently tugging.

Dani struggled for breath against the whirlwind sensations his touch ignited. "God, that feels so good." The words, whispered low, barely made it past her lips.

His eyes reflected in the lighting around them, hunger and need simmering in the neon depths. "I am your humble servant in every way." An edge of need sliced through his tone.

Dani was so turned on her body thrummed all the way down to the tips of her toes. "Then please me . . ." she said, savoring the moment. "Any way you want." Her words trailed off into a soft moan. Desire pulsed through her veins, filling her with a lust so strong that she felt it with every beat of her heart.

He treated her to a lazy smile, stroking one long finger over the curve of her breast, down her rib cage, going ever lower until reaching the line of her G-string. Kneeling as though he planned to propose, he bent forward, pressing a soft kiss by her navel. Moist, warm breath tickled her bare skin. Slipping his fingers under the elastic band, he ripped the tiny scrap of material off her body. The lace disintegrated, scattering tiny beads every which way.

A warm flush suffused Dani's cheeks. Because of the scarcity of costume she always kept her snatch meticulously bare, waxed down to nary a hair. Her nipples tightened into hard pink buds, and her stomach muscles contracted at the thought of his mouth and tongue exploring her sex.

"Good heavens," she gasped through an agonized groan of anticipation.

He planted a series of soft, slow kisses across the plane of her flat belly. "Do not think," he breathed. "Just feel." His hands slid up the insides of her thighs, hooking one of her legs over his shoulder for wider access. His mouth invaded the cleft between her legs.

Balanced against the pole for support, Dani thrust her fingers into his thick hair, holding on for dear life as he tasted every inch of her, his tongue flicking against her clit until her hips trembled.

Lost in the sensations, Dani pressed herself harder against his mouth, taking everything he gave. Her entire body quaked with an all-consuming carnality. She was so rigid that stopping now would shatter her completely. The need to come, to climax, was so pent up it hurt. The sensations he invoked in her body felt so good . . . so completely right.

"I'm so damn close," she grated between rigid jaws. The tremors began in small waves, climbing higher and growing more intense until every inch of her body writhed in the grasp of heated tremors.

Dani bit back a long husky groan. Strong inner muscles tightened and a delicious spiral of pure molten heat wound through her belly. Body pulsing, she concentrated on holding on to the delicious sensations just a moment longer.

Somehow her lover made it back to his feet, his mouth unexpectedly claiming hers with a teeth-clashing appetite.

Dani welcomed him willingly, tasting the spice of her feminine cream on his lips. *Delicious.* She was ripe, hot and ready for full penetration. "I want your cock," she breathed out through a vibrating moan. "I want you inside me." Her vision was clouded with need, unfocused. Her pulse beat through her head, dizzying her. Eager hands plucked at the buttons of his shirt.

When she couldn't undo the buttons fast enough, she tore through the material. Her hands explored the ridges and cobbles of his chest and abdomen. Hot muscle tensed beneath her palms. His erection pressed against the prison of his tight jeans, but she couldn't stop shaking long enough to make her hands cooperate.

Saner hands than hers assumed control. "Let me."

Taking his time, Butterscotch gave her a sexy grin before unbuttoning his jeans. The zipper crunched down. He wasn't wearing a stitch underneath.

Dani blinked, impressed. The shaft he freed jutted up toward his abdomen. Long and thickly ridged with veins, the cherry-red crown invited tasting. Droplets of pre-cum glistened at the tip.

The fragile hold she'd had on the last of her control slipped entirely through her fingers. Her gaze devoured every inch, and her brows rose. "Nice . . ." If he handled his cock half as well as he'd handled the oral, she was going to be one very happy woman.

Lust flared in the depths of his gaze, a look more intense than any she'd ever had from a man. "You approve, I hope."

Her heartbeat bumped up a notch, and adrenaline surged through her all over again. Her nipples jutted, hard little rosy beads. "In every way." If her nerves hadn't been jangled before, they definitely were now.

He also had a saner head, producing a small foil-wrapped item from the breast pocket of his shirt. "I hope you do not mind."

Dani shook her head, watching him expertly rip open the packet with his teeth. "That's confidence," she commented.

With an ease that came from a lot of practice, he rolled the latex condom down his raging erection. "Just being careful for both of us, my lady," he said, smiling into her eyes.

That made sense, and Dani was glad he'd thought things through.

Butterscotch reached for her, turning her around until she faced the pole. Hot breath scorched the nape of her neck. His lips were mere inches away from her ear. "I can please you in many ways."

Dani's fingers curled around the cool steel even as his hands settled on her hips. "I'll reserve any judgment until I've tested the matter for myself." Her hips automatically angled so the tip of his penis slipped between her thighs. The heated trickle of her desire mingling with his saliva provided a nice slick path. She tossed a smile over one shoulder. "If you don't mind."

One broad, strong hand reached around to claim her breast. Thick fingers plucked and rolled the tip of her nipple in a delightfully painful way. "Indeed, I am most honored you would grant me such liberty." Hips pressing forward, he slid his cock through the silky folds of her sex. The single thrust impaled, claimed and then conquered.

His act of wicked sensuality tore a gasp from Dani's throat as pure ecstasy stormed in from a million different directions, obliterating every brain cell in her skull. If she'd believed she was the one in control, she was so very wrong. The man who fucked her controlled her. Her body unanimously agreed. Deep inside, she felt eager flesh grip his ridged length. Lost in the sensations generated between their bodies, she closed her eyes and held on tight as climax propelled her into the stratosphere like a rocket taking flight. Losing all grasp on reality, rapture slithered through her veins like a speeding bullet injected through a fiery needle. . . .

Tonight, she'd enjoy his wild lovemaking, take whatever he was willing to give. She didn't believe their hours together would survive past the heat of a passion engendered by the flight of imagination she created on stage. Tomorrow her mystery lover would be nothing more than a divine memory, a one-night stand.

After all, Dani Wallace never let pleasure interfere with her business.

Never.

2

There were two things Dani Wallace hated more than anything else in the world: going to bed and, conversely, getting
out of it. Once she got up for the day, usually in the late after-
noon, she burned every hour down to its last second, determined to avoid the collapse inevitably arriving in the early
morning hours before dawn. Hitting the sheets in utter exhaustion bought the opposite thought. She was ready to crash,
snoozing the morning hours away in a room totally devoid of a
single shaft of light. In her mind the day shouldn't begin before
noon. Anyone out before one o'clock had serious problems.
Like a real job and a real life.

This morning was no exception.

Cracking open one sleepy eye, Dani looked toward the dig-
ital at her bedside. The blurry red numbers read half past noon.
Much too early to get up.

Yawning, Dani stretched and rolled over on her side, tucking her body pillow between her legs. Every muscle ached, a
testament to the vigorous loving she'd gotten last night. Not
only had her Butterscotch stallion kept her occupied until the

club had closed, they'd gone on to continue their private party when he'd offered her a ride home. She couldn't help but be impressed that his car had turned out to be a limousine, complete with a liveried driver. Taking the longest route possible to her home address, they'd had sex every which way possible in the back of that limo.

Mind-blowing. And surreal.

During their tryst, he'd hardly said a word to her. No words were needed, though. Their bodies did all the communicating necessary. If ever there was a man whose physical appetite matched hers, Butterscotch was the man. Every way he'd touched her had felt so good, felt so right.

Just remembering all they'd done last night caused Dani's inner temperature to rise. Her body still tingled in the places he'd touched, everywhere and often. She shivered at the memory of his intense lovemaking. He'd barely give her time to catch her breath or think straight before he was taking her again, each time more intense and fevered than the last. Orgasm on top of orgasm had twisted her senses. Good thing the window between the chauffer and the passengers was tinted or the driver would have gotten one hell of a carnal education.

Stamina. Butterscotch definitely had stamina.

Wrapping her arms around her pillow and snuggling closer to its familiar warmth, Dani felt moist heat pool between her thighs. The hunger for more still flared bright inside her. Since she was alone, she'd just have to make do with her hand and her imagination.

Dani sighed and closed her eyes. Her hand slipped down into the crevasse between the pillow and her body. Fingers slipping under the elastic band, she gently dipped into her creamy sex. Breath catching in a hitch, heavy awareness pulsed through her veins, a delicious accompaniment to the slideshow of images unspooling across her mind's screen. She hadn't taken a shower before going to bed last night, and his scent still lingered on her skin, musky and potent. It was easy to recall the smell of his heated flesh, the touch of his hands on her bare skin, the devouring kisses he'd given her even as his cock plundered her depths.

Breath catching in her throat, the electricity of craving shimmied through her. Fingers slipping deeper, she attempted to assuage the ache building inside. Need surged. She pushed her fingers deeper, desperate now to douse the flame of desire her mysterious lover had ignited. Strong muscles pulsed around her fingers. She was moist and wet and ready for the plunge of a proper cock.

Dani swiveled her hips so she could touch herself just the way she liked, two fingers inside while her thumb worked her clit. Her hips bucked against her hand. Connection with the right spot came a moment later. The tremors began in small waves. She quickened the pace, touching herself without relenting until the friction was almost unbearable. Climax rolled in like an avalanche, the thrill of stimulation sweeping her entirely away.

Hand slipping out of her panties, Dani rolled over onto her back. A long slow groan slipped over her parched lips. The honey-thick relief of climax mantled her body in delicious warmth. Pleasant little aftershocks rippled through her system. She wondered if she'd ever breathe normally again. Oh God. Talk about being überhorny. She'd just gotten herself off with a pillow.

Not a bad way to wake up, though.

Dani stretched her hands over her head, arching her spine. A few snaps and crackles answered. She'd been so worn and wrung out last night she barely remembered stumbling through the door and heading downstairs to the basement apartment she rented from her brother, Brenden. It wasn't the biggest place in the world and would by no means pass for the Taj Mahal, but it suited her single lifestyle. Meaning it was cheap.

Having gotten herself in deep with the credit card companies, she was simply going to have to forego the luxury of a loft with a view until she paid off her debt. Moving in with her older brother wasn't anything most twenty-one-year-old women wanted to do, but when times were hard and money was tight a big brother lending a helping hand was a godsend.

Not that Brenden Wallace was happy with her profession. A cop, he hated how she'd chosen to make a living. Working vice day in and day out, he continually warned her about all the bad things that could happen to a young, pretty girl. In his mind, men who came to watch a woman strip had nothing but dishonorable intentions.

Dani had to grin. Brenden was a prude, a fuddy-duddy and a stick-in-the-mud all rolled into one tightly strung package. Thank God he'd recently remarried. Despite her initial misgivings of Brenden's choice of a wife, Líadán had managed to fit comfortably into the family. Head over heels in love, Brenden wasn't such an insufferable prig now that he and Líadán were setting the sheets on fire every night.

As for setting her sheets on fire . . . Her mystery lover— whose name she still didn't know, damn it!—had promised he'd be getting in touch. When Dani had tried to give him the digits of her cell, he'd waved her offer off. After all, he knew where she lived.

She might see him again. Soon.

Anticipation whisked a thrill down Dani's spine. Her pulse kicked into high gear all over again. That simple thought was all it took to bring his sexy masculinity and her reaction to it flooding back. Even with his clothes rumpled and his hair disheveled from her exploring fingers, he still looked hotter than any man she'd ever laid eyes on.

The dampness between her legs increased. Stomach muscles coiling with need, her hands found her breasts, nipples erect beneath the cotton material. The memory of his touch threatened to make her climax all over again. At this point, she could lie in bed and fantasize. What he'd done to her would take a whole day to completely remember. No man she'd ever had sex with felt so good, so perfect, so right for her. Usually handsome men were stingy lovers, too. Not Butterscotch. He'd made her pleasure his priority. Being with a man that damn fine would make any woman think she'd died and gone to heaven. Hell, he'd even walked her to her door, cupping her chin in his hand and tilting back her head to deliver one final, sweet kiss before they parted. It was just as well. A harder, more demanding kiss would have had her dragging him down to the basement to ravish his magnificent body.

Dani drew a deep breath, trying to cool herself off. It didn't work. Hormones raging, she was hornier than ever. She closed her eyes, close to slipping back into a hazy daydream concerning what she'd like to do with Butterscotch when she had him all stretched out naked in a real bed.

An angry bellow snapped her right back to attention. "Goddamn it, Dani! Get your freaking ass up here right now." From the echoing sound of his voice, Brenden stood at the entrance of the basement. He rarely came downstairs if he could help it. He hated the way the ceiling grazed the top of his head, a drawback when you're over six feet tall in a space designed for short people.

Heart thumping double time, Dani bolted upright in bed. Unsure she'd heard correctly, she called back. "What's the matter that you've got to yell at me like a fucking banshee, bro?" She didn't hear the smoke alarm, so the place wasn't going up in flames. By the tone behind his words, he was pissed, super bad. *What the hell did I do?*

"Just get up here," Brenden yelled back at the top of his lungs. "Now."

Dani rolled out of bed. She could say for certain that he was definitely stressing. "Who put a burr up his ass?" she muttered to no one in particular. Dressed in only a white T-shirt and white cotton panties, she couldn't very well go marching upstairs half naked. "Will it wait while I catch a shower?" she yelled back up.

Brenden's answer was short and sweet. "No."

Eyes adjusting to the gloom, Dani dug around the mess in her room for a robe. She wasn't the best of housekeepers and most of her clothing usually ended up somewhere on the floor. It didn't help that the windows were blacked out with tinfoil. Not that the view was that terrific. Looking out her bedroom windows would give her a nice view of the cars parked in the driveway.

That's when it hit her. Her car wouldn't be there because she'd let Butterscotch drive her home. And one of his cop buddies had probably clued him in that her vehicle was still in the parking lot at work. Of course that would be enough to piss him off. First he'd bitch about the safety aspects of accepting a ride from a stranger, then he'd cite the statistics about how many women vanished without a trace—and what condition they were usually found in, if they were found at all.

Finding her robe in the mess, Dani slipped into it and belted it around her waist. Hating to be caught barefoot, she shoved her feet into a pair of slippers. "Oh, for the day when I can afford my own damn place," she muttered. As it stood, living with Brenden was still cheaper than trying to den up with a couple of her girlfriends. You couldn't beat a hundred bucks a month, all bills paid. He'd accepted that only because she'd insisted, then just redeposited it in a savings account in her name. Despite his grouchy ways, her big brother took care of her. He always had.

Rubbing the last remnants of sleep out of her eyes, Dani stumbled through the living room/kitchen combo that made up the front half of her apartment, returning to a somewhat normally lit area.

The view was no better, but the sliding windows were larger, allowing for a sense of illumination and space. Her cream Persian, Nilla, was stretched out on the table, basking in a shaft of sunlight. The cat flopped any damn place she wanted, taking no regard that humans might eat there. Dani didn't mind since she didn't eat at the table anyway.

The décor was pure boho—a futon, a mat for meditation, a small altar for practicing her witchcraft and tons of candles and incense burners. People outside her circle often did a double take when seeing the altar.

Dani found it amusing when she offended some people's religious sensibilities. Mention witchcraft to average humans and they would run screaming for their crosses and holy water, not understanding there were different levels to conjuration and ritual invocation. As a witch she neither sacrificed small animals nor partook in orgies. Anything strange and alien, like the practice of magick, was always seen as a threat to the unknowledgeable.

Dani Wallace was a witch. A Wyr-witch, to be exact. The Wyr belonged to an ancient clan called the *Gwyd'llyr,* or seekers of purity. Guardians against darker forces seeking to bastardize legitimate magick into twisted and foul things, the Wyr were bearers of light—guardians against the darker forces haunting this world.

The origins of the *Gwyd'llyr* stretched back to a time when the hours were uncounted and the earth's mountains and valleys were still covered by mists, an age when magick was a real and palpable force to those who would dare pursue the secrets belonging only to the gods. Both she and Brenden were direct descendents of the Wyr bloodline, through their Scotch/Irish heritage. It was something Dani had known since she was a small child, raised on stories of her Irish grandmother.

Dani had willingly believed her grandmother. Brenden had been a little harder to convince. Now, though, he was a firm believer in their origins and one of the most valued warriors in the Wyr army. His journey began with a spell. Well, two, exactly. A love spell and a destiny spell. When she'd done her spell work, she'd had no way of knowing Brenden would get hit with a double whammy in the form of the sensual Líadán Nimah.

Glancing toward her implements of the craft, Dani felt her cheeks heat. Her spells had a way of going awry, and those had definitely gone off track, landing Brenden smack in the middle of a vampyric cult. He'd been raped and tortured within an inch of his life before being turned into one of the demonic creatures by the cult's leader—and Líadán's master—Auguste Maximillian.

For Brenden, the entire experience had been a real eye opener, a true look at the unseen forces menacing this world. Already a cop, pledged to serve and protect, he took his new duties very seriously. He'd recently helped found a new branch of the force, cryptically known as the CCD (Cultic Crimes Division). Cases that didn't fit within the boundaries of normal police investigation were handed off to his team.

The fact that her spell had caused her brother more than a little grief sent a spike of belated guilt through Dani's conscience. But taking it back wasn't an option. She had to believe karma had its own mysterious way of working or it wouldn't have put the old spells in her path to begin with.

Brenden's bellow pulled her attention away from her altar. "Quit dragging ass and get up here. Now."

"I'm coming," she yelled back. She cast a final glance at the implements of her art. *Well, it all worked out, anyway.*

She really needed to start putting more effort into her witchcraft. Her instructor, Counselor Nash, wasn't happy that she'd let things slide since becoming a second-tier acolyte. The musty old bastard, Irish to the roots of his hair and devoted to the study of the occult, didn't understand that a girl needed to make a living in this world. The trouble with slaying demons was that it didn't pay very damn well at all.

After tripping toward the stairs, Dani stopped at the foot and looked up. Sure enough, Brenden stood at the top. Arms folded across his chest, he was the frowning picture of a perfectly controlled but seething angry man. He even tapped one booted foot against the tile floor.

A lump in her throat threatened to cut off her air. Uh-oh. Some shit had definitely hit the fan. Dani racked her brain trying to pinpoint what might have set him off. Brenden usually didn't blow easily, but when he did it was like Mount Vesuvius exploding. Best to duck and run for cover until he cooled down.

Dani pulled her robe closer to her body, as if the thick terry cloth material would somehow shield her from his wrath. "What is it?" Her innocence wasn't pretend. She truly didn't know what the hell was going on.

Fixing her with an assessing stare, Brenden frowned more deeply. "I don't know what the hell you've been up to, young lady, but you've got a lot of explaining to do."

Not knowing the reasons behind his pounce, Dani prickled. "Since when do I have to explain anything to you, Bren? I'm free, white and over twenty-one."

Her brother snorted. "There's a man here," he gritted through a jaw so tight the words might have shattered it coming out. "Asking for you."

Dani relaxed. *Ah, mystery man.* He'd shown up, as promised. She hadn't been expecting him this early in the day, but then again she hadn't really known when to expect him, if at all. She was more than a little pleased that he'd shown up. Most men were content to dump a girl after fucking her. At least Butterscotch was a man of his word.

She frowned. Her personal life wasn't any of Brenden's

business. "So what's wrong with him?" If she wanted to invite men over, well, that was her option. The basement was supposed to be her private space. And if she wanted to run naked and fuck until her brains sizzled, well ... maybe she'd remind him about the times he and Líadán set the ceiling above her head to rocking.

She crossed her arms, mimicking his defensive posture. "I've got a new boyfriend, thank you very much for asking. That's nothing to get your panties in a twist about, Bren. I am allowed to date, you know."

A pregnant pause ensued.

His gaze never wavered. "Oh, it's more than that, Danicia," he shot back. Using her full name was never a good sign. "Your, uh, so-called boyfriend is here claiming that you are his bride-to-be."

3

The scene that met Dani's eyes when she walked into the living room looked like a casting call for some off-the-wall fantasy movie. Since the sun was deadly to vampyrs—it wasn't even Brenden's normal time of day to be out—the drapes were drawn against the sun shining outside. All the lights inside were turned on, blazing like a Christmas tree in December. The whole sight had an unreal, stifled quality, too many bodies stuffed into too tiny of a space.

A quick glance around revealed a lot of faces, some familiar, some not at all. Líadán stood to the rear of the room, looking distressed as she held a tray of coffee mugs no one seemed interested in.

Counselor Nash was also present and accounted for, his expression going from disgruntled to pleased. Nash had a schoolmaster's demeanor that served only to enhance his shrewd analytical temperament. Brenden was his primary student in the occult arts, his star pupil. Dani, well . . . she knew he didn't think much of her haphazard approach to her cultic studies.

Nash was presently engaged in an animated conversation with a man Dani didn't know or recognize.

Cleary unhappy with the oddball invasion, Brenden snorted. "It's just as crazy as it looks." He elbowed her in a none-too-gentle way. "And there's lover boy." His words dripped with disapproval.

Dani swiveled her attention toward the group standing a slight distance away from the others. She gasped, blinked to make sure what she saw was absolutely real, then blinked again to make sure the entire scene wasn't some kind of mirage.

The man she'd made love to last night was there, but he'd changed. *Drastically.*

Gone were the nice tight jeans and casual shirt he looked so damn good in, replaced by a high-necked white shirt overlaid with a snug-fitting vest of black velvet, a pair of snug breeches and shiny knee-high black boots. A full-length laced Victorian-style coat lent a formal and commanding air to his already impressive physique. Beautifully cut and fitted, it was an impressive piece of tailoring. Despite the strange style of his costume, he wore it with panache—and looked pretty damn good in it, too. He appeared much taller than she remembered.

Every hair on Dani's head tingled with awareness. Just remembering how he'd touched her caused her nipples to peak under her T-shirt and robe. Heat suffused her body, intensifying as it settled into a hard knot inside her gut. Moisture seeped between her thighs, just hours ago spread wide to receive his magnificent erection. His very presence shot through her like a bolt of pure electricity, reminding her what had attracted her to him in the first place. The intensity behind his very presence made her pulse beat double time. She had no regret that she'd had sex with him. She'd probably do it again if given the chance.

And she hoped she would be given the chance.

By the serious expressions on everyone's faces, no one else

was entertaining thoughts about having sex but her. That fact didn't make her lust any easier to deal with. Good thing they weren't alone. Otherwise she'd have torn those fancy clothes right off his body and taken him right then and there.

Flustered, she cut her gaze to his companions, flanking him to the left and to the right. Apparently they were his bodyguards. At least that's what the broadswords strapped across their backs would lead one to think. As for their clothing, well, it didn't seem to belong anywhere in the modern world at all. Dressed in short-sleeved tunics, breeches and knee-high leather boots, they definitely had some Goth–medieval vibe going.

Brenden cleared his throat loudly to get everyone's attention. "And here's the lady you've all been arguing about."

All eyes turned toward Dani.

She squirmed. "Uh, what's going on here?"

Counselor Nash stepped forward. All eyes expectantly turned his way, waiting. "Allow me to introduce Prince Casedren Teraketh of Sedah."

Sedah?

She'd never heard of it.

Now formally identified, Prince Casedren stepped up and offered a slight bow of his head. "It is an honor to stand among you today."

Brenden Wallace had little use for people with fancy names or fancy manners. "Formal-talking bastard," he mumbled under his breath.

Dani gave Brenden a surreptitious poke. "I know you're pissed," she muttered out of one side of her mouth. "Just can it, okay?"

Prince Casedren's penetrating gaze swept over her from head to foot. Clearly pleased with what he saw, he smiled. "As promised, my lady, I have returned to claim you."

Under the scrutiny of Casedren's admiring gaze, Dani gathered her robe tighter around her body. Casedren was dressed to the nines, while she was decked out in nothing fancier than a robe and fuzzy pink bunny slippers. With her hair in a tangle and last night's stage makeup half gone, she probably looked like something the cat puked up. He didn't seem to mind a bit. Undaunted, he stepped a little closer. The connection between them was so strong it felt like some magnetic force was pulling them together. The air practically sizzled and popped between them with static energy.

Intensely aware of his presence, she blurted out the first thing that came to mind. "I wasn't aware you'd be showing up with a marriage proposal."

A wide grin broadened his face. "I know what I want when I see it. You are the woman I intend to take as my bride."

Heart in her throat, Dani swallowed hard. "I, ah, forgive me if I don't know what to say." Her voice sounded foreign to her ears, strangely husky and throbbing with a longing she found difficult to mask.

Casedren laughed, his pale eyes lightening with mischief. "Yes would be nice," he said softly.

A soft growl emanated from her brother. "Let's not take things too damn fast," he warned. "She isn't agreeing to anything just this second." A mass of suspicion, he stared Casedren straight on and refused to be budged.

For a moment she felt sharp resentment toward her brother. How dare he meddle in her business! *I wish he'd leave us alone,* she thought irrationally. Another thought tread sharply on the heels of the first. *He's just trying to protect me.*

Perceiving a threat to their liege, the guards reached for their swords. Dani winced, silently wishing her older brother would zip his fucking lip. His overprotectiveness was turning him into an overbearing lout. He'd better put a cork in it or he might find his head rolling around on the floor, courtesy of a very sharp blade swinging into action. The thought seemed to have occurred to Brenden as well, and he wasn't smiling.

Casedren sensed their move without even turning his head. "At your ease," he ordered firmly.

Gracing her brother with a benign smile, he stepped back until the distance between them was wide enough to be acceptable. As he moved, his muscles rippled beneath his clothing, setting off all sorts of erotic images in her mind. The memory of his heated flesh beneath her hands sent her inner mercury soaring.

Watching him, Dani felt as if she were on fire. His presence seemed to enter straight into her veins like a narcotic, a high that delivered the sweetest of agonies.

She shivered. His presence alone made her feel more alive than ever. Were he to leave now, it would be like having all the air sucked out of her lungs. She'd collapse.

The man who'd been conversing with Nash gave them no chance for further confrontation. He bustled over and planted himself firmly in between his liege and the rest of the group. He was short, balding, and his dark, long-sleeved, narrowly cut tunic identified him as cleric of some kind. No doubt about that. His step and manner were disciplined and punctilious. And by the look on his stern face, he would brook no nonsense.

Nash bowed slightly in acknowledgement. "This is Minister Gareth, of the high council to King Bastien," he said by way of introduction. "Now that Prince Casedren has declared his intent to take Danicia as his intended, Minister Gareth has come to finalize the details of her dowry."

"She hasn't got a dowry," Brenden snapped. "And we're not offering one—or her."

Minister Gareth shook his head. "You don't seem to understand. By Jadian custom, the groom-to-be settles the bride's price with her guardian." He spread his hands and smiled. "I think you will find Prince Casedren's offer more than generous."

The minister snapped his fingers. The prince's guards jumped to attention, retrieving a small chest near the front door and placing it near Brenden. One flipped its lid open. A cornucopia of gold coins entirely filled its depth, not an inconsiderable amount.

Dani's eyes widened. Holy shit! She'd never seen that much gold in a jewelry store, let alone sitting right in front of her.

Noticing the look on her face, Gareth smiled. "I pray you find Prince Casedren's offer satisfactory?"

Dani gulped, unsure what her response should be. Diamonds might be a girl's best friend, but cold hard cash guaranteed a lover all access.

The thought caused her cheeks to heat all over again. Okay, okay. So she was a material girl. And it was just as easy to love a rich man as it was a poor one. Whether or not she wanted to admit it, the balance was tipping in Casedren's favor. He was good looking; rich; an honest-to-God royal; and, better yet, an excellent fuck. Most women would call her crazy not to bite that hook.

Except lust was one thing. Love was another.

After the money was spent and the sex worn thin, would there be anything left to sustain the attraction? The last thing Dani wanted was to be trapped in a loveless union. Brenden's first marriage had plunged him into hell and misery. She didn't want to make the same mistake. The man she married had to be *the one*. Once she took those sacred vows, she intended them to last until her final breath. Her parents had stayed married to the day they died, perishing together in a head-on collision. They'd loved each other to the end.

An ominous tremor whisked down Dani's spine. She wanted that kind of marriage for herself. She'd even been prepared to kiss a lot of frogs to find her prince.... Now her prince seemed to have appeared virtually overnight.

Talk about being swept off your feet. She couldn't help but be impressed.

Brenden's abrupt reply pulled Dani out of her thoughts. "My sister is not for sale. She's not a piece of property to be sold to the highest bidder. The answer is still *no.*"

The elderly minister offered a courtly bow. "The prince wishes to assure you that he is most serious in his claim," he said, lifting one gnarled finger not to Dani, but to Counselor Nash. "He insists most vigorously that consensual intercourse has taken place—and that he and Danicia are in fact now legitimately affianced under Jadian law."

Hearing the man's words, Brenden Wallace turned five shades of crimson. "Oh my God. You had sex with a strange man?" he asked, making a show of giving her a disapproving stare.

Dani's cheeks went hell-furnace hot. *Uh-oh. He's busted me for a slut.*

Right now would be a good time for the floor to open up and swallow her. If there was one thing her brother didn't need to know about, it was her sex life. In his mind she was still the little girl in pigtails and braces, perpetually twelve years old and as pure as the driven snow. Of course he knew Dani wasn't a virgin, but knowing it and actually getting all the dirty details were two different things.

Casting about for an explanation that would assuage him, she found none. Time to confess, and take the consequences for her actions. She'd obviously gone and gotten herself in some very big trouble.

Question was, how could she gracefully get out of it?

"Um, yes," she slowly admitted. "I did have sex with Butterscotch, uh, the prince." She hastened to explain, "I honestly didn't know who he was—"

Brenden interrupted. "I don't want to hear another word."

He waved his hands, shooing everyone away. "I think these people need to get the hell out of my house." His voice broadcast loud and clear.

Dani cringed. No mistaking her brother's stance in the matter. However much she disagreed with the tactic he took, she did secretly wish they'd all do just that. Leave. She needed time to think, to gather her wits. *To talk to Nash alone and find out what the hell's going on.*

That clearly wasn't going to happen.

Counselor Nash unexpectedly took charge.

Catching both Dani and Brenden by an arm, he pivoted them toward Líadán, who still waited patiently with tray in hand. Freed of her vampyr master after centuries of servitude, she had blossomed into the average suburban housewife. That is, if a vampyr could be an average suburban housewife.

"Both of you settle down and listen to me," Nash hissed under his breath. "Right now we're in the middle of a diplomatic negotiation that could mean the difference between war and peace between our kind and"—he subtly cocked his head toward the visitors—"theirs."

"I don't get it," Brenden started to say.

Nash hushed him by shoving a coffee cup toward him. "Just drink this and listen a few minutes." He turned to Dani. "Better grab yourself a cup, too."

Líadán smiled. "It's still hot, I hope," she offered. "I've been standing here for ages, but they won't touch it."

Brenden leaned over and gave his wife a quick peck on the forehead. "Fuck 'em, babe. They'll be leaving soon, anyway."

Líadán grinned, clearly in love with her husband of six months. "Don't be so hasty," she whispered back. "They are serious in their mission."

Taking a cup for himself, Nash nodded. "That's for sure."

Dani grabbed a familiar mug, the one with her favorite motto emblazoned across its face: A HARD MAN IS GOOD TO

FIND. She hadn't even had time to wipe the sleep out of her eyes before being shoved into this mess. A jolt of caffeine would help clear the cobwebs out of her head. Then she'd be able to think about something besides how hot Casedren looked in his attire.

And he's a prince to boot! her mind filled in with secret delight.

Not a bad score at all.

Now about this marriage thing . . .

She sipped her coffee, still marginally warm. She grimaced. Líadán's brew was strong enough to be declared a deadly weapon. It could definitely use some sugar and cream, but no time to dither. "So who exactly is Prince Casedren? I've never even heard of Sedah."

Nash took a healthy drink of his coffee. "Sedah is the dimensional world interwoven throughout our own," he explained.

A light dawned in the back of Dani's mind. Now she understood why Casedren's strangely accented words and manner seemed so foreign. He didn't belong to her society at all.

Brenden immediately cocked a brow in thought. "Then they're not human?"

Chuckling, Nash shook his head. "Though they share many of our characteristics, the Jadians are not human in the sense as we know it. For one thing, they are extremely long lived. Their lifetime stretches centuries to our years. Another is that they are expert in the ways of magick—it comes as naturally to them as breathing. And, of course, they are shape shifters. Their internal physiology is a little different than ours, but on the whole all the parts meet up just as our creators intended." He tossed out that last piece as if it was something everyone should already know.

Brenden's brow darkened. "I don't like the sound of these *things.* Aren't they what the Wyr are fighting?"

Nash released a copious sigh. "In the old days, it was so. The Wyr and the Jadians have a long history of clashing," he explained patiently. "That fortunately came to an end and the treaty between our people, the *Evania Isibis*, has stood for more than eight millennia."

Brenden fought to keep frustration off his face, and failed. "What kind of treaty?"

Nash answered with terse directness. "In return for not robbing, raping and pillaging our world, we Wyr allow them access to choose select females as mates. While humans and Jadians can propagate quite nicely, they can father only male heirs. Therefore to continue their species, they need our women."

The prospect clearly dismayed her brother. "Sounds more like you're sacrificing virgins to appease the gods," he grumbled. "It would probably be better to let the bastards die off."

Choosing select females for mates . . .

"That all sounds very feudal." Dani gulped and curled her fingers around her mug. "I take it I'm one of the selected?"

Nash smiled kindly toward Dani. "It's to your credit that you have captured the eye of the next heir to the Jadian throne, Danicia. I had no idea you had moved into a courtship. I'm proud of you, girl. You far exceeded my expectations of your abilities."

The bottom immediately dropped out of Dani's stomach, as though she were riding in a hot air balloon suddenly burst by some sharp object. The landing was going to hurt like hell. Counselor Nash was actually encouraging the match!

"I did?" she asked in confusion. "I mean, I didn't know I was being courted."

Nash patted her arm, clearly undisturbed that she'd had sex with Casedren. "In the Jadian culture, a man declares his intent to engage a woman by having intercourse with her." Her mentor chuckled. "The prince obviously found you worthy or he would not have made such a bold advance so quickly."

There was a moment of awkward silence before Dani recovered her composure. "I had no idea. I mean, well, I just met him last night."

Brenden's palm connected with his forehead. "Oh God, if I have to hear any more about your sex life I'm going to puke." Hand coming down, he fixed her under a laser beam stare. "Jesus, Dani, you're supposed to get to know a man before you sleep with him."

His words didn't set well.

Squelching the urge to kick the massive Neanderthal in the shin, Dani gritted her teeth and smiled back. Her gaze swept over her brother, and then his wife. "Tell me again how you met Líadán?" she inquired sweetly.

Líadán blushed ten shades of scarlet before ducking back into the kitchen. So did Brenden. He'd ended up sleeping with Líadán the night he was supposed to be busting her as a whore.

When her brother didn't answer, Dani mused, "Funny how those things can come around to bite you on the ass."

Brenden's mouth twisted briefly, cynically. "Touché," he granted through tight lips. "But it isn't my ass in the sling right now, Dani. It's yours."

Dani glanced toward Nash. "Isn't there anything you can do, like tell Prince Casedren I'm flattered but I'm not ready to be engaged?"

Nash's face assumed a cautious blank. "You aren't going to like hearing this, Dani, but it would be considered a great insult for you to refuse Prince Casedren's offer." Then, in a lower, more sober tone, he continued, "Were he not so highly placed, there might be a way we could graciously refuse by suggesting he seek a bride among the regular populace. But this man could be the next Jadian king, and as such he requires a consort of impeccable pedigree."

The coffee in Dani's stomach turned to lead. She'd believed there'd be an easy way out, that she could simply say no and that would be the end of Casedren's shocking proposal. "Me? An impeccable pedigree? You're making me sound like a bitch to be studded."

Nash's rejoinder came with the smoothness of practiced diplomacy. "As a Wyr, Dani, I assure you that your bloodline is above the average. It also helps that you are a witch, aware of the uses and practices of the craft."

Dani could hardly believe her ears. "Am I hearing you right, or were you actually suggesting that I accept his proposal?" Surely he didn't mean for her to actually marry a man she'd had sex with on a whim of her hormones.

Counselor Nash nodded vigorously. "I am not only suggesting it, Dani, I'm absolutely and wholeheartedly encouraging it."

4

Hearing Nash say the words was one thing. Actually following through with them was another. Especially since her brother wasn't going to let her go without an argument.

"Now, wait a minute!" Brenden Wallace protested. "It seems to me that you're being awfully quick to encourage this union. I'd like to know more about this bargain the Wyr have struck with these-these—things." His obvious scorn withered.

Dani found herself half wishing that she'd never cast the two original spells that had shown her brother his true lineage and path in this world. Sometimes it was easier to go through this world blind, deaf and dumb. Not better, but easier.

As if her thoughts were somehow transmitted his way, Prince Casedren Teraketh cleared his voice in a manner loud enough to draw attention his way. "Forgive me for rudely interrupting, but I could not fail to overhear your conversation given the small space of these quarters."

"Then you pretty much know how I feel about the entire matter," Brenden shot back without hesitation.

Casedren fended off his verbal attack gracefully. "Indeed, I am aware of your feelings on the matter, sir," he said, in the politest of voices. "I feel I must speak up and declare to you that my intentions toward Danicia are entirely honorable."

"Honorable means keeping your hands to yourself and your dick in your pants!" The anger in Brenden's words penetrated deep.

Casedren's stillness and lack of reaction at such a slap in the face was uncanny, a schooled bit of control that said he would not stoop to the level of being drawn into an unnecessary confrontation. "I did not have to force her. Your sister made her willingness very clear. Several times."

Brenden Wallace made an obscene gesture. "I have two words for you: Get out. There's no way in hell you're hijacking my sister as a brood mare."

Casedren sighed, and with a resigned gesture said, "If only it were that easy." His voice had taken on a flat, oddly muted tone, as of defeat.

The look on his face was one of such complete resignation that Dani felt her nerve endings tingle with alarm. His silvery blue gaze settled on hers and she caught her breath as a thought from his mind seemed to streak through hers.

You are our only hope, Dani. . . .

The words echoing inside her skull came and went before she even had time to compute their existence, much less figure out who they really belonged to: him or her. The tension linking them went up another notch, until the space between them practically crackled with it.

In the space of seconds, her vision tunneled, some unseen force pulling her toward an unknown destination. A flash of the future rose in front of her eyes, as surreal as it was soul chilling. She saw the earth, its skies shrouded under a miasma of rolling fiery clouds. Below the clouds was a landscape shrouded in a gray, gloomy mist, enveloping and devouring the remnants of what had once been a city, a great city. Giant fanged reptiles slithered through the ruins, wrapping their long cold bodies around people unlucky enough to be left alive in the wake of a great and terrible apocalypse . . .

Dani froze, feeling herself begin to sink, as if forced down by some invisible force. "Oh my God." Barely aware she was speaking, the words slipped past her numb lips. Dizzied by the intensity of the mental picture that had smacked her straight between the eyes, she swallowed hard, the empty coffee mug slipping from her numb fingers. She blinked, slipping into complete darkness seconds before her body pitched forward. She would have hit the floor in a heap had Casedren not swept her up into his arms at the exact moment her legs collapsed.

Casedren carried her to the nearby sofa, gently laying her in a comfortable position. "Are you all right, my lady?" He knelt and took her hand as everyone else gathered around, concern etched on every face.

Brenden muscled his way through, hovering over her. "Dani? What the hell happened?"

Dani slowly opened her eyes. Despite the blur lingering around the edges of her vision, everything seemed normal, okay. She pressed a hand to her forehead, clenching her jaw in an attempt to beat the nausea threatening to rise from her tangled guts. "I-I'm fine," she said, voice shaking more than a little. "I just got dizzy for a minute. . . ."

Brenden shot a none-too-happy glance toward Prince Casedren. "You're not pregnant, are you?" he grated out between gritted teeth.

Still keeping a firm grip on her with a hand that felt cold and heavy as concrete, Prince Casedren quickly shook his head. "I assure you we used all precaution."

His words didn't seem to mollify Brenden in the least.

Dani raised her gaze to her brother. "I saw something," she said half audibly. She paused, fighting for self-control as she reluctantly recalled the hellish scene. "I-I looked at him"—she vaguely gestured Casedren's way—"a-a-and I saw..." Her words trailed into silence. How could she admit that such a terrible thing had come from a man she was so intensely attracted to?

"What?" Counselor Nash urged, his features pale and creased with an anxiety she hadn't seen before. "You must tell us what you saw, Dani. It's important we know."

Casedren gave her hand a gentle squeeze, meant to reassure her. "It is very important we know what you saw, my lady. Your vision could very well be the key to a prophecy none of us want to see fulfilled." His words held a strange sense of prescience.

"I looked at you," Dani said slowly, trying to cope with what she had to tell. "And I saw the end of times."

Counselor Nash gasped and clasped his hands in front of his body. He exchanged a frightened glance with Minister Gareth. Casedren, too, looked deeply disturbed. Brenden just looked puzzled.

Dani looked at them all, intensely aware of the ripple of fear her words had set off among the Jadians and her own teacher. Nash had always told her that one of the true gifts of a Wyr was the ability to pick up psychic impressions from people and objects. She had a bit of psychic intuition, enough to prove useful when car keys were misplaced or to know when the phone was going to ring before it did. But she'd never had such a mind-blowing, knock-you-on-your-ass, honest-to-God psychic vision of such intensity.

There was no doubt in her mind that what she'd seen was all too real.

"So it has come to the beginning of the end," Nash said, and laughed a little ruefully. "We all knew it would have to happen. We just didn't know when."

"The end of days," Brenden protested. "That's kind of kook talk, isn't it?"

A tremor shimmied down Dani's spine. "What I saw wasn't anything to make fun of," she insisted. "It was real, Bren. I speak the truth when I say that for a moment I stepped into the future. The demonic things I saw would make a nonbeliever find his faith. Not only did I see the end, I smelled the terrible stench of sulfur emanating from burning clouds, and I heard the cries of the damned as they were consumed by serpents."

Hearing the final word, Casedren's face went a shade whiter than normal. His hand tightened subtly around hers. "It sounds like a fate worse than death," he murmured.

Nash studied the big cop coolly. "Brenden, I know you're a lapsed Catholic, but there's got to be a bit of Sunday school teachings still left in you."

Brenden shrugged. "About the end of times? Who really believes that?"

"You should believe it because it is true," Prince Casedren broke in quietly.

Minister Gareth piped in, "Your people and our people have a history that has been intertwined since the beginning of life on this planet we share."

Brenden shook his head. "I'm not getting it."

Counselor Nash looked to Minister Gareth. "Should we tell them?"

Minister Gareth sighed, then nodded. "Because the success of this joining is so vital, we must." He paused, then affirmed, "We must."

Nodding his own agreement, Counselor Nash hurried to retrieve the briefcase he'd arrived with. Popping it open, he retrieved a large tome from inside, beautifully bound in dark leather with gold trim around its edges and pages.

Brenden quirked a skeptical brow. "Is that a Bible?"

He hefted the weighty thing. "Not quite. This is the *Gwyd'llyr* version of historical events pertaining to otherworld forces. From the time of man's creation, we've been harried by beasts of all shapes and sizes. They want our bodies, our lives, the very planet we call home." Opening the book, he flipped its pages until he found what he wanted. "Does anyone recognize this?"

Everyone looked at the lavish illustration drawn by an unknown medieval artist. The technique was crude, but the subject was easily recognizable.

"It's Adam and Eve in the Garden of Eden," Brenden said.

"And what else?" Nash urged. "Who else is there?"

Dani felt her blood go cold. "The snake wound in the Tree of Knowledge . . . it's like the ones I saw in my vision."

Counselor Nash nodded. "That's right. The devil himself, in serpent form."

As her mentor spoke, cold awareness washed through Dani's senses, bringing a chill so terrible it felt as if someone had shoved her in a meat locker and closed the door. What Brenden seemed to be missing all came together in her brain. After all, she'd touched the source that had sprung the terrible vision upon her: Casedren.

Breaking through the paralysis holding her, she quickly snatched her hand from his grip. "It's you!' she accused. "You're the Beast that will bring mankind down."

Visibly wounded by her rejection, Prince Casedren climbed to his feet. "I am not the Beast," he said slowly. "But he is close to me." He looked to Minister Gareth. "We might as well tell them everything. They need to know, to understand the great struggle we have ahead of us."

Grimly, the old man nodded. "I agree."

Brenden broke in. "If you think my sister is marrying the devil, you have another thing coming. That's not going to happen in this lifetime." His totally inappropriate outburst brought a chuckle to Jadian lips.

"I assure you that I am not the devil, nor even a demon," Prince Casedren said. "However, I am the product of Lucifer's promiscuous whims with Lilith, believed to be the first wife of Adam." His even neutral voice betrayed nothing. "As you are the progeny of one creator, so we are the descendants of another."

"It is true," Minister Gareth followed up. "We were evil things, the spawn of hell itself. Then came the age of reasoning, when the Jadians began to realize they, too, were a people of soul and conscience and could, in fact, fight their demonic natures and assume a more civilized existence. The *Evania Isibis* was created, the treaty named for the Jadian king who first set it in motion. It has stood to this day, unbroken. We have kept a peace that has allowed our interlinking worlds to co-exist, and thrive."

"And I'm supposed to be thrilled about that tidbit of information?" Brenden shot back sarcastically. He rolled his eyes. "Why is this going from unbelievable to just plain bat-shit crazy?"

Counselor Nash closed his book and set it solemnly aside. "It's hard for someone still very much an outsider in the Wyr culture to believe, much less accept on faith."

Minister Gareth pressed his hands together, palm to palm, as if intending to pray. "Faith has tested the best of us, but through it all the treaty has held firm."

"Then why break it now?" Dani asked.

"With the ascension of a new monarch comes the ceremony of renewal, when the Wyr and Jadians meet to renew the terms of the *Evania Isibis*," Gareth said. "Each king determines how his rule shall go. And as their king goes, so does the Jadian people."

"And when this Prince Casedren is king, he doesn't intend to renew the, uh, whatchamacallit treaty?"

Dani hadn't missed a word of the conversation. "The *Evania Isibis*," she corrected, attempting to say the words with the same strange, soft accent the Jadians spoke in.

Casedren smiled down at her with obvious appreciation. That little smile was sexy enough to melt steel. Dani swallowed hard and her heart skipped a beat before settling back into its natural rhythm. His presence, at once overwhelming and magnetic, threatened to send her swooning all over again.

Whatever he's got, he's got it in spades, she thought. The fact that he should be a direct descendant of the wellspring of all evil wasn't even a deterrent to her attraction. There was a reason they'd been drawn together. That was as clear as her own name.

Casedren drew a deep breath. "Were I to become king, I would renew the treaty without hesitation so both our worlds could continue in peace. But I am not assured that honor. My brother, my *twin* brother, Cellyn, intends to make a challenge for the throne based on the claim I am unfit to rule. He is not as kindly disposed toward the human race as I am. He sees the treaty as the betrayal of our own true origins."

"Remember, even the prophecy of Revelations speaks of the appearance of twin beasts that are the product of the dragon," Counselor Nash reminded. "Of the two, a leader will rise, one of whom is destined to plunge this world back into chaos. No human soul left on earth will be spared the torment."

Casedren nodded vigorously. "I know my brother's heart to be black as night, but he hides it well. Were Cellyn allowed to take the throne in my stead, I believe he would tear the treaty to shreds, piece by piece, until he has eradicated it entirely."

"Then he needs to be stopped," Brenden said, settling his hands on his hips in a defensive posture. He bared his teeth, his incisors blooming into a beautiful set of deadly sharp fangs. "I'm ready to take names and kick ass anytime." He cocked a brow toward Casedren. "I'm sure you recognize a kissing cousin courtesy of your Big Daddy."

Dani resisted the urge to roll her eyes to the ceiling. Ever since Brenden had gotten the hang of whipping out his fangs at the drop of a hat, no one had been spared a demonstration.

"Very nice," Prince Casedren returned smoothly. "But I can top that." He lifted a hand, passing his palm briefly over his chest. Words no one understood passed from his lips. He vanished, disappearing and reappearing in the space of a single blink.

A large powerfully built serpent occupied the space where he'd stood, its massive hooded head easily rising above the rest of the men in the group. Its body was thick as a log. Jaws unlatching, its mouth opened to reveal a set of fangs a saber-toothed tiger would envy. Black and red, it had faint, pale orange bands crisscrossing down the length of its scaled body.

Dani's heart leaped all over again, threatening to hammer its way completely out of her chest. "Oh God!" she cried aloud with the impact of fear and extreme mental agony. Right in front of her eyes was the serpent of the terrible apocalypse. "That's what I saw. Thousands of them, everywhere."

Casedren instantly shifted back to human form. Distress and regret mingled on his face. "Please, I meant no harm in showing my alternate face." As hard as he fought to keep his voice steady, something of his inward struggle communicated itself to Dani. She looked up quickly and, for a moment, their gazes locked and she knew his struggle, and his pain.

Prince Casedren had no desire to rule his people.

You must, Dani pleaded back silently. *I've seen what will happen if you're not . . .*

Guilt filling his eyes, Casedren slowly shook his head. He deliberately averted his gaze away from hers, breaking the connection.

More than ever before, Dani felt destiny knocking at her door. In the space of a single night's sex, she and Casedren had somehow developed a mental link to each other's minds. They need only look at each other to activate it.

A grim quiet hung over the room. Too quiet. No one knew what to say.

Brenden tucked his fangs away. "Nice set," he said with an admiration that broke the ice. "Must be a hell of a job to keep those things brushed up all nice and shiny white." The frost seemed to be thawing between the two men now that they'd compared balls and found each had a set that hung nicely.

Everyone laughed. The relief was welcome, but it wouldn't last long.

Once the moment had passed, Counselor Nash continued. "Prophecy isn't always set in stone," he reminded everyone. "Dani was given a warning of what might come if we don't take proper precaution. We know now Prince Cellyn can't be allowed to succeed in his challenge toward Casedren's ascent to the Jadian throne. Forewarned is forearmed. To keep the peace between our worlds, Casedren must become king."

Casedren shook his head sorrowfully, all but defeated in spirit. "For me to become king, I must present myself at my father's court with a suitable consort." A small smile crept onto his lips. "I thought I had the time to court Danicia properly, but my mother's recent unforeseen death has hasted my father's decision to abdicate."

The acid rising at the back of Dani's mouth tasted bitter. "I'm just a second-tier acolyte," she reminded everyone. "I wield no great power myself. What use could I possibly be?"

Prince Casedren failed to conceal his smile. "All I need is a woman willing to stand at my side and pledge to my father she is my willing and avowed consort." His bright gaze slipped briefly over her body, probing every inch in seconds.

Wracked by the sexual hunger burning behind his eyes, Dani felt completely exposed. No doubt about it. Casedren wanted her, with or without the shadow of doom hanging over their heads. An unexpected tingle ranged through her entire body.

Fighting to keep her composure, Dani demurred and dropped her gaze. She shifted uncomfortably, sitting up on the sofa to tuck her legs under her body. The quick movement delivered a brief but potent whiff of her sexual heat. Her inner core burned hotter than a furnace in midsummer, making her slick and ready for him. Had he parted her legs and slid a hand between her thighs, he would have found the crotch of her panties soaked completely through.

Breaking his eye-lock on Dani, Casedren continued staunchly. "As for myself, I intend to fulfill the duty to my people that I have been forsworn to carry through since birth."

Always the skeptic, Brenden Wallace wasn't entirely convinced. "It can't be that easy. There has to be a catch."

"There is a catch, and it is entirely in my favor," Casedren answered. "Once my father is satisfied that I am qualified to assume my duties, my coronation can go forward. After I am king, Danicia may release herself from our pending union by publically declaring she finds me unfit to satisfy her needs."

Dani swallowed hard when she heard his words. That would be more than a little difficult to truthfully declare. So far, he'd satisfied her completely. Enough that she looked forward to going back for another serving. "I would have to do that in front of everyone?"

Minister Gareth nodded. "Before the chamber council, yes. But that would release you from engagement and you would be free to return to your world. Prince Casedren would also be free to pursue another consort to become his queen. If nothing else, he must provide heirs to the Teraketh bloodline."

"And that would be it?" Brenden asked. "Dani would be out of your family's infighting?"

Casedren nodded. "Cellyn has two strikes against him in that he is still the younger by more than ten minutes and he is not wed. Only my death would qualify him—something the assassins who I am sure strike by his word have not yet succeeded in. As king I would have the right to imprison him. Were he to be set into ice for eternity, it is a justice I would feel served."

Brenden whistled under his breath. "Harsh, though probably fitting. But for the sake of conversation, let's say this treaty were to be somehow broken." He turned to Counselor Nash. "We are Wyr, right? The ones who win."

Counselor Nash gave him a rueful smile. "Listen to me and listen closely." His tone, carefully controlled, was tinged with an underlying urgency. "Were we to actually engage in battle, I fear our side would be the losing one." He shivered more than a little. "As Wyr, our numbers have grown alarmingly thin these last few centuries."

True. Very true.

Dani remembered how hard it was to recruit her own brother to the cause. That was a bitch. Brenden hadn't been willing to admit the truth behind his heritage. Like his parents, he'd always scoffed at their grandmother's tales as nothing more than an old woman's stories from the Old World. The Irish were full of blarney and the Scottish were too damn sensible to believe in a narrative set in the far distant past.

"So they could kick our collective asses if they really wanted to?" Brenden asked tersely, eyeing the visitors.

Colin Nash nodded. "Most likely with their eyes closed and with both hands tied behind their backs. And they would have more than one reason to come." His voice quaked more than a little. "Don't forget, theirs is a place where females are not readily available. In our world, women outnumber the men ten to one. That makes us a very tempting target, don't you think? As the codicils in the treaty stands, a woman must be willing to join Jadian society. To take a woman by force is explicitly forbidden. How will it be with a Jadian ruler who holds the opinion that our people are little more than insects, our women mere chattel?" What he left unsaid spoke volumes.

Dani shivered as she listened to Nash speak, a dozen different thoughts warring in her mind, all terrible and all tinged with the blood of the innocent. Did she really want her refusal to stand with Prince Casedren to be the source of a confrontation between two very different worlds? The lives of uncountable millions could hang on her decision.

Panic clutched her throat with chilly hands. She'd been in the grasp of pure evil once, when Auguste Maximillian had kidnapped her with the intent to use her abilities as his own. It was an experience she never wanted to repeat—and never wanted another person to have to experience.

Guilt roared in next, hammering her conscience hard as the desire to do her duty as a Wyr guardian beckoned. She had pledged her life, her burgeoning abilities as a witch, to keep the forces of darkness at bay. To turn her back on it all now because what she'd accidentally stumbled into didn't suit her would be a betrayal of everything she believed in.

She was hemmed in, with no escape in sight.

Who would have thought that in broad daylight, in a house in Dordogne, Louisiana, on a street where children could play after dark, the ascension of the future sovereign of a civilization she hadn't even dreamed existed rested on the shoulders of Dani Wallace—a twenty-one-year-old stripper who couldn't keep her hands off credit cards or hunky men with hair the color of butterscotch.

Before she could consider the consequences, Dani opened her mouth and the words tumbled out. "I'll do it," she said, voice as shaky as her knees. "Whatever it takes to keep the peace, we have to stand with Prince Casedren. If that means I have to become his consort, then so be it."

5

The limo wound its way through downtown traffic, heading toward a destination unknown.

Dani Wallace sat beside the man who would go before his father and declare her his bride-to-be. Ordinarily a girl would be thrilled by the idea of her fiancé informing his family of his forthcoming nuptials. Under other circumstances, she would've been entirely delighted to accept a proposal from Casedren Teraketh.

This, however, wasn't anywhere close to a normal engagement. When they went before Casedren's father, it wouldn't be as a young couple declaring their love for each other. No, there would be deception behind their act, a calculated move to keep his twin at bay.

It seemed too damn incredible to be believed, yet here she was. Her! The woman who couldn't balance a checkbook was about to be plunged headfirst into the intrigue of a foreign world. Nothing would ever be the same for her as a Wyr-witch. She'd been unwittingly thrust straight in the Grandmaster's game. She'd have to play like a pro and pray she made no missteps.

Dani glanced over toward her companion. Casedren sat as far away from her as physically possible, hands laced in his lap, staring straight ahead. Her travel bag, the sole thing she'd been allowed to bring, sat between them like a soldier on guard. She'd been assured that she'd need only the bare necessities. Anything else she might require would be lavishly and amply supplied by the prince.

Her brother had tried to talk her out of the whole insane scheme. Brenden had even threatened to lock her in the basement and nail the door shut to keep her from going. That didn't make much sense as she could've easily climbed out one of the windows, but she caught the gist of what he was trying to say. Not going, however, wasn't an option. Both Counselor Nash and Minister Gareth had done their best to impress upon her brother the importance behind the covert mission to secure a consort for the prince. After an additional hour's argument, Brenden finally relented. Casedren had even promised she would have a guard by her side at all times, a necessary precaution.

Before letting her go, however, Brenden had given Prince Casedren an explicit order: Keep his hands off! He'd demanded it through a face full of fangs and the righteous anger of an older brother looking out for a younger sibling. To Dani's absolute astonishment—and dismay—Casedren had promised not to lay a hand on her and swore to be a complete gentleman. He had to, she supposed. Brenden had threatened to tie his "scrawny snake ass" into a knot.

Dani peeked toward Casedren again. He was clearly very uncomfortable, sitting so formally rigid that he'd probably shatter if touched. In a way, she felt terrible for him. They shared a secret, one he had probably never dared say aloud. Not that she could be entirely sure she'd read him correctly. For all she knew she'd imagined the whole thing.

Some nagging in the back of her skull insisted it was true. *He acts out of duty and no true desire. It's the right thing to do, but nothing he wants.* In her mind that was his measure and worthiness as a man. The ability to stand up and do the job no matter the sacrifice of personal desire. That alone made him doubly desirable.

She still lusted for him, despite the fact he'd left her entirely and deliciously sated less than twenty-four hours ago. The idea of making love to him again sent a nice hot rush of desire straight to her core, the beginning of an ache she couldn't easily ignore. Her tight jeans rubbing against her crotch didn't help matters one bit.

Shifting in place, Dani crossed her legs, giving a little squeeze of her thighs to ease the taut material. The move only served to agitate her clit, sending need to an entirely new level. She was halfway tempted to reach for one of Casedren's big hands and guide it between her legs. *If my brother thinks I'm going to play by his stupid rules, he's dead, damned wrong.* Should Casedren invite her to his bed again, she'd gladly go. And if he didn't invite her. . . . She decided she'd have to seduce him with a sexy lap dance. She had every woman's secret weapon to help her out: She already knew what turned him on.

She cleared her throat. "Sorry about that," she said as a way to break the silence between them.

Casedren turned his head ever so slightly, as though he dare not look at her full on. "Sorry about what?" he inquired politely.

Dani snuffled a half laugh. "My brother."

He nodded politely. "I can understand his position, my lady. He wishes only to protect you."

She resisted the urge to roll her eyes. "Isn't that the truth?"

Letting out a heavy sigh, Dani uncrossed her legs and settled back against the plush leather seat. The limo was tricked out with every conceivable luxury the automaker could shove into so limited a space. Not that it had stopped them from taking one hell of a wild ride. Last night they'd made love in every conceivable position the seat allowed, and then some. Amazing what a couple could do when driven by hormones and the desire to get their hands on each other. Such was the power of raw, purely physical sex.

Not that anything was going to happen now. Casedren had gone all formal on her, speaking only when spoken to and leaving a wide berth around her. She doubted he'd look twice if she stripped buck naked right then and there.

At a loss for something else to say, she looked out the window. By now they'd exited the city, heading out onto the highway. The city receded into the distance, the view changing to the pine forests, cotton fields, wetlands, and waterways marking the outskirts of Dordogne. Both of Casedren's bodyguards followed the limo on motorcycles, a matching set of huge Harleys. No driver passing the bizarre entourage seemed to notice their odd way of dressing or the fact that both men had broadswords strapped across their backs.

Apparently sensing her thoughts, Casedren spoke up. "A blindness spell," he said as if answering a question she'd spoke aloud. "To human eyes, everything about them looks perfectly normal."

Surprised, Dani turned her head toward him. "You can read my mind?"

Casedren nodded slowly. "Yes, we have that ability. Although I try not to enter other minds without invitation, sometimes I cannot help catching stronger thoughts and impressions. Human thought is often like noise escaping through a wall, something I cannot miss even if I wished to."

Considering what she'd been thinking about a few minutes ago, Dani felt heat creeping into her cheeks. "Then you know—" she started to ask.

Amusement colored his smile. His eyes drifted over her in an intimate way. Interest sparked in the depths of his gaze. "That you were thinking about what we did in here last night?" He glanced around the interior, licking those sensual lips of his. "I have fond memories of that myself."

Heart speeding up, Dani gave him a teasing smile. With a not-so-careless hand she knocked the travel case separating them onto the floor. Path clear, she slid over beside him, not caring if she was too forward or too aggressive. She wanted him and that was enough. "Care to relive a few of them?"

"Here?" Casedren glanced toward the driver in front, who smiled into the rearview mirror. "Now?"

The smoky glass window immediately buzzed into place, cutting off front from back.

"I think we have all approval." Dani fingered the lapel of his coat. The smell of leather mingled with his own heated scent, creating an enticing aroma. It reminded her of wild things, dangerous things. "That is if I can get you out of these damned clothes."

Angling his body toward hers, Casedren eased her back against the plush seat. A good position for making out. "Why don't we not worry about my clothes and concern ourselves with getting through yours?"

Beneath her bra and T-shirt, Dani's nipples pebbled to immediate attention. Every time she took a breath the material rasped against the sensitized tips. "I could agree to that," she breathed in anticipation. "In fact, I highly encourage it." Every nerve in her body tingled.

Casedren leaned forward and flicked his tongue against the seam of her lips. "Good." The breathy heat of his mouth so close to hers tickled.

Dani groaned and let her head fall back a second before his mouth covered hers, the beginning of a slow, luxurious kiss. A tingle of warmth spread through her, settling deep inside her sex. She stretched out, offering him full access to do what he wanted. Knowing what he could do, she was in for a treat.

Breaking their kiss, Casedren settled his hand just below the fullness of her left breast. "I cannot believe how lucky I am," he murmured. "I feared I would never find you."

Dani barely suppressed a whimper as his hand slid up, cupping her. His thumb brushed over a hard nipple. Desire steamrolled her, submerging every cell in molten lava. "Are you just saying that because you really wanted to fuck me?"

Casedren obviously fought to swallow past the tightness in his throat. "I would still want you even if I could not lay a single finger on your body." He drew slow circles around the little peak, his erotic touch burning through the cotton material and sending a tremor all the way up her spine. "Fortunately that is not the case."

The sensations of his fingertips skimming round and round her nipple felt wonderful. Her senses purred. "You have me. All of me. Anytime you want."

His brow quirked in that sexy manner. "Despite the fact your brother would tie me into a knot if he saw us right now?"

She grinned, tilting her head to one side. "So who's going to tell Brenden anything?"

Casedren chuckled. "Definitely not me." He set to work easing her T-shirt out of her jeans. When he'd freed the stretchy material, he pushed it up over her breasts. "You are dressed in less than I am and you're harder to get to," he said, frowning at the bra snuggling her breasts.

"So do something about it," she teased.

"I definitely intend to." Tracing along the lines of the plain underwire lingerie, he inserted one finger into the left cup, tugging it down. A rosy nipple popped out, raising its pebbled head with definite interest.

He tweaked the tip approvingly. "Now this is something a man can feast on." His head dipped, his lips capturing the beaded tip.

Dani arched her back against the seat, encouraging him to suckle her deeper, harder. Her fingers tangled in his thick curls as a soft whimper stole from her throat. Rich, bubbling sensations poured through her, heating her senses like a shot of straight tequila.

Arousal ignited into blazing life. "Casedren, please . . ." She hooked her fingers against his shoulders when he gently nipped the quivering peak. Inwardly she cursed the limitations of the vehicle, preferring to imagine their bodies completely naked, limbs twined together, his cock buried to the hilt in her sex. Craving skin-to-skin contact in the heat of full on lovemaking made anticipation that much more painful.

Soon, she thought through her dreamy haze, wanting every inch of his lithe, muscular frame covering hers. For the moment, she'd have to settle for heavy petting.

"Yes, my lady?" His tongue drew slow, lazy circles around the dusky peak.

Her clamoring senses rang like a nine-alarm fire bell. "I need more," she gasped, aching to have his powerful hands take complete control. "Touch me, all over. . . ."

He smiled. "I can do that." He skimmed one open palm down her flat abdomen. His hand connected with the top of her jeans. Experienced fingers worked the single button open. The zipper crunched down.

Temples pounding with blood, Dani felt her mouth go stone dry. The haze of sensuality blurred her vision. Everything around her seemed to fade away until only the two of them remained. "Oh my," she breathed as his hand slid under the elastic of her panties, pressing for deeper access between her legs.

Voice hoarse with desire, Casedren gave a sexy order. "Spread your thighs, love."

Through the wild spin of her thoughts, Dani spread wider. She gasped a soft sound somewhere between a whimper and a moan. She glanced down. The absolutely sensual sight of her half-exposed body met her eyes, sexier than if she'd been completely naked. One breast out of its cup, his hand down the front of her jeans. Just looking almost made her climax right there.

She grabbed for self-control. "Don't make me come too fast," she breathed through gritted teeth.

Casedren leaned into her. Mouth settling on the straining cords of her neck, his lips created a moist warm path to her ear. "Isn't that the point?" he murmured, catching her lobe between his teeth and suckling.

Her gasp came out as a strangled laugh. "If I get any hotter I'll explode!"

Another slow suckle at her lobe followed. A tiny shiver of delight raced down her spine. "Oh, you are definitely going to get hotter, my lady." The heel of his big hand settled on her Venus mound. One thick finger slipped between the silky folds of her creamy sex, and stroked. "You are so damn wet. Have you been thinking about my cock inside you?"

His blatant question made Dani's body tingle all over again. Her hand rose, twisting the sensitive peak of her exposed nipple. She released a little moan. "All morning, damn it."

"Yours is a body made to please a man." He crooked his finger, and the tip made delicious contact with her clit. "I love watching you respond to every touch, every stroke."

Electricity sizzled through her. Gasping in a breath of air, she arched off the seat with a squeal. His blue gaze devoured her reaction. "Oh my!" she gasped. "I felt that all the way to my toes."

Stroking the tiny organ with his fingertip, Casedren gave her a slow, lingering kiss. "Good. You are supposed to."

Dani moaned as the first searing sensations of carnal delight crawled through her nervous system, little sparks of magic fire consuming her from inside out. "That feels so good." Desperate to give him better access, she pushed her jeans down over her hips. "Inside me." Scrabbling hands reached for his fancy breeches. "I need you inside me."

Casedren bit back a moan. Underneath his tight trousers, his cock was rock hard and ready. "No time, my lady," he murmured. "My hand will have to suit you."

Barely able restrain her need, Dani threaded her fingers though his hair and guided his mouth to her nipple. "Hard," she urged. "Hard as you can."

"As you wish." Casedren's mouth captured her nipple. At the same time one finger invaded her rippling depth. A second finger soon joined the first, creating a thicker, more fulfilling effect. He made little effort to be slow or gentle, sensing her desire to be enslaved and conquered by his touch.

Wild with lust, Dani thrust her hips upward. Her body shuddered under his unrelenting hand. She sacrificed herself to the moment, her fevered emotions crackling with a mind-bending intensity.

Climax seized her like a giant hand from behind, lifting and tossing her into an all-consuming abyss of pulsing energy. A strangled moan scraped over her lips. She arched her back, crying out as the ferocity of sexual delight incinerated every cell in her body.

Dani came back to earth slowly. Her skin was slick with sweat, and the air around her was pungent with the fragrance sex. "Wow. Just wow."

Casedren's mouth quirked into a pirate's smile, the kind that stole hearts. "Is that good?"

She smiled up at him. "It's excellent."

Casedren eased his hand out of her jeans. His fingers traced her mouth, dampening her lips with the cream of her arousal. "I'm glad you enjoyed yourself." His mouth followed, giving both a taste of her musky feminine spices. "I certainly did."

Licking her lips, Dani laughed hoarsely, exhausted, basking in the marvelous afterglow. "I can't believe you've worn me out again." She tugged her clothes back into place, wishing she could take them off completely instead of put them back on.

Settling back against the seat, Casedren took several deep breaths to compose himself. Despite having a cock hard as a crowbar, he'd managed to hold his own arousal under control. "I have not even begun to," he said with the intensity of a starving man. "You have no idea what you are in for once I get you all alone in a more convenient place."

She rolled her eyes in an exaggerated manner. "Heaven help me then. I don't know if I can survive a full night in your bed."

Casedren had no time to follow up on her comment. The limo made a sudden turn off the main highway, following the craggy path of a utility road cutting through the trees.

The car pulled to an abrupt stop, flanked by the two guards on motorcycle. Trees stretched as far as the eyes could see, thick and impenetrable.

Dani's sense of gratification vanished like a puff of cigarette smoke as a nagging thought wriggled into her head. No one would see them here. No one would know if these men shot her in the back of the head, dug a hole and buried the body.

She swallowed down the morbid thought. That was Brenden whispering in the back of her mind, warning her to see the worst in people—human and inhuman alike. Perhaps her brother hadn't been at all remiss in installing a sense of cautious wariness in her. She would definitely be needing that "gut feeling" to get through this trial by fire.

Casedren noticed her unease. "Time to say good-bye to your world. The vehicle and motorcycles have to go."

Puzzled, she looked at the prince. "Go? Where?"

"Away. Such mechanical luxuries are unknown in Sedah." Opening the door, Casedren stepped out of the limo. Except for his slightly mussed hair, he looked perfectly composed. She, on the other hand, looked and felt like a damp rag mop.

Dani frowned. That didn't sound promising. In her world such luxuries were an absolute necessity unless you wanted to hotfoot it to your destination. Given her recent expenditure of energy, she sure as hell didn't feel like walking any great distance. All she wanted to do was roll over and take a nap.

The driver hastened around the car to open her door. "If you would, my lady," he invited. Out of manners, he kept his gaze discretely averted.

Dani grabbed her small travel bag, full of the necessities she absolutely couldn't survive without: toiletries, underwear and her iPod. No way on earth—or in hell—she'd go anywhere without her music! She barely had time to set her feet on the ground before the limousine and motorcycles winked out of sight, leaving not a single hint of their presence. Good thing she'd settled on a sensible pair of running shoes. It looked like they would definitely be putting in some walking time.

The driver reached for her case. "Let me, my lady," he offered.

She hesitated. The case was her last tangible link with her world.

"Let Enoch take it," Casedren said, a tad impatiently. "His purpose as a member of the royal household is to serve you in every way. You do him a disservice by not letting him do his job."

Dani handed the case over. The driver accepted it with a smile and a bow. "So why are we here?" She glanced around, expecting to see something mystical in the destination. There were a lot of trees, and a lot more of nothing else. A whole bunch of nothing going nowhere about summed it up.

Casedren saw the faint surprise and hesitation in her face. "We've come to one of the gates leading into the spellbinder's continuum."

Confusion replaced hesitation. "Spellbinder's continuum?"

Casedren made a brief circular encompassing motion with his hand. "The thoroughfare leading between my world and yours," he explained patiently. "The entire planet is wormholed with dimensional gates that go everywhere—different places, even different points in time. It is easy to get lost if you do not know your way around."

Dani smiled faintly. Well how else had she expected to enter Sedah? Why was it magick looked so damn easy on *Bewitched,* and was so damn hard in real life? It would be so much easier just to be able to wriggle her nose. "That's comforting."

He shot her a glance. "It is quiet easy to travel once you get the hang of it."

The wicked smart-ass side of herself raised its head. She smiled sweetly. "I'll believe it when I see it."

Brief amusement crossed his face. "To see is to believe, I suppose." He raised his left hand, palm out. "Oh, guiding spirit I beg your clarity, lend me your focus and your charity, lead me where I need to be. . . ."

The pressure around them built slowly, almost imperceptibly at first. A low tone, just barely perceptible, settled into a maddening hum.

Dani became aware of a pulsing rhythm around her, thumping against her senses the way her heart beat in her chest. A small prick of light began to form a few feet away from Casedren's palm, quickening and brightening as it set to expanding into a huge vortex of hurricane-like proportions. Mist-hazy shards of light and crawling colors wove through its circumference. It whirled on and on, a ceaseless tidal sea with the power to consume everything in its path if not controlled.

Hey eyes widened in disbelief. "Fucking awesome," she breathed.

Casedren held out his hand. "Are you ready?"

Swallowing hard, Dani shook her head. Hell, no, she wasn't ready. Her feet felt rooted to the ground. There was no way she wanted to walk into that devouring depth. She looked around; the guards and driver seemed perfectly calm, eager even. And why wouldn't they be? For them, the gate led home.

Fear surged up inside her like rock striking flint. "Is this the only way?" she quavered. All she wanted was to go home, climb back in bed and forget the whole matter entirely. It had to be a bad dream, something she'd conjured up in the midst of sleep. If she pinched herself, she'd surely wake up.

Dani pinched her cheek. Hard. Ouch. That hurt. Dismayed, she frowned. It also proved she wasn't caught in some terrible nightmare. She was wide awake—and all this was real. She eyed the colossal gate. *Too damn real.*

Casedren nodded patiently. "Yes." Sensing her fear, he added. "I will not let you get lost, Danicia. I promise you will be fine."

She hesitated. "Do you promise?"

Gazing straight into her eyes, Casedren smiled in that heart-stopping way of his. "Yes. I do." For an electric moment they stood, doing little more than gazing at each other. That's all it took to set off an internal reaction. Her entire body thrummed with desire, her internal temperature spiking back into the danger zone.

Ah, Butterscotch. All hot and sticky sweet. She couldn't stop the thought any more than she could stop her need for oxygen.

Sensing her arousal, Casedren briefly ducked his head in embarrassed self-depreciation. "You will be absolutely safe," he said, clearing his throat in a way indicating he also struggled to keep his own carnal yearnings restricted. "Otherwise your brother will hunt me down and kick my ass," he mumbled under his breath.

Catching his words, Dani laughed. "Yes, he probably would," Tamping down attraction to a manageable degree, she mentally gritted her teeth. Damn it, he had her all tied up in knots. Such a strong attraction to one man had never happened before. She suddenly understood how women could drop everything in their lives to follow a man to the proverbial ends of the earth—and beyond.

"Are you ready?" His outstretched arm didn't waver.

Dani stared at him. There was no more time for hesitation. "I think so." Taking a deep breath, she reached for his hand. Her stomach clenched as strong, warm fingers curled over hers. His grip was firm, secure.

Casedren pulled her through just as a cold shiver ran down her spine. *Don't think, just go.*

6

Stepping through the dimensional gate was like stepping in front of a freight train and being hit head on. The forces within the vortex were trying to push her away, spit her out like something foul and terrible.

Struggling to keep hold of Casedren's hand, Dani clenched her eyes shut against the wave of nausea ripping through her. Dimensional currents spun around her, shards of light and psychedelic colors slashing through her lids, invading her brain. The ground disappeared beneath her feet. Casedren's hand slipped from hers as another force seized hold of her. Invasive claws dug into her bowels, even as strange flashes of illumination smacked her eyes from inside her closed lids.

The gate wanted her out. The gate wanted her gone.

Dani struggled against the force, but the alien rhythms continued to batter her from all sides, stretching and kneading her body and mind into unnatural shapes and sizes.

She opened her mouth, hardly aware of the moan rippling up from her throat. Somehow her agony broke through the barrier of otherworldly energies, shattering the eerie paralysis holding her prisoner. Abruptly, there was a dazzling flare of red-hot flame, followed by a sense of fusion. The struggle to break free had felt like an eternity. In reality, only seconds had ticked by. The physical sensations were like the bad side effects of an overdose of LSD.

Dani opened her eyes and blinked. A monstrous three-headed dog with a snake for a tail and snakes twisting down its back like a mane sat in front of her. More terrifying than its fearsome countenance was its size, as huge and wide as the average house. Chained to a dull gray wall stretching high into a phantom blackness, the hound bared long, vicious fangs. Yellowish strings of saliva dripped from its mouth. There was nothing else around but the hound, the wall and a sky that didn't seem to exist.

Cerberus.

Dani's guts twisted painfully, and her blood immediately turned to icy water. She felt a sickening sensation, as if she'd unknowingly stepped onto a mire of quicksand. Oh shit. This couldn't be a good thing to see.

The fucking thing's going to eat me up and spit out the bones . . .

Lowering all three of its massive heads, the hound snuffled at Dani's clothing. Catching her scent, it emanated a low growl from deep inside its chest. The head to the left and the head to the right both bared fangs in a menacing manner. The head in the middle, the largest of the three, loomed closer yet.

Dani caught a whiff of something terrible and gagged. A stench emanated from the beast, like a pile of animal carcasses left out in the sun to bloat and rot. "Shit," she muttered under her breath. "Get a mint."

The beast opened its mouth and spoke. "Do you wish to pass me?"

Dani stood rigid and still, not daring to move, barely daring to breathe. Nobody had bothered to fill her in about the talking dog. This, she felt, might have been a nice piece of information to have. Right now, though, she wasn't sure what she was supposed to say.

Feeling like a rat that has just stepped into the trap, she nearly jumped out of her skin when a hand settled on her arm. She turned her head just enough to see Casedren standing beside her. "Is that"—she indicated the dreadful hound with the slightest twitch of her head—"what I think it is?"

Casedren settled a calming hand on her arm. His manservant and guard stood a few feet away, waiting patiently. "It is just the guardian at the gates of the city."

Dani eyed the massive wall behind the beast. There seemed to be no break in its face nor end to its length or height. *What gate?* She didn't ask, though. She supposed she'd find out soon enough. "So what am I supposed to say to it?"

"If you want to proceed," Casedren advised, "you must tell it, '*Of my own will,*' otherwise the hound will not let you enter Sedah."

Given she'd just been metaphysically ripped to shreds and reassembled in a way that didn't even feel completely whole or right, Dani wasn't sure she wanted to enter Sedah. "Why?" she asked.

A small smile crooked Casedren's lips. He angled his head, sending a spill of blond hair into his eyes. "It's a precaution of sorts, for your protection more than ours, really. You see, all our mates are taken from the human world. But we can neither force nor coerce a woman into coming to Sedah unless it is her own decision." He paused, tightening his hold on her arm. "If you want to say no, now is that time."

Dani glanced up, catching the shadows lingering behind his calm blue gaze. He was afraid she would not go any farther. "What'll happen if I say no?"

Eyes going narrow, he quirked his mouth at one corner in a dubious smile. He didn't want to answer, but did. "Cera will send you home. You'll be back in your own bed, and none of this will have happened."

She picked up on his unease. "My memory will be wiped?"

He nodded. "Just altered a little, a necessary precaution. I am sure you understand why."

Dani frowned. "I suppose I do," she said slowly, even though she didn't like the idea. It made sense that some women, while successfully wooed by a Jadian male, might want to change their minds when confronted with the truth of their origins. Her own knowledge of the cultic realm sent a cold prickle down her spine. She hesitated before she admitted, "I don't like it, but I understand it."

As if to move things along, the impatient hound gave her a prod with its center wet snout. "Do you wish to pass me?" it thundered a second time, with more insistence.

Casedren looked to her. "Well? You can proceed no farther until you give Cera your answer." He left the rest hanging, unsaid. He would go on without her, face what he must. Alone.

And I'll never see him again. Everything about him, their incredible lovemaking, would be excised from her brain. Gone. For good. That idea alone set a desperate frustration to gnawing at her heart. She swallowed hard against the lump rising in her throat. Damn it, she couldn't remember wanting another man as terribly as she wanted Casedren. If she let him go now, everything they'd shared—that brief moment of ecstasy— would be erased, forever.

I'm not willing to lose that . . . at any cost.

Regrouping, Dani raked both her hands through her untidy hair. Somehow the band holding her ponytail had come undone, sending a long spill of half-tangled platinum tresses around her shoulders. She'd made it this far. Backing out now would be stupid. More than staying with Casedren, this was her chance to carry out the purpose she'd been sworn to as a Wyr and as a witch of the clan of *Gwyd'llyr.*

After scrubbing a hand over her face, Dani lowered her hands and squared her shoulders. "Of my own will." Her shaking voice held enough firmness to be believable.

The great beast dipped its head. "Enter freely into joy and prosperity."

And then it was gone.

The hound and the solid, immovable wall faded away to invisibility. For a moment there was nothing. Seconds later a new view transitioned in, incredible and astonishing as the world of Sedah revealed itself to her eyes.

Sedah was ice and stone.

The architecture was a strange blend of the Romanesque and Gothic styles—all stone, all austere and all part of an ancient realm existing through centuries uncounted. Composed of a range of icy peaks, the landscape stretched as far as the eye could see. Clouds, heavy and dark as lead, blotted out the sky, or perhaps they were the sky. A clinging wet purplish-gray mist shrouded ground and building alike.

Shivering at the foreboding sight, Dani curled her arms around her body for warmth. Her palms made contact with a velvet soft material.

She glanced down. And gasped.

Her simple T-shirt and faded jeans had somehow turned into a long-sleeved, black silk A-line gown. Cut low in the front, decorative lacing pulled the velvet material taut across her full breasts. Her running shoes had vanished, replaced by a delicate pair of black leather lace-up boots with a thin sole and thick heel. A flowing cloak covered her shoulders, extending all the way down her body and sweeping the cobbled ground beneath her feet. Her long hair tumbled around her shoulders, spilling over breasts that themselves threatened to spill over the edge of the tight bodice.

Eyes wide, she stroked the material. "It's beautiful," she murmured. She glanced up at Casedren. "Is it real?"

He nodded. "It's more appropriate for you to wear the styles of our women. You won't be so obviously an outsider."

"That makes sense." She looked at the manservant carrying her bag. That, too, had changed into something of a more fitting style for the strange era Sedah seemed to exist in.

"Everything you packed is inside," Enoch assured her.

The mist cleared, shifting the scene around them into something more recognizable. For the first time she saw they were standing in some kind of courtyard. A turreted castle, a behemoth of stone, stood at a distance of perhaps a quarter of a mile away. The grounds, the gardens, the fountains, everything surrounding the entire place appeared to be fashioned out of stone and ice. From the most delicate blade of grass to the most exquisite flower, all were frozen in rigid perfection. Exquisite to look at but frigidly untouchable.

Dani cocked her head. "Your world is beautiful, but strange."

Casedren cast his gaze to the overcast sky and frowned. "Believe it or not, normally it is green, lush and alive."

"This must be winter, then."

Shaking his head, he sighed heavily. "Unfortunately our world reflects the mood of its crowned head. My father still mourns my mother with a heavy heart. He is in darkness, and so our world becomes desolate, frozen. His misery punishes all, and until he passes the *Scepter of Inara* to his successor, Sedah will be a world encased in ice and rock." He sighed again, heavier than the last.

Dani didn't want to imagine what Sedah might look like under a monarch brooding war instead sorrow. She'd already glimpsed a world where the sky boiled red fire and the earth below was scorched bare.

She settled her hand on Casedren's muscular arm. "I'm sorry to hear of her passing. He must have loved her dearly."

Casedren attempted to find a smile and failed. He clearly wasn't happy to be home. "He did. They were married nigh on five centuries. With her passing I am sure he feels as if a piece of his soul has disintegrated." He glanced around. "In fact, it has. Never before in my entire life have I seen Sedah in such desolate straits."

Dani's stomach lurched. She remembered Counselor Nash mentioning that the Jadians were extremely long lived. That thought gave her pause now. Fixing her eyes on his profile, she considered her companion, this man she'd made love to but didn't yet know anything about. Like how old he might be. She did some quick mental calculations based on what she perceived of his looks. Casedren appeared to be in his late twenties. Surely no more than thirty—if he'd even reached his third decade.

"How old are you anyway?" she blurted out.

Amusement glittered behind his intelligent gaze. "I'd wondered when that would occur to you to ask."

Dani snorted. "Well?"

"I am almost two centuries old, give or take a few years."

The term *older man* suddenly took on a whole new definition. "You're a little mature to be hanging around a girl my age, aren't you?"

Catching her hand, he tucked it deeper into the crook of his left arm. "Not at all, my lady. My father was well into his second century when he married my mother, a lady merely twenty-three years old."

Dani shook her head in disbelief. "The numbers don't add up. The human life span is so—"

He quirked a brow. "Short?"

She nodded. "Yes."

"It is true our kind are hereditarily inclined to outlive human beings, but we are by no means everlasting. We do age, however decelerated the process. And when we take a human mate, we can slow down aging through our venom."

She eyed him dubiously, hesitant to accept that the fountain of youth could be obtained through a shifter's venom. "You're not going to turn into a big snake and bite me, are you?"

"That is how they did it in the old days," Casedren teased.

Dani felt an inborn chill spread through her. She'd seen how damn big those fangs of his were. Those fangs were not penetrating her skin. Uh-uh. No way. "I think I'll pass on the immortality bite then."

He gave a quick, artful wink. "Despite the look of our world, we do not exactly live in the Dark Ages. Nowadays we know how to harvest the venom and inject it using a simple syringe. The venom contains antibodies that stimulate dormant genes in the human body, slowing the aging process to a near standstill."

Interesting. And provocative. Dani wanted to ask more about the process; however, further query had to be put aside. They were no longer alone.

A group of heavily armed soldiers marched toward them. They kept a steady pace, five rows, each with half a dozen men. A helmeted figure on horseback led the formation. Nobody needed to speak a name to identify the figure leading the squad.

Dani felt Casedren tense. His guards started to draw their blades and step in front of them. Her breath froze in her lungs. It looked like the prince wasn't going to live long enough to present a challenge to his twin. A few against five times their number hardly seemed to make for a reasonable fight. More like slaughter. A slaughter she'd probably be a victim of.

Casedren's expression turned grim. "Hold steady," he said firmly, ordering his men to stay in their place. A muscle jumped in his jaw. Other than that small facial tic, he betrayed no other unease. "They may serve my brother's interest, but his is not the time to act. For now they must keep their blades at bay. Later they may see my blood on their hands, but not today."

Clutching his arm tighter, Dani looked up at Prince Casedren with pure admiration. Though his entire body had gone solid with anticipation, he neither flinched nor showed a whit of fear. Perfect control strengthened his precise words. He was definitely braver than her. Insides turning molten, she was sure the knocking of her knees would reveal her less than courageous stance.

The soldiers came to a stop perhaps six feet away from where Casedren and his men waited. The lone horseman guided an enormous ebony stallion around the group, bringing the horse to a standstill in front of his men.

Dressed in full body armor reminiscent of something a medieval knight would wear into battle, the horseman slid gracefully off his mount. He lifted the helmet off his head, tossing it to one of his soldiers. "At your ease." He stepped up to Casedren, giving only the slightest nod of his head. "Forgive me for not being here to greet you on your arrival."

Dani could hardly believe her eyes. Casedren's twin, the man who'd shared the same womb with him before birth, was his literal mirror image. Save for the scar angling across Cellyn's brow and cheek—it appeared someone had intended to take out his right eye—the men looked exactly the same.

Past their physical resemblance, there was nothing else the same about them. She could take one look at Cellyn and see he was an entirely different man than his brother. His narrowed gaze was hard, aloof and cruel. *Detached* was the word best used to describe the mental distance he obviously kept between himself and others.

Dani didn't like him on sight. She didn't trust him, either. *Sinister* would be the word best chosen to describe him. Devious thoughts simmered behind his crystal blue eyes, icier than the wintry landscape presently surrounding them. His jaw, too, was set rigidly. And while his mouth offered a smile, there was no joy behind the gesture of greeting and welcome. He did it because it was expected, because it was protocol. For the time being he would play along with the cordial manners one would expect him to offer a future sovereign.

For the time being . . .

Casedren returned the nod. "That is quite all right. I see you are busy with your regiment. You march them as if off to war."

Prince Cellyn Teraketh's smile was tinged with a feral cast. "It hurts not to keep our skills honed to their sharpest," he said with more than a little condensation coloring his tone. "A great unrest simmers in the hearts and minds of many, and dangerous times approach from all sides. Readiness to respond will keep us the superior race." The glint behind his eyes wasn't entirely that of a sane being.

Dani tightened her grip on Casedren's arm. How could anyone fail to see the man standing before them was pure, unrelieved evil? *Superior race.* Hell, he talked like a fucking Nazi general. She almost expected his troops to give a high-handed one-arm salute. Every man she saw was a study in physical perfection. They all looked the same: lean, mean and hungry for the fight, for the conquest.

She shivered. She didn't have to close her eyes to remember the chaos she'd witnessed in her vision of what the future could possibly become if Prince Cellyn succeeded in his quest to assume the Jadian throne. Her psi-senses suddenly kicked up a notch, a whisper of foretelling crept into her mind. *The conflict begins here this very day. Two will seek but only one shall rise triumphant. Beware your own safety and step carefully through the web.*

She knew then that her decision to support Casedren had been the right one.

Instead of calling a spade a spade, Prince Casedren merely offered an approving nod. "Keeping your men at their sharpest is a wise move, brother."

Cellyn nodded in reserved agreement. "One cannot be sure when an assassin's blade will strike. If only father had heeded my warnings, our mother might still be alive."

Casedren's own gaze cooled considerably. "If only," he grated in agreement.

"We hunt," Cellyn said. "Yet still the assassins continue to elude us."

Casedren's lips thinned, but he said nothing. No one had any doubt whatsoever the assassin eluded Cellyn's men precisely because they weren't looking too damn hard.

Cellyn continued his verbal prodding. "This civil unrest amongst our people needs to be settled—and soon. Now that our father is no longer in a position of strength, the agitators are seeing their chance to seize power and take a new direction."

This time Casedren didn't let his brother's provocative remarks pass. "Which I intend to quell once I take the throne," he said, verbally thrusting each word in a pointed manner.

Cellyn had to smile, despite the penetration. For the time being he had to show a position of support. "Of course you have my support—and that of my men—in every way."

"Of course."

Cellyn's probing gaze turned to Dani. His eyes widened with delight. Oh, he clearly liked what he saw. For an instant she saw a naked and cruel lust lurking in the depths of his gaze. And by the way his mouth curled up at one corner, he undoubtedly anticipated a taste for himself.

Dani gathered herself. All she wanted to do at the moment was run, as far and as fast as her feet would carry her. The low cut of her dress made her feel more exposed than ever as his gaze ranged over and settled on her breasts. No doubt he liked his sex rough and brutal. "This is a surprise," he said, for the first time acknowledging her presence.

Casedren made the introduction, as was expected and proper. "This is Danicia Wallace, a lady of the Wyr and a witch of most extraordinary talent."

Cellyn's brows rose, first with surprise and then with envy.

"She is Wyr? A rare find, indeed." His words simmered jealously.

Having honed his verbal blade, Casedren thrust it in for the kill. "Danicia has also agreed to accept my proposal of marriage. On the morrow I am prepared to go before our father and declare it so."

Cellyn's gaze dropped at least twenty degrees. "You have—" he started to ask.

Casedren notched a brow. "Carnal knowledge? Oh yes. We have consummated our union, as the lady will testify."

Dani saw her chance to fire off a shot and took it. She couldn't help it. That bastard brother of Casedren's needed to be put in his place. "Most vigorously," she said, smiling. She made a show of squeezing Casedren's arm. "And in the most pleasing ways."

Cellyn's smile completely vanished. "Is that so?"

Dani tilted her chin in a saucy manner. "Your brother is a most delightful lover." Her answer went all over him like a bad rash.

"Perhaps inexperience would lead you to believe so," Cellyn returned smoothly. "You would not be the first innocent he has misled into the belief that he is a man of worldly experience." He chuckled darkly and his wicked smile returned. "I know for a fact my brother prefers the feel of a cock in his hand over a pair of firm breasts."

Casedren gave his brother a narrow look. He said a few sharp words in a language Dani didn't understand before switching back to English for her benefit. "That is quiet enough," he repeated firmly, making it clear what the gist of his scolding covered. "What I prefer—or do not—is most decidedly not an appropriate topic of conversation, especially in front of the woman I intend to take as my wife."

Cellyn blinked innocently, as if unfairly attacked. "Then it doesn't bother you, my lady, that my brother prefers his own sex?" he asked Dani, clearly determined to deliver every verbal smackdown he could despite his brother's anger and embarrassment.

Dani's heart hammered, long pounding beats. "I don't mind what well the prince has drawn his experience from," she said airily, as if all her lovers were butt-pluggers. "As long as I am satisfied." She could keep up the verbal sparring as long as he could.

Except that Cellyn's took on a dangerous edge. "I am delighted my brother has such an open-minded fiancée. He has told you, of course, of our custom of mate swapping," he said, his tone growing confidential. "Given the grievous shortage of the female sex in Sedah, it is not unknown for the married males in a family to share their wives with a brother, or two. Or three."

Bowels knotting painfully, Dani struggled to work through the implications Cellyn had presented. *Whoa! Wait one minute.* This was definitely something Casedren hadn't told her about.

Casedren curled a lip in disregard of the entire subject. "The decision of which rests entirely with the woman in question," he countered without a flicker of distress. "If she desires, she may take as many lovers as she likes."

Cellyn's gaze lost some of its malicious glitter. "If she desires," he repeated with the strength and conviction of a punctured balloon.

Thank heavens!

Ass pulled out of the fire, Dani breathed a silent sigh of relief. Like a cat stalking a mouse, Cellyn was clearly trying to box both of them into a corner. He probed for weakness, cracks in the façade of their dual unity. They would have to stand together, each watching the other's back.

In an instant an old saying came to mind: Keep your friends close and your enemies closer. Especially if that enemy happened to be a future in-law. She didn't like Cellyn, and not because she'd been warned about him beforehand. Oh, he was good looking enough. Even the scar on his face did nothing to detract from his apparent attractiveness. His manner was the biggest deterrent, too stiff and too formal in a society seemingly already stifled and hamstrung by both—as if by acting civil the Jadians could somehow prove themselves enlightened despite their inauspicious origins.

While such a manner fit Prince Casedren in the most charming way, it fit Prince Cellyn like a badly tailored suit. Cellyn acted like society expected him to, not as he truly wished. Were he to break out and reveal his true nature, all hell would probably break loose. As it was he was too tightly wound. The vibrations surrounding him were there, a subtle current easily masked from all but those possessing a true psychic sense. No spell was potent enough to mask the sixth sense of the third eye.

By attempting to stifle his true nature and inclination, Cellyn inadvertently revealed himself to be a cold, calculating being. To be impartial, to be distanced from emotions, would've be an excellent trait in any monarch, were he not a war-monger in his heart, a man who'd surely resurrect old hates and prejudices in the name of recovering his people's true demonic natures.

Making an effort to assuage ruffled feathers, Dani smiled her widest, most alluring smile. Keeping the peace was vital at this point. "You can be rest assured, Prince Cellyn, I'll think about it."

Casedren's twin looked at her with close calculation. A forewarned enemy was a dangerous enemy. She'd have to tread carefully around him, give away nothing. *If a Jadian queen isn't invulnerable to the maneuverings behind an assassin's blade, I'm not, either.*

The restless prancing and snorting of Cellyn's horse recaptured his attention. "Belal grows anxious to continue our ride."

Casedren offered a brief nod of his head. "Please do not allow us to delay you longer, brother."

Reclaiming his horse, Cellyn put one foot in the stirrups and swung up on his mount with the grace of a practiced rider. Positioned high above them, he sneered down his nose. "As if I would allow it," he said, detaching himself from an uncomfortable situation. Before reining his horse around, his lips stretched into a final smile—wide, insincere and utterly chilling in its confidence. "I will see you on the morrow, my brother. It will be a very interesting day, I think."

Casedren's mouth pressed into a paper-thin line. "Very," he agreed with zero enthusiasm.

Conversation cut to the quick, Cellyn spurred his horse hard, setting the massive ebony stallion into motion. A cry rallied his waiting soldiers to follow. His determination to take what he wanted at any cost was crystalline.

Watching the heavily armed soldiers disappear, Dani shivered. No doubt the soldiers serving his command would follow him past the gates of Sedah . . . and beyond.

7

If Dani found the landscape of Sedah to be icy and unwelcoming, then she could definitely say with conviction the living quarters were equally inhospitable to comfort and warmth.

Having glimpsed the great castle from the courtyard, Dani had assumed Casedren lived there. Not so. He occupied quarters perhaps half a mile away, a great stone edifice that couldn't decide if it wanted to be a temple or a manor. The odd architecture puzzled as much as it intrigued. On one hand the Jadians seemed to be leaps and bounds ahead of humans, having the command of supernatural forces at their beck. They traveled the dimensions as easily as she walked across the street. But where her world had advanced into an age of technological wonder and scientific discovery, Sedah remained frozen in a single medieval age, like a prehistoric insect preserved in amber. Comparing Sedah and earth was like trying to compare apples and oranges. Each offered its own unique flavor and attraction.

Still, the idea of existing in a world enveloped in the grip of icy gloom definitely put her off. Why would any right-minded, sane woman want to give up the modern world for a mysterious, threatening underworld?

They say love is blind, Dani decided. But it would also have to be deaf and dumb to make it appealing. Nothing about it impressed. Depressed would be a more accurate description. As for Casedren's so-called home, it left a lot to be desired.

Hands on her hips, Dani surveyed her new quarters with growing horror. There was nothing in the chambers—no furniture, no carpeting, just blank walls and bare spaces. Illumination from no readily apparent source lent a harsh, unrelenting glare. If what she'd seen of the great castle was accurate, the royal family appeared to spare themselves no luxury. Why Casedren lived in a big, blank bunch of nothing left her at a complete loss.

Noticing her dismay, Casedren laughed softly. "It is empty because it awaits your command to fill it."

A frown tugged at her lips. "What do you mean, my command to fill it?"

He raised an eyebrow. "Are you not a Wyr-witch, able to spell out what you desire?"

Convinced his mental marbles had spilled out and were rolling around loose, Dani gave him a funny look. "Um, I don't know what kind of spelling your people do around here, but where I come from you just don't wave a wand to furnish your house."

That seemed to puzzle him. "So what do you do?"

Considering his origins, Dani really wasn't sure just how much time Casedren had spent in her world. Surely enough to be familiar with the basics. Of course, if she had the power to whip up anything she desired at will, she doubted she'd be familiar with the concept of shopping. "Well, we usually go to a furniture store," she said slowly, "and buy what we want."

Casedren's face lit up. "Ah, commerce. The trade of goods and services for pieces of paper and plastic." He shook his head in wonder. "I still do not understand how your people attach value to their possessions through the exchange of such an intangible thing as cash and credit."

Dani sighed, silently wishing her credit card balance was an intangible thing she could just wish away. "Don't the Jadian people have a system of trade to get the necessary items for living?" She eyed the empty space. "Or do you just levitate in the middle of the room for comfort and eat air for sustenance?"

Casedren smiled. "Why don't you try a little wish-craft."

Dani blinked. "What?"

"Wish-craft," he said again, then explained. "Many of the women we take as mates have no cultic training. It is simpler for them to learn wish-craft. As you are a witch, you should be able to command the homunculi with ease."

Her mental antennae swiveled to attention. "Homunculi?" she questioned. "Isn't that a—"

He nodded slowly, smiling. "A witch's servant. Yes. They merely wait your command."

Dani stiffened, visually searching every nook and cranny. She didn't like those little bastards one bit. They were sneaking, devious things. "Where are they?"

Offense colored his features. "Embedded in the stone, of course. The little buggers are too unpredictable to let run loose. Given free reign, they hardly mind."

She shivered at the idea that the walls had eyes and ears. "I take it as, uh, Lucifer's nearest and dearest that the Jadians have access and command of all the little beasties in hell?"

Casedren laughed and attempted to explain. "The homunculi are not sentient, but more like a mechanical device. They perform a function. They have no feeling, thought or individual identity. It is like flipping a light switch. The electricity produces light. Here, the homunculi are the energy that powers your wishes."

She was beginning to catch on. Suddenly it didn't sound so

bad. The material girl inside perked up. "So whatever I wish for, I get?"

He grinned. "Within reason. The homunculi can only provide things that will contribute to your physical comfort."

Dani pursed her lips in frustration. "So wishing your brother would drop dead is out?"

Obviously having considered the option himself, Casedren shook his head. "Afraid so. *Drulal'elyn*—the practice of black magick—was outlawed many centuries ago. By the law governing the Magus, anyone caught practicing the darker arts faces immediate execution." Judging from his tone of voice, the threat of capital punishment didn't do enough to detour offenders. There were many who would defy moral and spiritual laws, at any cost. Even death.

Dani turned that piece of information over in her mind. "So you're not immortal?" she asked slowly.

Casedren laughed as if horrified by the idea. "Absolutely not. In that respect we Jadians are every bit like you humans. We bleed when cut and can die when lethally wounded. We're just a little harder to kill because we do have some internal regenerative capabilities." He pointed to his head. "Our bodies are not internally arranged like a human's is." His hand dropped, hovering somewhere near the base of his rib cage, where she'd expect the stomach. "Our hearts are actually here."

Seeing him point to an entirely different place gave Dani pause. Counselor Nash had mentioned that some of their internal organs were arranged a bit differently. How very deceptive. Anyone who didn't know that would aim for the upper left section of the chest. She tucked the vital piece of information away.

Just in case.

His words failed to quell the knot of fear writhing in her belly. "The more I learn about your people, the more I wonder how we poor humans have ever stood a chance against such an ominous legion."

Casedren sighed. "Despite our origins, we are not all beasts of demonic desires."

Dani didn't have to think hard on that one. "If your far distant forefather was Lucifer, what does that make you then?"

"Unlike a demon, which is created to serve a conjurer's bidding, we are Magus—of free thought, and free will. That is the way and the right of all men born." He hesitated, then continued. "It is a difficult path to walk, knowing you were created by an entity of such destructive origins. Our natures are dark by virtue of our creator. On the other hand, can human beings claim to be any less violent or destructive?"

Dani shook her head. "I suppose there are times when mankind seems a plague on this planet, too."

Casedren nodded. "Despite our genesis, it is conscience alone that sets us apart from those who seek the ways of darkness. It is, if you will, the battle eternal. Only the side we take determines the worth of our souls, in this world and whatever may come next."

Icy claws clamped shut deep inside her belly. "Your brother has already chosen his side," she said quietly.

Casedren nodded. "I have been aware of that since we were children at our father's knee. Between us, though, my father sees me as the son who has disappointed him, and another who serves his people honorably."

That statement surprised. "You? A disappointment?"

Casedren nodded slowly. "Nothing I have ever done has pleased my father. He is more like Cellyn and has always ruled with an iron fist. Were it his choice, Cellyn would follow him to the throne. However, where my father is firm, but fair, Cellyn would be a tyrant. It is only by benefit of birth that I can stop him from taking that step. As for my own suitability . . ." Words trailing off, he glanced down at his hands, fingers tightly clenched together. "The day I had hoped would never come has arrived with startling swiftness. . . ." His words trailed off into silence.

Dani sensed again that strange tentative outreach of contact, like a knock directly on the outer walls of her skull. This time she knew she wasn't imagining it. "Why?"

Casedren shook his head. "I am a scholar, preferring my books, my studies, my travel through your world learning the cultures. Your people are so alive, so vibrant and still so very innocent of this universe you live in." He hesitated a moment as if reluctant to reveal more, then said, "Compared to it, my own world seems so cold and stifling. Not to mention that it takes a smart head and strong hand to rule the Magus. More than Cellyn, so many Jadians seek a return to the unenlightened ages when your kind was little more than sacrifices to feed our hungers. Even if Cellyn were to present no obstacle, I would still feel unfit to quell the civil unrest threatening to tear our people apart."

Dani found it strange that a man born of such a fierce race would possess such a gentle spirit. Surely, though, the gentleness was tempered with a backbone of steel. No matter his misgivings, Casedren Teraketh had proven himself fully prepared to step up and fulfill the obligations of monarch—even if it meant hijacking his bride a mere day before he would be obligated to step up and assert his rightful claim to the Jadian throne.

And I'm his choice as queen consort. What could that possibly indicate? If he felt no qualification, she'd definitely claim the same. In this case it felt like the blind leading the blind. Neither really knew what they'd be walking into. *At least I'm not having to go through this alone.* Come through successfully, Counselor Nash had assured her, and she'd be an acolyte of the first tier.

Yeah, right. She felt more like an amateur than ever.

Forcing herself to squelch her negative thoughts before Casedren sensed them, Dani licked dry lips. "For what it's worth," she said, "I believe you're more than qualified." The job of keeping herself under control, performing the duties of a consort as instructed, was strictly up to her. Supporting Casedren in his claim was vital.

Casedren's clear blue gaze met hers. "Let us hope you are not deceived." He turned his attention to the blank space around him. "But let us think of other more pleasant things—like filling this terribly bare room."

Letting him off the hook from what must have been hard to confess, Dani looked around the forbidding chamber. "Where do I even begin?"

He prodded. "You can wish for anything you like. Just say aloud what you want."

Mulling his words, Dani pointed to a blank spot. "So if I say I want a couch there, it'll appear?"

"Yes. The plainer your order, the plainer the item you will get. Since you are a witch, you should be able to work on a higher level, using mental visualization to affect physical manifestation."

Dani demurred. Visualization and manifestation was a technique for the advanced conjurer. She'd dabbled, and not always successfully. "I could try it," she said, then hurried to add, "but don't expect it to look terrific."

Casedren smiled his confidence. "Anything you want is fine. This is your private space to decorate as you desire."

She shrugged. "Sounds fun." She already had something in mind, having spent hours decorating her dream apartment. Nobody wanted to spend their whole life in a cramped basement.

Focusing inward, Dani mentally pieced the rooms together, laying them out as she'd always imagined she would when the time came. To back it all up, she quietly whispered the few words of the spell she'd been toying with. "This simple idea is mine to cast, a bit of magick to make it last—"

She sensed rather than physically felt a shifting in the space around her. For an instant nothing existed except the blank, cold space. Slowly, it began to shift, expanding and filling with light and color. Right before her eyes, a spacious room took shape, exactly as she'd imagined it.

Hardly able to believe her eyes, Dani gave her head a little shake. Plush oriental rugs; a crewelwork canopy-covered, king-sized, pencil-post bed; a mahogany inlay dresser; a late nineteenth-century wardrobe and blanket chest, and an antique sofa decorated the room. An ample hearth ready to have a fire stoked in its depths claimed one wall. Opposite the hearth, a large picture window softly draped with gauzy curtains over-looked the back expanse of the castle, the gardens there frigid with wintry perfection. A door newly formed in another wall opened onto a full private bath in a vaguely Romanesque style.

Surveying her handiwork, Casedren quirked a brow in surprise. "I'm impressed," he complimented.

Pleased her first spell had worked so successfully, Dani breathed a sigh of relief. Of course she knew she hadn't done all this herself. The homunculi had provided the majority of the energy and done the work to make the images they'd plucked from inside her skull into tangible items. Still, she'd call it a success all around. Even the harsh lighting had dimmed to a more acceptable level, replaced by the illumination of scented candles. The wonderful woody aroma of sandalwood mixed with rich, dark musk scented the air. The dim lighting and intimacy of the chamber hinted of romance, of soft whispers and softer caresses.

"What do you think?"

His smile took on a suggestive cast that made her insides warm with anticipation. "I think it is perfect." He gave her a suggestive look. "Do you think you could—" His words cut off as he cleared his throat. "Could you possibly be happy here, with me?"

His question caught her by surprise. "What, ah, what are you trying to say?"

Casedren stepped closer, the glowing of candles washing his elegant features in soft light. His hand found her face, gently stroking her cheek. "In my very clumsy way I am trying to ask if you would consider my proposal in a more serious manner."

Her eyes widened. "You mean, actually marry you?"

His feather-light touch traced the curve of her jaw. "Yes. Believe it or not, I meant to court you in a proper way."

Surprise filled her. She hadn't seen that coming. "You did?"

He nodded. "I honestly did not expect that my father would suddenly wish to abdicate. Even before my mother's untimely passing I had decided to seek your affections."

Feeling the oxygen drizzle out of her lungs, Dani licked dry lips. "I didn't know."

"You were always my choice, Danicia." He laughed softly under his breath. "My only choice, actually. I've known of you since you were a little girl."

"How could you—" she started to ask.

He rolled his eyes, amused. "Don't you remember when you were a little girl, sneaking into your grandmother's spell books, looking for love spells? That one you found . . ." Tracing her lips with the tip of a single finger, he softly quoted. *"With a witch's will and hallowed vision, thou canst capture thy otherworld lover with precision."*

Her mouth tingled enticingly where he'd traced. "I cast that spell half a dozen times when I was a kid," she murmured. "Nothing happened."

Casedren pressed the pad of his finger to her mouth, shushing her. His steady gaze never veered from hers. "Something did happen. I heeded your summons, and I answered it." His accented voice was warm and low, dangerously seductive. "I just had to wait for you to grow up."

8

All the pieces suddenly dropped into place in Dani's mind.

Now she understood why none of the men she'd dated had ever managed to hold her interest for more than a few weeks. In working her grandmother's old spell, she'd unwittingly created a connection to the one man destined to answer her call: her soul mate. No other would satisfy or suffice. She and Casedren were destined to be together. *He* was the otherworld lover she'd spelled for all those innocent years ago. That one reckless night she'd made love to him was supposed to be something more, mean something more . . .

A curling ribbon of heat unfurled in her core, reaching straight to her clit. No wonder she couldn't control her body's responses around him. She'd been primed for him to make love to her since she'd cast the spell. There was no sense in denying it, either. A spell once cast could rarely be undone.

She caught Casedren's strong hand, guiding the tip of his finger into her mouth. Lips pursing into a tight circle, she gave it a long, slow suck. "I think I'm all grown up now." Heavy awareness pulsed through her veins. Her chest heaved, breasts rising and falling. Her nipples were hard, swollen, against the tight bodice keeping them firmly bound. She licked the tip of his finger again, tracing it the way she would the crown of a penis.

Mesmerized, Casedren slowly drew his finger away from her mouth. His blue eyes sparked with anticipation. His full lips broke into a smile. "Yes, you are." His hand slid under her chin, tilting her head back to the desired angle. "And I intend to take full advantage of the fact, as many times as you will allow me."

Dipping his head, his mouth captured hers, the beginning of a long, slow kiss. Their tongues met and waltzed with perfect synchronicity, dancing the dance of lovers in no hurry to explore each other's bodies. Dani inhaled the scent of him, soaked in the heat of his body pressing against her.

"It's been so long," he murmured when their kiss had broken. "The waiting, the wanting. The damn years dragged on, slow enough to drive a man insane."

Dani sighed when he pulled her tighter against his body, melting against him. She no longer thought to question how she'd come to be here, holding him. "You really wanted me?" Her voice was breathy.

"Most desperately," he admitted. "Your eighteenth birthday was the hardest to let pass, but you weren't ready yet."

She tilted her head to one side, exposing a creamy slice of her neck and breasts, about the only part of her the dress didn't cover. "I'm ready now," she breathed in sensual invitation.

Casedren's warm mouth found her neck, the pulse banging double time. "Indeed, you are," he rasped against her sensitive skin. Kissing the soft bend between neck and shoulder, he traced a fiery path up her chin and the delicate curve of her ear.

Uncontrolled lust seized control of Dani's body, the feel of his lips sending surge after surge of tiny electric vibrations through her. The sound of her heart beating in her chest nearly deafened her. The craving she felt for this man was stronger than anything she'd ever experienced in her life. No alcoholic beverage had ever intoxicated her half as strongly as his caresses did.

A soft moan escaped when he slid his palms up her rib cage. An erotic pulse settled in her stomach, sending silken ribbons curling around her nether regions. "Every time you touch me, I melt. It's like you cast the spell on me." Temperature rising, the mercury was definitely in the red zone. Another minute and desire would surely incinerate her.

Casedren chuckled in the back of his throat. "I assure you my touch is driven only by desire, my lady." He cupped her firm breasts with both hands, relished the feel of them. His fingers found and teased the pebble-hard tips. "If that enchants you, perhaps my chances of persuading you to remain at my side will be even better."

Cursing the restrictions of her tight bodice, Dani felt her nipples peak even more under his touch. She ached for him to taste and suckle, but her body was constricted by too much clothing. She wanted to get everything off. Both of them.

Dani sucked in a much-needed breath. "Discussion in the middle of seduction is highly unfair," she gasped out. It was true. Right now she'd follow him into the grave if that's what he wished.

"I am doing my best to persuade you," he said, the warmth in his tone edging toward her was strained. His rigid cock pressed obviously against the front of his skin-tight trousers, straining the way a wild beast found to escape unwelcome chains.

Dani shook her head. "Fuck me now. Persuade me later." Catching the lapels of his heavy coat, she closed her eyes and gave a silent command in line with the sensual images her brain had began to conjure of Casedren. *I want this gone.* Much to her delight the heavy material dissolved under her fingers, vanishing completely.

Casedren glanced down. "You catch on fast, my lady." The light in his eyes was one of pure happiness.

Dani grinned up at him. "I'm a quick study. It seems to me that you've seen all of me and I've seen almost none of you. That's about to change." She batted her eyes. "If you don't mind, my liege."

He grinned down at her in delight. "I am most willing to grant all access." He eyed her like a buccaneer contemplating valuable treasure. "Though you are the one I'd rather have naked." As he spoke the words, her cloak faded away.

"Why don't we take it one layer at a time?" Dani's fingers plucked open the pearl buttons on his vest. Once she'd undone the last, she slid it off his shoulders, down his long arms. It landed in a heap on the floor.

Casedren reached for the laced bodice of her dress. The intricate lacing stretched across her breasts, all the way to her waist. "That sounds fair. I've never gotten the chance to properly undress and ravish you." He worked upward, pulling the silken cord free inch by erotic inch.

Dani breathed easier now that the tight bindings were loosening. She hadn't had any idea how impossibly a woman was bound into a gown of such antiquated style. Thank goodness she wasn't bound into a corset, too! "Ravish, you have." Her face heated. Cream welled inside her, a warm moist trickle. "And quite well, thank you."

Talented fingers unlaced, relieving the pressure binding her breasts. Tight bindings fell away, and he tugged the front of her gown downward.

Dani made a quick grab for the falling material, but he tugged harder, pushing it over the flare of her hips and down her legs. She obligingly stepped out of the pile. She glanced down, hardly surprised to see that all she wore was some sort of thin silky chemise, a pair of provocatively cut panties and those laced granny-style boots that were so damn sexy on a woman's foot. At least he'd left her a bit of clothing.

Dani took another turn, working to get his shirt over the tightly bunched muscles of his shoulders. As she discarded the unwanted piece of clothing, her gaze skimmed chiseled pectorals, tightly ridged abdomen, the muscular thighs supporting legs that stretched on endlessly. "Nice," she murmured in appreciation.

Casedren's gaze locked with hers. His pale, compelling eyes lingered on her like a passionate caress. "Does the way I look please you?"

Mouth going bone dry, Dani nodded and pressed her palms flat against his warm skin. Her hands skimmed over his hairless chest. Curious fingertips circled dusky male nipples, flat and round, with a hard little bead in the middle. "You're so close to human," she marveled. It amazed her that simply touching him caused her clit to pulse with an eager fluttering response.

He raised an amused brow. "You expected something else—cloven hooves for feet perhaps?"

"Yes . . ." A tremor rippled through her when she realized the implications. Casedren's people had been bred by an entity opposite what she considered to be her own heavenly creator. The images she'd seen depicting the fallen angel of light showed a horned monster with hooves and a slash of a tail.

"You forget," her otherworld lover whispered softly. "All accounts say he was the most beautiful and enjoyable of all angels. As you are the product of your creator's vision, so are the Jadians. And though we were born into very different worlds, we are not all that far removed from each other. No matter how you put the pieces together, our origins all spring from one single mighty source."

Tracing the solid planes of his abdomen, Dani pursed her lips. His skin was flawless. Oh, he was so damned good-looking, so perfect. His words, too, made complete sense. From the

Alpha to the Omega, the energies of all creation sprang from a single life-giving spark. "I never thought about it that way," she admitted.

"We have proven our kind can coexist, and have done so for centuries. Why my brother's heart is so frozen against continuing the peace, I do not know."

His mention of Cellyn sent a tremor rippling through her. Meeting Casedren's twin had unnerved her more than she cared to admit. "I don't see how you can take the way he prods you. I'd slap him into next week."

Casedren grinned. "I would like to, badly enough." His smile vanished. "It would only drag me down to his level, something I refuse to countenance."

Dani tipped her head to one side, idly tracing her fingertips down the ridged path of his abdomen. "He needs his ass kicked in a serious way."

"That he does," Casedren agreed. "But I'd rather think of other things—" Fingers tangling in the front of her lacy chemise, he tugged it away from her breasts. The flimsy thing disintegrated in his big hand. "Like getting you out of this."

Dani gasped. Her breasts jutted, the tips solid and flushed a deep blushing-red tint. She shuddered at the violence behind his grab, the possession in his touch when he slipped a strong arm around her waist.

Casedren pounced, his warm mouth settling on hers even as his free hand found one of her breasts, cupping its weight in his palm. His thumb brushed softly against the erect nub, showering Dani all over with dozens of hot sparks. A fresh sense of intensity powered his kiss, his tongue sweeping past her lips as if impatient to drink the life out of her. There was nothing gentle in his touch now. His desire—his demands—would be sated at any cost.

Before she knew what was happening, Casedren swept her up. He headed for the bed, tumbling both of them onto its softness. His body half covered hers, giving him complete control. Capturing her wrists, he pinned her arms down. His head dipped, sucking one tented peak into his mouth.

"Oh, goodness!" Head lolling, Dani closed her eyes and savored the feel of his tongue laving over her sensitive nipple. Gently nipping the little bud between his teeth, he followed the brief pain by drawing it deep into his mouth.

Casedren raised his head briefly. "Goodness is not what I have in mind for you, my lady." He flicked the flushed tip with his tongue. "In fact, it is all badness."

Arms trembling under his hold, Dani's ragged breath threatened to deprive her lungs of oxygen. "What are you going to do?" she gasped out, aware that he didn't intend to hurt her and perfectly willing to play along with the erotic game.

Keeping her wrists pinned with one big hand, Casedren smoothed his open palm down the flat of her belly, teasingly dipping into her belly button. "I am going to have sex with you," he said in a slow lazy drawl that thickened his other-world accent. "Thereby proving to you I do not prefer the feel of a cock in my hand more than I desire a pair of breasts in my hands."

Dani lifted her head as far as her captive position would allow. Curiosity prodded. "Is it true, that you've slept with other men?"

Casedren's finger circled her belly button. "We were not sleeping, if that is what you want to know." The thick tip delved into the shallow depth. "Does that bother you, to know I have been with other men?" His ragged breathing and the tremble in his hand indicated his unease with his confession.

Dani bit down on her lower lip. God, his move was so sensual, so suggestive, mirroring the descent of a cock into her anxious sex. Surprisingly, the idea that he'd been with other men wasn't a turnoff.

Casedren was a handsome man and she had no doubt that

his partner would be as equally well endowed. She could al-most see the picture in her mind's eye. Two beautiful males, cocks stiff and dueling, taking lascivious delight in each other's muscular bodies. It was easy to imagine adding herself in the middle of the duo, her naked skin soaking up the pleasures dual lovers could impart.

Dangerous, she thought. *But, oh, so very tempting.*

Dani sighed like he was sinking his cock into her silky depths. "I think it's sexy," she murmured.

Surprised, he lifted a single brow. "Do you?"

"Mmm, I do." Dani twisted her wrists against his iron grip. His hands were so damn big that he only needed one to hold both her wrists. "Almost as much as I love the idea of being ravished by such a sexy beast."

Shifting his weight off, Casedren's hand slid lower, tracing the line of the saucy panties hugging the curves of her hips like a second skin. He pressed a palm against her thigh, silently urg-ing her to spread her legs.

Dani willingly spread.

The barest trace of a smile touched his lips as he brushed the tips of his fingers across the silky crotch. Tiny darts of desire went straight to her heart. "Because women are the minority in Sedah, it is customary for a young man to take a male lover. Usually it is one of the drones, those born to no class or rank." His finger delved against the dewy material stretched tautly across her sex. "This allows us to learn the ways of lovemaking and eases a lot of the tensions that can build in an almost en-tirely male society."

Dani stifled a moan. Her panties clung, soaked completely through. The smell of her arousal enticed, turning her on in a way she'd never imagined. "That makes sense," she gasped out, barely able to concentrate on his words when his hand had made a vital shift in position.

He hesitated a beat. "Although I enjoy being with a man,

my preference is women. There is something so much more pleasing in the female form, so much more satisfying."

Dani had to laugh. "You don't have to explain your past to me." A blush rose to her cheeks. "I'm not exactly innocent in that area."

Meeting her gaze with an amused one of his own, Casedren smiled. "I know." Pressing his fingers to the damp silk, he stroked with a slow, steady motion, inducing an exceptionally pleasing sensation of tiny pulses to her clit.

Dani closed her eyes, arching her back against the mattress as the pulsing within her struck up a stronger beat. "God, I'm going to come. . . ." She trembled, shivering with the need for deeper, more inclusive fulfillment. She wanted him inside her.

Casedren's hand slipped away. "Not yet, my lady. We're just getting started."

"I don't think I can wait much longer," she gasped.

Pushing his hand inside her panties, Casedren worked it over the curve of her hips and down her legs. His touch branded a delicious trail of heat into her skin. He flicked the panties away.

A shot of pure molten heat poured through her core. His move left her dressed in nothing more than a pair of boots. "You've still got too many clothes on," she hinted about his breeches and boots.

Casedren gave a sexy grin. "Patience." He slipped down between her spread legs and ran his wide palms down the insides of her legs. "I want to take my time with you." His hands slid insidiously back up the plane of her inner thighs.

Knowing she was in for a treat, Dani pulled her legs up, bending them at the knees. She pushed herself up on her elbows so she could watch.

Still between her legs, Casedren settled an arm beneath him. His other crooked at the elbow, palm settling under his chin. He eyed her with appreciation. "That's how I love seeing you."

"I take it you like staring at pussies?"

His hand came down, gently stroking her silky labia. "Oh yes," he said agreeably. "The mysteries of a woman's body can get a man to thinking for hours about the ways he'd like to please her."

Dani's head dropped back as he worked the tip of his thick index finger through damp folds. "You must think a lot about it," she bit off, the edge in her tone unmistakable.

He brushed her small hooded sex with the thick pad of his finger. Warmth immediately curled around her clit. "Oh, I do." His head dipped. The heated, moist sensation of his tongue followed.

Hips bucking against her will, Dani felt red-hot darts of fire take aim, then strike, with startling intensity as he employed his lips and tongue to compel her on to newer, fiercer cravings. Kissing, nibbling and licking, he tormented her with a merciless tongue.

Drowning against the tempest of desire consuming her, Dani reached down, tangling the fingers on one hand in his thick hair. Her lower body pressed against his face, silently begging and pleading for more. Chest heaving, her swollen nipples strained hard and taut. "Fuck me, damn it," she ground out. "Make me come."

Casedren drew away, refusing to be hurried. A smile twitched across his lips. "Patience, my lady."

His reply sent her frantic nerve endings on edge. "Please," she moaned in supplication. "I need more."

His grin turned devilish. "Something like this?" He eased a finger inside her.

Dani gritted her teeth. "More. Please." Her breath came in short, ragged gasps, underscored by her soft pleading. A light sheen of perspiration glazed her pale skin. Candlelight wavered around them, giving the shadows dancing on the wall behind them a strange, surreal life.

A second finger joined the first. His fingers slipped in and out as his thumb worked her sensitive clit.

The tremors began in small waves.

Dani's hips trembled with an intensity bordering on desperation. But it wasn't enough. She wanted him inside her. Not his tongue, or his finger, but his cock. Ever last inch of it, stuffing her to the brim, pounding her until her thighs trembled and her legs ached. Nothing less would do.

He was half naked now. Unbuttoning the front of his trousers was all it would take to release his straining erection. A second tremor shook her that had nothing to do with the cold but everything to do with getting this man fully naked.

She sat up, reaching for him.

Giving a devious look, he dodged her grab. "I'll do the giving if you do not mind, my lady." His hands shot out, neatly flipping her onto her stomach. Going to his knees, he grabbed her hips and pulled her up on her knees. Big hands kneaded her ass cheeks.

Dani's stomach muscles tightened, and her fingers dug bunches into the comforter. "I need you," she whimpered. "I want your cock inside me."

Casedren gave her left cheek a playful squeeze. "If you insist."

She sucked in a breath. "Oh, I definitely insist."

"Then your wish is most definitely my command." The last pieces of his clothing melted away, giving her the first flesh-on-flesh contact. His penis felt as long and rigid as an iron bar. Nuzzling into the crease of her butt, its crowned head seeped with the first droplets of pre-cum.

Positioning her hips just so, Casedren guided his shaft between her legs. Instead of entering her quickly, he stroked the broad head against her dewy labia, lubricating himself with her cream. The tip of his penis was smooth, promising easy entry.

Dani whimpered, pushing back against his body, trying to entice him to enter. "Are you going to make me beg?"

His breath seized with anticipation. "I am taking my time," he whispered. "As is a king's right." His free hand slid around to fondle her breast. Trapping her nipple, he tugged it gently. Each pull of his fingers sent sparks of pleasure ricocheting off her heightened nerve endings.

Dani squirmed, barely able to catch her breath. "Future king," she said through a moan. Lifting up against him, she felt the solid ridges of his chest against her back. The rub of his naked skin against hers was sweeter and hotter than the delicious blaze he'd lit inside her soul.

Recovering the nipple, he tugged and rolled the tip in a particular way, giving her a taste of erotic pain. "Tease." Her sex rippled, creaming harder, burning hotter.

Dani's hands scrabbled behind her, fingers digging into the flesh of his hips. Her head settled back against his shoulder. She closed her eyes, giving her senses free reign to respond to his touch. "Oh God, hurry up, Casedren. I can't wait much longer."

Hot breath scorched her cheek. "Do you know how long I've waited for this?" His hand skimmed down her stomach until reaching her mound. He dipped a single finger between her labia and stroked the tiny organ. Her clit was engorged, stoked with thousands of nerve endings. A gasp broke from her lips when the end of his finger settled on her damp center and stroked.

Dani dug her nails deep into his skin, making her frustration painfully apparent. Her peaked nipples tingled, as she remembered the delightful suckling he'd given them. "Damn it," she growled, hand digging her nails in. "I want you inside me."

Casedren chuckled. "As my lady wishes." He entered her from behind, his thick, powerful shaft easily filling her to the brim. Their bodies fit together perfectly. "You are so wet and tight, it is like having a virgin." He pulled back briefly, taking a deep breath to control his need. "Holding myself back will be difficult."

A groan close to frustration crept up Dani's throat, working its way free. "Then don't," she grated. "Fuck me until I scream."

Casedren's hip bucked upward, sheathing his erection as far as the limits of their bodies would allow. "You will scream so much my brother will hear your cries of pleasure," he promised.

Heart pounding frantically in her ears, Dani closed her eyes and pressed her body against his. Cock stabbing from behind, Casedren rubbed his finger over her clit, softly at first, then applying more pressure until another grating whimper broke free. "Is this what you wanted?" His words sounded sensuously carnal as he slowly ground his hips against hers.

The ability to speak coherently abandoned her. "Yes, oooohhhh . . . perfect. . . ." Strong muscles clenched together, claiming him with a rippling intensity that went all the way to her toes. She felt every inch of the ridges covering his erection, felt the pulse of a man on the verge of spilling his seed. The pressure intensified, deep and full inside her—and he wasn't wearing any sort of protection.

Her eyelids fluttered shut. *Do I really want this . . .* The answer came almost unconsciously, without much contemplation. Yes, she decided. She did. Even if her body were to be sated today, she knew without doubt she'd desire him again and again. Her gut warned she wouldn't be satisfied until their union was complete.

Between them, they settled into a gliding, rocking motion, reveling in the sensations building between them as momentum climbed toward the peak of orgasm. Her heart thundered, so forcefully she feared she'd pass out from the sheer pleasure he instigated.

As the final moments closed in around them, one of Casedren's hands lifted to her throat, drawing her head back. Her pulse hammered beneath his palm, out of control. His other hand settled across her belly, fingers splayed apart. He leaned back slightly, hips shifting to spear her more deeply than ever before. His final thrust slammed pleasure through her. "Come for me." His erotic order shocked. The unexpected ferocity in his voice pushed her over the edge.

Gasping at the brutal delight behind his last body jolting stroke, Dani felt her sex tighten around his, the searing bands of orgasm coiling into a tight ball deep in her gut. Stomach doing a perfect backflip, the last barrier inside her melted like hot wax. A flood of sensation swamped her.

Helpless to do anything but take the ride to its wild conclusion, Dani barely had time to snatch a breath before orgasm swept through like a hurricane making landfall. Pleasurable waves of tidal force swept in, picking her up and tossing her into a chasm of a pure and delightful bliss. . . .

9

Dani woke to a frosty, overcast morning, the kind of chilly gloom that sent sleeping in straight to the top of her list of things to do. Last night she'd been so depleted from the events of the day—not to mention most vigorous lovemaking—she'd collapsed straight into a dreamless void.

Lids drifting shut, she rolled over and burrowed back under the warm cocoon created by the blankets. Warm, naked male flesh connected with hers. Casedren was curled beside her, his chest rising and falling with the gentle regularity of a deep and wholly contented sleep. She lay for a moment, simply listening to him breathe, a lulling, steady sound.

It felt comfortable to be stretched out beside him, sharing a bed with him. She couldn't imagine a better way to wake up.

A little smile stole across her lips. She could imagine a better way for him to wake up than ball scratching and eye rubbing.

Slipping an arm under his, Dani snuggled closer to her lover. Breasts flattened against the rigid plane of his back, she spread her palm against his lean abdomen. Pressing her face in the soft hollow between his shoulder blades, she inhaled. His odor, skin scented with the mingled scents of perspiration and sexual musk, teased her nostrils. His smell was exotic, hinting of shadows and forbidden secrets.

Her grip tightened. Somehow it felt right to be beside this man—one she'd known a few days. Within that relatively short span, they'd not only become lovers, they'd become conspirators in a common cause. At first she'd been afraid of the challenge he presented, walking alone into an unknown minefield armed only with her wits as a witch and her wiles as a woman. When he'd kissed her, all those fears melted away. She wasn't alone by a long shot. Casedren had made it perfectly clear he intended to stay right beside her.

Curled against him, lulled by the sound of his gentle breathing, she would have sworn she'd been with him not a single night, but dozens. His touch, so new and exiting against her skin, also felt strangely familiar. Admittedly the sparks of attraction had ignited into an unstoppable wildfire. His physical appeal was certainly undeniable.

Yesterday there hadn't been any time or energy to devote to second thoughts. Now that she had a quiet minute to think, Dani sorted through the reasons why she should have refused Casedren's strange proposal. There were dozens, each shot down with a mental arrow as they passed through her mind. The man was like a magnet, some inner force drawing her inexorably into his orbit. He need only crook a finger and she would come running. Embrace her in his arms and she melted. His caress was pure liquid fire, and a single touch incinerated.

I've been charmed came the single giddy thought. It had to be an enchantment, not just the wishing of a twelve-year-old girl spelling to find her one true mate.

So why the hell did everything about him feel so damn right? She'd never even liked sharing a bed, preferring to get up, dress and go home rather than spend a night in a lover's arms. Not that she didn't like sex. Intercourse was fine and well.

Sometimes good, sometimes bad, but rarely spectacular. Orgasms were few and far between, most of them induced by vibrator rather than the skill of her partner.

Casedren.

Oh, he knew how to lay his hands on her in all the right ways. Just the way he looked at her set her heart to thudding. There was a particular spark in his eyes going beyond desire, or even lust, into a place less cerebral and driven by pure instinct alone. A place where the heart ruled the head, and damn the consequences.

Pressing her lips to the curve of his shoulder, she let out a shaky breath. The look in his eyes scared her. A lot.

Not because she didn't appreciate it. Any woman would. It scared her because she wasn't sure she could return the emotion and the affection such adoration engendered. Truth be told, she'd always been a little bit selfish, a little bit remote with the men in her life. She liked the feeling of power that came with being a beautiful woman. She liked stripping, the rush it gave her to watch otherwise intelligent men reduced to slobbering fools.

All for what? A flash of tit and a peek of bare ass? Yes, there was true power in being a woman. A man might have a dick, but she had a pussy. And one pussy could get all the dick in the world. All she had to do was promise to spread her thighs and a man would do anything for her. She knew that power and she used it, extracting cold hard cash. Stripping freed her from the guilt that came with being a predator. Marrying for wealth wasn't a goal, either. She'd always planned to follow her own rules, blaze her own path, as a woman and as a witch.

Wiser heads warned about making plans. The grandest designs of mice and men frequently went awry. Dani hadn't been expecting to be stonewalled by tall, blond and handsome.

Oh, and he wasn't even human.

Too many conflicting thoughts, too many confusing things were beginning to fill her brain to overflowing. Stuff one more in and her skull would surely crack from the pressure, spilling her brains out into a gooey puddle. The path she'd chosen to walk had changed in the blink of an eye. She'd agreed to take the new direction. Where it would lead, she didn't yet know. Finding out would be the adventure of a lifetime. She barely knew Casedren, but one thing was already crystal clear. She was in deep. She'd been brave enough to take the first step. Taking another . . .

Closing her eyes, Dani forced herself to focus on a dark cool oasis in the back of mind, the place where she could find and center her thoughts. No more chaos, no more doubt. There was only Casedren, limp in sleep. The gentle rise and fall of his abdomen under her splayed palm attuned her to the rhythms of his body. With each rise and fall, she couldn't help to be reminded of his cock, of the in and out motions as he'd claimed her. The thought not only enticed. It aroused.

I'm a goner. Casedren had captured her hook, line and sinker. Reeling her in hadn't been difficult at all. Her mouth quirked down in a frown. The strength of his magnetism still unsettled and surprised her. This profound, fierce attraction was totally insane and she knew it. *I'm just the kind of sucker who'd drink the damn Kool-Aid.*

Well, at least the shit would taste good on the way down.

Almost as good as gooey, sweet butterscotch.

She sighed and nuzzled as close as physical limitations would allow. His steady breathing coupled with the warmth of his body banished all her bad thoughts, replacing them with a single good one.

Dani slid her palm lower. Her fingers found and curled around Casedren's privates. His penis, limp and flaccid, just waited for a female to awaken and arouse it.

Lightly nipping his shoulder, she supplied a little hand action, slowing jacking up and down his silky length until a full hard-on raged against her palm.

A low moan broke from Casedren's throat, warning her he was awake—and very aware of her sensual abuse. "No one has ever woken me up like this," he murmured, his dulcet voice still drugged with the aftereffects of deep sleep.

Dani nuzzled the back of his neck. She could barely close her thumb and forefinger around his cock's circumference. "Mmm, thought I'd give it a try and see how you liked it."

Casedren rolled over to face her. Face splitting into a wide grin, perfect white teeth flashed. His blue eyes were twin pools, endlessly deep, warm and inviting. "I like it a lot."

The words slipped out before she had a chance to check them. "I'll do anything to please you." She kept up the slow steady stroke, feeling thick veins rippling along his shaft. Her body responded, nipples drawing into tight buds even as a trickle of moisture seeped between her legs. Her thighs ached from the pounding he'd already given her, but all she could think about was the need to feel him inside her, spearing her sex until she screamed with delight. "Anything at all."

Casedren flipped the covers off, fully exposing their naked bodies. "I can think of a lot of anything," he murmured. His hand came up, tracing the softness of her mouth, the curve of her chin, then her neck. Lower still until his clever fingers found and plucked a waiting nipple. His touch sent a shiver down her spine as muscles deep inside her core tightened with unbidden ferocity.

Face to face they lay still, gazing at each other, content to stroke each other softly. Soon Casedren's father would call him to court, questioning his suitability to be the next head to wear the crown of Sedah. Cellyn, petulant and burning with jealously, would lay his own claim to the throne in no uncertain terms. Such a challenge would undoubtedly lead to violence. It was possible the danger could cost one or both of them their life.

Dani didn't want to think about any of that. She wanted to enjoy this moment, basking in the brief lull of peace and contentment it offered.

Dazzled by the beauty of his exquisite features, she had to wonder how a man so handsome could be descended from such a dark creator. He appeared more angelic, his blond locks shining against the snow-white pillowcase beneath his head. His lithe body simmered with untapped strength. To touch him, to be taken by him, hadn't been any sacrifice on her part. It was a pleasure, one she looked forward to enjoying again.

And again.

Casedren broke the lull by gently tugging her peaked nipple. "All I want to do is make love to you again." He raked his fingertips down her abdomen. Finding the crux between her thighs, he slid his hands between her legs. Her clit pulsed with immediate attention.

Dani caught her breath, turning it into a sigh. "Ohhhh . . ." She bit her bottom lip when his thick fingers found the tiny cluster of sensual nerve endings.

Pressing his fingers against her clit, he smiled. "Feel good?"

Dani rolled her hips against his hand, a hint she wanted more. "Very," she breathed. Sparks of pleasure poured through her veins.

He delved, slipping a finger inside. Strong inner muscles rippled and clenched. "You are so wet."

"Am I?"

His hand slipped away, then two fingers penetrated. "Oh yes."

Dani shifted onto her back, spreading her legs wider. "That's because I'm waiting for that nice hard cock of yours to be put to good use."

Dragging his fingers out of her creamy depth, Casedren

chuckled. "I can do that." Rolling on top of her, he supported his weight on outstretched arms as he eased his naked body atop hers. His cock settled against the soft nest of her smooth belly, stiff and ready to penetrate her sex.

Dani slid her arms around his waist, settling her palms on the curves of his perfect ass. "Much better."

Hair spilling over his face, he grinned down at her. "I am glad you approve."

She dug the tips of her nails lightly into his skin. "Oh, I do."

Casedren lowered his head as she lifted hers. Their mouths came together, the beginning of a slow, sweet kiss promising to weave into something more erotic, more intense.

Too bad it wasn't destined to last. Their lovemaking was rudely spoiled by a loud chiming sound.

Groaning low in his throat, Casedren cursed against the pillow of her lips. "Damn."

"What?" she murmured back, still nuzzled against him.

The chime sounded again, coming from nowhere, yet filling the entire room with its melodic sound.

Casedren sighed and rolled away, taking his beautiful cock with him. The distraction had already begun to play havoc with his desire. "A message is on the way."

Barely able to think through the erotic haze enveloping her senses, Dani had to make a grab for her brain. "A message?" She looked around, wondering where those damn chimes had come from. She didn't remember conjuring any when decorating the room.

The answer appeared right before her eyes.

A tiny speck of light winked on, hovering a few feet above their bodies. The light glowed, spitting out a series of sparking green flames. For a moment they flared with such intensity that Dani had to look away. When the light faded, a small iridescent creature fluttered in its wake.

Dani blinked. Roughly the size of a kitten, the creature

looked like some kind of horned toad gone mutant. Leather wings webbed with eerie luminescent veins of a particular crimson shade beat the air with slow strokes. Aerodynamically the damned thing shouldn't have been able to hover, but the normal rules governing physics didn't seem to apply in Sedah. A scroll was clenched between two rows of impressively sharp fangs.

She shook her head in disbelief. "Is that what I think it is?"

Casedren retrieved the scroll with a casual and familiar ease. He obviously didn't mind that the flying lizard could snap a finger right off. "Yes," he said, unrolling the parchment. "It is a dragon courier." He scanned the message, written on thick parchment.

She eyed the ugly beastie a little closer. "That's a dragon? An honest-to-God dragon?"

"Yes, it is."

She squinted. "Are they really that little?"

He shrugged. "That is about as big as they get."

She extended a tentative finger. "Will it bite?" Curious, the critter hovered closer. It seemed to want to be petted.

"They like a good chucking under the chin. Go ahead. You can pet it."

Half-afraid, half-fascinated, Dani crooked her index finger under its little chin and scratched. The little dragon automatically raised it head to enjoy the treat. A kind of trilling purr rumbled from its throat.

She smiled. "It's kind of cute."

"See? Not everything about Sedah is all terrible."

Tired of scratching, Dani let her hand drop. Startled, the miniature dragon flitted back, hovering. "I never said it was terrible. Just . . . different. Way, way, way different." She managed to pull her attention off the messenger long enough to glance at the note in his hand. Brow wrinkled in consternation, he didn't look pleased. "What does it say?"

He flicked the paper with more than a little annoyance. "It is from my father. He sends his greetings—and a summons. He expects us in his private chambers within in the hour. I was hoping he would allow us a few days to settle in, but he is clearly impatient."

His words sent her heart into a double-time step. "An hour," she croaked. "It takes me at least three hours just to get out of bed."

Casedren shook his head. "We will have to make haste then." He glanced at the waiting messenger. "Tell my father we will be there, as he expects."

The minidragon bobbed its horned head. Instead of taking flight right away, it hovered, waiting.

"What does it want?"

"Ah, I forgot." Casedren held out the parchment.

The dragon puffed, fire streaming from its nostrils. Flames devoured the page, consuming it so thoroughly not even ashes remained. Seemingly satisfied, the winged courier turned tail and vanished.

Dani slowly shook her head. "That was totally bizarre."

Casedren smiled. "Dragons have to have something to do nowadays."

"That's cool. Dragon Courier Service." She snorted an unintended giggle. "I can see the commercial now: We deliver, to hell and back." Damn. She'd certainly stumbled into a strange place. An alternate world, a three-headed beast, rooms with invisible servants and miniature dragons delivering the mail.

Casedren cocked his head good-naturedly. "So you think Sedah is hell?"

"If it's not, it's pretty close to what I'd imagine." The moment the words came of her mouth, Dani felt a stab of guilt. She hoped she hadn't just stuck her foot in her mouth. Shoe leather wasn't her favorite snack.

Good humor draining away, his expressive eyes cooled. He studied her a long moment before he spoke. "Sedah is an entirely self-governing dominion. Our dimensions have been intertwined since, literally, the beginning of time. One would not exist without the other. And while the battle lines between our people have been drawn for ages uncounted, not all Jadian men are so demented as to want to see both realms drowning in the flames of destruction," he said after a long pause. "We are neither immortals nor eternal. Destroy your world and we would also effectively obliterate our own. If we have no mates, there would be no children. No children would eventually lead to the extinction of the species. I cannot speak for all of us, but I am certainly not suicidal or homicidal. Those who are—we deal with them as we have to, as we must to ensure survival."

Time to back off pointing fingers, especially as precious minutes continued to tick away. "I didn't mean to insult or offend you," she said by way of an apology. "That makes sense. You'd think anyone with a half brain would think about it."

Expression warming again, Casedren gave her a rueful smile. "There will always be a snake in the Garden of Eden." He hesitated a moment. "Recognizing the enemy is half the battle."

Her gaze settled on him, probing and intent. "I don't know why you belittle yourself, Casedren," she said softly. "You seem to be a very wise man."

He took her hands in his own, caressing her palm with long, cool fingers. "I am not a wise man, just one who wants to live."

Casedren's touch smudged her palm with the lingering traces of ash from the message he'd burned. Curiosity niggled. "Why burn the message?"

He brushed the smudge away with his thumb and a quick kiss. "Private communications between the king and his subjects are always destroyed." He shrugged. "It is just the way my father works. His methods have kept him on the throne over five centuries. He is the eighth king to rule the throne since the accomplishment of the *Evania Isibis,* the law of which only the king is above."

She drew in a rattling breath as her gaze trekked over his face, searching for the truth and hoping she wouldn't find it. "The king alone can break the treaty?"

Casedren smiled thinly. "That, or whoever deposes him and seizes the Scepter of Inara."

His words struck home with a stomach-turning jolt. Dani mentally applied palm to forehead. Oh, and mustn't forget the vengeful twin who wants a shot at kicking Casedren's ass so he can seize the throne and obliterate the rights and liberties of human beings and return planet earth to the chaos under demonic rule. "The scepter has that much power?"

He shook his head. "Like a crown, it is only a symbol. A king's true power lies in his ability to be as ruthless as he is merciful." He sighed, deeply and fitfully, clearly disturbed by the thought. "The games of intrigue and assassination are clever maneuverings I am not sure I could ever sustain. The odds are overwhelming, and eventually mistakes are made."

A gut-level sense of unease knotted in her bowels. "Your mother—" she started to say.

Casedren's eyes narrowed, his blue gaze turning hard and unpleasant. "Yes, my own mother," he managed to say before his voice disappeared in a tangle of disbelief and grief. A deep breath pulled his composure together. "Taken down by a dream-spell as she slept."

The hair on the nape of Dani's neck rose. "A dream-spell?" This sounded ominous. She'd heard of entities able to invade people's sleep, but never one able to inflict a harm as terrible as death.

"Mind-walking is a gray area of magick, not exactly forbidden because it allows communication to take place between the

Magus on a deeper, more intimate level," Casedren explained grimly. "Usually it is done between those sharing certain intimacies, or those who wish to keep communications private."

"But?" she asked, knowing it would only get worse.

It did.

"There are certain spells enabling a conjurer to walk into others' minds when they are at their weakest—sleeping or otherwise unconscious—and invade their dreams. Once the invading entity assumes control on the astral level, he can convince his victims that what is happening is absolutely real."

Dani's heart lurched, not the first time since entering this twisted landscape. And probably not for the last time. "So if they kill me in my mind and I believe it, I'm dead?"

Casedren nodded slowly. The shadows of sadness flickered in the depth of his eyes. "Even if there isn't a physical scratch on you. If the invader can convince you that what is happening to you is real, it is. The only defense you have is your sense of self, to have a will stronger than your assailant."

The image of crimson-tipped claws tearing out her throat flashed through her brain. Everyone had a panic button, a certain fear that would send them straight over the edge. In the hands of an enemy, the unreal could be exploited. The idea of being trapped inside her own mind terrified her.

How do you fight something that can step into your skull?

Dani licked dry lips, a slick sheen of perspiration rising on her naked skin. Shivering, she reached for the comforter, pulling it up to cover her breasts. She suddenly felt open to the elements, an exposure traveling past the physical and straight into the metaphysical. "My God," she blurted. "Can anyone defend themselves against that?" Just a few hours ago she'd been snoozing like the dead.

Casedren sensed her fear, his demeanor suddenly changing from one of anger to protectiveness. He reached out, giving her bare shoulder a suggestive stroke. The goose bumps chilling her skin scurried away. The heat of desire in his eyes and the need behind his touch was enough to keep an arctic storm at bay.

"It is not as terrible as it sounds."

She fixed him with a pointed look. "Oh? Sounds pretty damn bad to me. Very disturbing, in fact. Given the power of your people it's a wonder any of you survive a day, much less centuries."

He gave a small, sad smile. "An uninvited entity can enter your mind only if there is a weak spot or hole in your aura," he said softly. "Intoxication, extreme mental distress, negative emotions such as hate—even extreme exhaustion. All of these things can leave you vulnerable to attack." He grimaced. "In my mother's case it was a simple sleeping potion in her wine."

His expression resigned, Casedren shrugged helplessly. "I know what you are thinking," he said perceptively. "Is it any wonder I have dreaded the arrival of this day? Become king and I will have to surrender my entire life to preserve our world in a civil manner." He broke off. Unable to look into her eyes, he turned his gaze toward the fire snapping in the hearth.

What Dani saw within those snapping flames offered a picture as dismal as it was terrifying. Heart thudding dully in her chest, she struggled to swallow past the lump in her throat. "Step aside and you sacrifice mine," she murmured.

10

At the appointed hour, Dani Wallace and Casedren Teraketh presented themselves in the private chambers of King Bastien III, supreme ruler of the Jadian people.

As this was to be a private meeting between a father and his sons, no council members of the king's advisory cabinet were present except for Minister Gareth. No formal or public announcements would be made until a single question could be answered: which twin was to follow in his father's footsteps? Until then, it was a private matter to be settled behind closed doors. It was also an unprecedented one. While other grabs had been made to unseat the Teraketh bloodline from the throne, never before had brother challenged brother for the right of ascension.

As before, Casedren was dressed in clothing similar to those he'd greeted Dani in. Resplendent in the strangely mixed styles of other ages, Casedren looked confident. Except for looking a bit pale, he didn't seem bothered by the pressure knuckling down on his head.

Dani was dressed far more formally than she'd been the day

before, wearing a sort of princess gown with long flowing sleeves and split overlay of sheer fabric, linen under skirt and velvet bodice. The muted ivory shade reminded her of a wedding gown. Except her shade wouldn't be pure white because she wasn't a virgin. The style of the dress certainly marked her as a scarlet women. The bodice was cut down to her nipples, almost to the point of her breasts spilling over. She had to take care not to step on the dress as she walked, otherwise her tits would come tumbling out for all to view.

Far from hiding her under modest clothing, Casedren seemed to be showing her off. She'd glimpsed a few women as they'd traveled to meet the king's deadline and most were dressed in a similar way. The Jadian males appeared to be very proud of the females they'd acquired as mates and didn't hesitate to show off their assets.

Standing to their left, and as far away as the physical limitations of the chamber would allow, Cellyn had chosen to take another route. His dress reflected a more military leaning, right down to the sword strapped at his side. He would neither look at Casedren nor acknowledge Dani's presence. The brief glance he'd cast her way slashed right through. She didn't have the right to exist in his world.

Though Cellyn wouldn't give her the time of day, she had plenty of opportunities to get a good look at him. Lean and muscular, he was every bit as striking as his twin. Booted feet planted slightly apart, hands clasped behind his back, he stood as rigid as stone. The set of his mouth and the tension in his jaw lent a pitiless cast to otherwise pleasing features. He didn't have to speak a single word to reveal his state of mind. Jealousy oozed from every pore like poison.

Dani had no doubt that he'd been behind his mother's assassination. Without a doubt Cellyn possessed ambition. Cold-blooded murder probably wasn't beyond him if it would advance his personal agenda within the Jadian court. She sensed he felt stifled but was close to breaking free. Through most of his life he'd bided his time, gathering his confidants, building a cadre of men who'd blindly serve his visions of destruction—even if they, too, were destroyed in the rush to assert racial superiority. Time and time again, history had proven it to be the strategy of a fool and a psychopath. Countless lives lost, countless souls sacrificed. The toll mattered not as long as the madman could survey the carnage and believe he'd won the battle.

Cellyn was that kind, willing to plunge them all into hell to reclaim a power he believed lost to his people.

Dani forced herself to stop sneaking glances at Casedren's twin, instead focusing her attention on the chamber around them. She definitely felt out of her element as she stood before King Bastien. His private chambers were fashioned out of what appeared to be pure crystal. The glass had been cut in prisms that refracted the light outside, giving the whole place a dark, almost gloomy cast. The walls around them were decorated with luxurious tapestries and banners, emblem of the Teraketh bloodline.

King Bastien sat upon a lounge draped with silk in a rich cerulean shade. He was dressed in an ensemble of white shirt, vest and tight breeches cut off at the knee. Black boots polished to a shine took up where his breeches left off. A three-quarter-length frock coat fashioned out of dark velvet completed his outfit. Silvery-blond hair stretched past his shoulders. His piercing gaze missed nothing.

At a glance he looked to be in his late fifties, certainly no more than barely past middle age. By the look of him he was still a vital, vibrant man. The lines etched at the corner of his eyes and mouth were the only signs of his bereavement. Grief over his recent loss had taken its toll. Mouth set firmly, he clearly wasn't pleased with the matter at hand.

Pale and drawn, but straight and dignified, Minister Gareth indicated it was time to proceed.

"We gather here today to designate the next heir to the Jadian throne," he said, solemnly addressing King Bastien. "As you are in the unusual position of having twin sons, we must have your word on which will be the next king."

Head barely moving, King Bastien looked from one son to the other. Outwardly he was solemn, as befitted this most serious of occasions. His face was impassive as he looked at Cellyn, silently considering the younger of the twins. Though no smile crossed his lips, the glint of satisfaction in his eyes spoke silently of his regard for his second son.

As for Casedren . . .

King Bastien next glanced to the eldest of the twins. His mouth betrayed him, settling into a deep frown as his gaze ranged over Casedren. He clearly was not pleased with the young man standing in front of him—or the decision he would have to make.

Watching from her place, Dani noticed the fine beads of perspiration forming on Casedren's hairline. She knew he did not want to be here, did not want to take the throne. He did it to preserve the uneasy peace in his world and to salvage the future of hers.

You cannot choose Cellyn, she thought, desperately focusing to make her thoughts clear so her message could be heard. There was a chance, a slim chance, King Bastien would hear her silent plea.

Closing her eyes, she silently tried to transmit her thoughts toward the old king, hoping he would realize what Casedren was doing, the sacrifice he was making, to serve his people.

"What say you, my liege?" Minister Gareth prodded.

King Bastien stared at his sons for a long moment before he found his voice. "It is my declaration that Casedren become my successor," he said quietly.

Hearing his words, Dani's heart skipped a beat. Oh, thank heavens! The old man wasn't senile or out of his mind, as she'd feared. He seemed perfectly capable of making the correct decision and following through.

But it wasn't to be that easy.

Casedren had already warned her Cellyn would protest, as was his right by law. Like a prosecuting attorney, he had the right to present an argument and prove his brother unfit.

Pleased, Minister Gareth turned to Prince Casedren. "By the law and custom of our people, he who is to ascend the throne must have a consort of agreeable lineage. My lord, have you a woman who will stand at your side and swear she is to be your queen?"

Casedren nodded steadily. "I have chosen the woman I believe will make a most suitable queen to the Jadian people. She is Wyr and a witch, a most advantageous conquest."

The first spark of interest lit King Bastien's eyes. "Is it true you have found one of these rare creatures?"

Dani blanched. *Rare creatures?* She wondered if she'd sprouted a horn in the center of her forehead. King Bastien spoke with the reverence of one who'd glimpsed a unicorn.

Casedren inclined his head in respectful reverence. "That is correct." He caught Dani's hand, giving it a quick squeeze for reassurance before leading her closer to the imposing figure. "Father, this is Danicia Wallace." He paused, clearing his throat. "She is the woman I intend to wed."

King Bastien skimmed Dani from head to foot. He clearly liked what he saw. For the first time a hint of a smile turned up one corner of his fine mouth. For a gentleman of indeterminate age, he was a handsome fellow himself. It was easy to see where his sons had gotten their looks.

The old monarch lifted an approving brow. "I had feared my eldest would never find a suitable wife." Rising from his place, the king offered his hand. "You may approach."

Having been prompted by Casedren, Dani stepped forward. Taking his hand between her own, she gave a brief but formal bow, an acknowledgement of respect for his position by a visitor. "It is my honor to stand before you today," she said, hoping the words Casedren had hurriedly pressed her to memorize came out correctly.

Having done as she'd been prompted, Dani stepped back and folded her hands demurely in front of her. She glanced down at her bosom, relieved her breasts hadn't escaped the confines of her gown. God, how did the women stand wearing these ridiculous things? Right now she'd have given her right arm for a comfortable pair of faded jeans, her favorite Baby Brat T-shirt and a well-worn pair of sneakers. Though the witchy-Goth leather boots she wore were sexy enough, they were killing her feet.

As for the idea of actually marrying Casedren, everything in her rebelled against the idea of exchanging her modern twenty-first-century world for this forbidding realm locked in ice and gloom.

Yet if she said yes, there was no doubt that she'd have a husband who would love and cherish her unto the end of her days. The thought of going back to her old life after having had Casedren seemed equally unacceptable. If only she could have Casedren *and* live in her own world. That would be perfection, paradise achieved.

Her mouth quirked down at the thought. Casedren probably wouldn't want to live in a basement apartment beneath her brother's house.

Well, that was something to be worked out at a later time. Right now, she needed to concentrate on matters at hand and not let her attention wander toward fanciful daydreams.

From beneath her lashes, Dani sneaked another glance at King Bastien. He looked impressed. "I am most pleased with your choice."

Dani breathed a sigh of relief. Good. *This just might work.*

All she had to do was continue to play her role in the manner Casedren had outlined. Cellyn could challenge, but winning reconsideration in his own favor would be tough.

Bastien considered Dani for a long moment, then gave Casedren a small, knowing smile. "You have, of course, carnal knowledge of this woman and have found her suitable?"

A blush creeping to his face, Casedren nodded tightly. "Yes, lord." He slipped his hand into Dani's, offering another small squeeze of unity. She squeezed back to let him know he had her full support. "I have engaged in physical relations with this woman and found her to be most pleasing."

Bastien studied their not-so-subtle move, appearing intrigued. Eyeing her with pure admiration, he pursed his lips. "My lady," he began most graciously. "I know you are unfamiliar with our ways and laws, though I am sure my son has given you some idea of what you would be facing when you agreed to become his consort."

Her fingers tightening around Casedren's, Dani nodded. "I am aware, my lord," she said, smiling easily.

Another step in the right direction. "Good. Then I must ask if you find my son to be a pleasing lover?"

Though she'd been warned as to the personal nature of some questions she might be asked, Dani blinked at the question. She was unprepared to unfurl her private life in front of strangers, share every intimate detail.

She decided to be diplomatic. The less details, the better. "I have," she said simply. There was no way in hell she'd tell any of the men present about Casedren's magical ability to deliver orgasms that made her scream with delight.

Bastien grinned, appreciating her brevity. "If the lady is satisfied, then so am I."

Casedren smiled, relief in his gaze. "Thank you, father. My only desire is to fulfill my duties to the crown. I a-am—" He stumbled but quickly recovered. "I am prepared to serve the Jadian people in a manner that will continue to preserve their rights and liberties as free-thinking beings."

An inelegant snort of disgust interrupted.

"Fine words, indeed, from a man who has never shown a single day's regard for the rights and liberties of his people," Cellyn muttered, speaking in a way that indicated he fully intended his words to be heard.

"You speak out of turn," Minister Gareth started to warn.

Annoyance flashing across his face, Bastien cut his minister off with a savage gesture. "I am already well aware of Cellyn's protest against Casedren's ascension." He sighed and cocked his head, clearly weary of the whole matter. "You may continue, Cellyn. The sooner you are heard out, the sooner this can be settled."

Dani struggled to stifle a groan. She had a feeling once Cellyn got to talking, nothing would be settled soon, or easily.

11

Relishing his time in the spotlight, Cellyn stepped forward. "By law and by blood, it is my right to speak out against Casedren inheriting the crown based solely on the fact that his birth precedes mine by a mere ten minutes." He held up his hands, spreading all his fingers. "Ten minutes is his only qualification. By that alone he is seen fit to become a ruler. But is it enough?" His hands clenched in a move meant to add drama to his words. "In this instance I firmly believe it is not."

Minister Gareth broke in. "I beg to differ, but our laws clearly state the firstborn son. Given those ten minutes qualifies your brother, unequivocally."

Cellyn smiled a shark's grin, all teeth and no mirth. "Definitely, from your point of view, but not irrevocably from mine. By the law, a future sovereign may be removed from the line of succession if he is found to be mentally, physically or morally infirm."

Minister Gareth interrupted. "All of which are nullified in Prince Casedren's case."

Cellyn sniffed. "Be you so sure, Minister?"

Gareth stood firm. "Of course. I would be the first to recommend Casedren's removal had I found him to be inadequate in any way." He lobbed a visual warning toward Cellyn. "Just as I would were the positions reversed."

Cellyn smirked. "Just as I hope you will once you have fully heard my argument. While it is true that Casedren has no mental or physical defect, I will argue that he does have a moral one—one that may prove to be the deadliest of all."

King Bastien's frown showed his distaste for the entire scene unfolding before his eyes. "Although I am not pleased with your claim, Cellyn," he said heavily, "I am prepared to hear you out and render judgment."

"With all respect, my liege," Cellyn said deferentially, "I act as my heart tells me I must."

"Something tells me it is more than his heart," Casedren muttered in a low tone.

Cellyn turned on his brother. "You will not speak so irreverently once I finish what I have to say."

Casedren returned a smile that barely escaped insolence. "No doubt we will hear everything you can think of to smear my character."

Cellyn sneered back. "Of course you would mistake the facts for an attack."

Minister Gareth's voice rumbled through. "Both of you are out of line. I suggest you put bickering aside and continue as civilized gentlemen. If you are incapable of further restraining yourselves, you will both be removed from the presence of the king."

Both brothers immediately retreated from the argument. King Bastien's face had returned to its former blank and unreadable state. His forehead ridged a little, but no more emotion escaped him. Again the long silence settled on the chamber, as emotions stretched too tightly for anyone to consider speaking.

Cellyn finally inclined his head in reverence to his father. "Forgive my display of emotion, father. It will not happen again."

Bastien nodded. "Continue what you had to say."

Cellyn drew a long breath, then spoke. "Just to be eldest son, as we both know, is not enough. A king requires a queen. In this case, Casedren has scrambled to make himself a more desirable candidate by acquiring a harlot of supposed noble Wyr blood."

Hearing his reference to her, Dani felt hot sparks of anger ignite inside her. Aware an outburst of any sort would be unwelcome, she clenched her hands into tight fists, fighting to hold still. How dare that goddamn asshole take a high hand with her. Given the chance she'd be glad to slap the smirk off his face.

Although she hadn't meant for it to, her anger apparently poured into Casedren. Eyes sparking, he immediately rounded on his twin. "How dare you call my chosen a harlot. Such a slur against her character is out of line and completely uncalled for."

Cellyn stood, rocklike and patient. "Forgive me for calling your intended a harlot, brother. The word was entirely inappropriate."

"You are damn right it is," Casedren steamed.

Cellyn unleashed a shark's grin. "What I meant to say was *prostitute.*" He turned to Dani and dug in. "Is that not a more correct term in your world for women who fuck men for money?"

Mouth dropping open, Dani felt her heart take a plunge straight to her feet. Although she'd been paid to dance privately for Casedren, she didn't consider having sex with him also tied into the exchange of money for her professional services. Others might misconstrue the truth, and rightly so.

Refusing to be shamed for her impulsive desires, she raised her chin. "I'm not a whore," she grated in her own defense. "I slept with Casedren because I wanted him, not because he paid me." Nevertheless the damning accusation was a deep stain on her character, not to mention the poor light it cast on Casedren. It appeared as if he had neither time nor inclination to find himself a proper bride.

Cellyn ignored her outburst and continued his attack. "To meet his eligibility, Casedren has claimed this female as his consort." He pointed a damning finger at Dani. "A woman he met and seduced barely a day before his return to stake his claim."

Minister Gareth shrugged, trying to minimize the damage of the blow Cellyn had dealt. "By law, Prince Casedren must only have carnal knowledge of his future consort. How long he has had the knowledge of her is irrelevant. Love—" he chuckled dismissively "—is not always an equation in marriage. All that counts is their satisfaction with each other."

Cellyn rolled his eyes in mock exaggeration. "By the law he qualifies still," he sneered. "But it is by those same laws I may challenge his right. Birth order alone isn't a qualification when twins are concerned. In such an event, one must consider a man's entire life—not the impulse of a single day. You must ask yourselves now: Has Casedren truly fulfilled duty to his kingdom and fellow citizens?"

Having removed himself from the argument over Dani's suitability, King Bastien leaned forward in his seat. "You argue your points well, Cellyn," he conceded grudgingly. "More and more my eyes are opening as to the truth in the matter."

Pleased, Cellyn flicked his hand in clear dismissal. Already he had the attitude of a king, if not the actual title. "I have studied our laws extensively, as one would expect a future sovereign to be knowledgeable of the treaty and constitution governing the Magus."

"That is clear," Bastien allowed.

Cellyn smiled "Then compare my life to my brother's and you will see clear discrepancies in our characters. I have spent most of my life in armed service, ferreting out those who conspire against our beholden laws in their seeking to bastardize legitimate magick." He pointed to his brother, the callous light of the fanatic dwelling in his gaze. "Casedren has not drawn even a blade from its sheath, much less spent a single hour searching for the assassins who so cruelly deprived us of our queen and mother. Instead he has chosen to devote himself to his studies, preferring musty old books to the solid experience of action on the field of battle. Moreover he has spent most of his years living out of Sedah, seeking out the company of humans to his own people."

Dani winced. That sounded pretty damning to her. The way Cellyn was framing his brother, Casedren was an irresponsible, uncaring lout, interested in satisfying his own needs and impulses to the detriment of everyone else. Countering such an argument would be almost impossible.

Doubt crept in, uninvited and unwelcome. Given the circumstances, she didn't need this little imp to show up just now. But it wouldn't go away, persisting in perching itself on her shoulder and whispering in her ear all the things she dare not think. Opened, the floodgates in her mind couldn't be closed. Like opening Pandora's Box, too many things were let loose, never to be recovered.

Prince Charming's armor was beginning to show signs of tarnish. Moreover, it looked like he was about to be unseated from his valiant steed by the black knight.

Wasn't this just her luck? Once again one of her damn spells had gone off-track, hooking her up with some half-assed prince of an underworld domain. Casedren might be a nice guy, but there was truth in the saying that nice guys finished last. Oh yeah. They also got their dicks knocked in the dirt.

Charging in with guns blazing, Cellyn was doing a stellar job blowing his twin out of the water. Had the fight been physical, Casedren would probably be watching his teeth drop out of his mouth like Chiclets. Cellyn wasn't just taking names. He was kicking ass. Badly. If he kept it up, Casedren wouldn't have a shred of dignity left. Not that he had much now.

Dani shot a look at her pseudosuitor. *He'd better have some damn good tricks up his sleeve.*

"Cellyn makes several strong points," Minister Gareth conceded. "But are these points truly enough to disqualify Casedren as your successor?"

Cellyn scoffed in rebuttal. "Isn't it clear Casedren's interests, his sympathies, are with the inferior race? He truly forgets how great a people we truly are." He fixed his father under a hammering gaze. "Something I believe we have all forgotten. All our days of glory have truly dimmed to nothing more than memories. It is a sad day when our people forget their fighting hearts and fierce spirits."

Dani clamped down on the bleat of a laugh threatening to sneak past her lips. She had to stop herself from giving a dramatic eye roll. Oh damn. Cellyn was really hitting hard, appealing to their patriotic spirits. Nothing funny about it, though. Those were the kinds of words that could very will tip the balance in his favor.

Not good. Not good at all.

Dani didn't have to wonder what it would be like to be on the losing side if the Jadians decided to wage war against humankind again. She'd already been given a glimpse of that future, and it was a bleak one.

But the future wasn't carved in stone. Minister Nash's book of prophecy was a guide, not an absolute. There were always two paths to choose between. The wise took heed and prepared.

As if sensing her thought, Casedren briefly smiled her way. His calm magnetism flowed out to envelope her, reminding her all over again why she'd been attracted to him in the first place. When he looked her way, his eyes lit up as though seeing a goddess in the flesh.

Remembering the way he'd touched her, caressed her naked skin, Dani felt a hot flush steal into her cheeks. Closing her eyes she could envision his hard body mantling her soft one. A shivering ripple spread through her. Closer than their bodies could come together, though, she remembered sinking into him, the two of them blending briefly into a single unit. Touching, surging, responding, mouth to mouth, breasts to chest, his cock filling her eager sex.

Somehow, for some reason, she belonged to Casedren. Where the future might take them, she still didn't know. All she did know was that they'd have to face it together. Her decision was made half-consciously, driven more by instinct than any cognizant thought.

Having heard Cellyn's argument in its entirety, King Bastien looked at his eldest son with weary patience. Troubled shadows brewed in his eyes.

"Your brother presents a solid argument against you, Casedren," he said in a tone displaying no emotion. "Truth be told, I am fully aware you have never aspired to walk in my footsteps."

A spasm of panic clutched Dani's throat. Fear grabbed at her heart with small, steely fingers. *Oh shit. This isn't good.*

Cellyn turned to her, a gloating smile on his face. The space between them buzzed, taking on electric life as the lines of psychic communication opened. A strange pressure slammed into her forehead and a sudden spark flared as their minds connected. Cellyn knew what she'd been thinking, and he was ready to respond.

It will be better, the wolf snapped, lips drawn back in a bestial smile, *when you belong to me.*

Dani reeled, fighting to steady herself. Remembering what Casedren had said about the Jadian ability to mind-walk, Dani immediately clamped down on her mental defenses. Fear had lowered her defenses, letting him creep in through the cracks.

I'll never belong to you, she screamed into the void between them.

Cellyn scowled darkly, sending a strike that penetrated her brain with fiery shards. The sharp, dizzying smell of sulfur pinched her nostrils. *You will,* he silently taunted back. *And when I have you, I'll fuck you in ways my brother could not even begin to imagine.*

Grinding her teeth, Dani signaled back. *Never going to happen, asshole!* Determined to force him out, she envisioned a steel wall slamming down hard and cutting off the unwanted invader. She backed it up with a quick spell of self-protection.

In the shadow, evil hides, trying to draw me from love's side. Send evil away, send evil astray, never again to pass my way.

Their mental connection disintegrated in a burst of sparks, then the rush into a black void. The blood clearly drained from Cellyn's face. He hadn't been expecting her to counter his assault so fiercely. Fully realizing the extent of her retaliation, his gaze turned icy, chilling her with the sudden rush of hate powering its intensity.

He would get even. Not a threat. A promise.

Clamping down on the cry scraping her throat, Dani licked dry lips. It had lasted only a second, two at the most, but she felt totally drained, as if something had attached itself to her soul and begun to suck away her life-force. With grim sureness she found herself thinking that this initial trial was only the beginning of a longer, harder road for Casedren—and for her—to walk. It would all be uphill from now on.

Oblivious of Cellyn's sneak attack, Casedren and his father continued their argument.

"But father," Casedren started to say.

Bastien held up a commanding hand. "Let me finish, boy."

Chastised, Casedren nodded solemnly. "Yes, sire."

Bastien's dark features momentarily held great conflict. He quickly shook it off, slipping on the impassive mask of the composed monarch. "It is true you would make a reluctant monarch. Therefore I ask you now: Do you wish to step aside in favor of Cellyn?"

Dani's breath stalled. Surely Casedren wouldn't say yes.

He didn't. "Absolutely not. I will fight him every step of the way to stake my claim as rightful heir to the throne."

She relaxed. Thank God. Despite his gentle demeanor, Casedren did have a spine after all.

King Bastien looked to Cellyn. "And you?"

Cellyn's jaw tightened. "I will fight it to the end as well. I do not believe Casedren morally fit to take the Jadian throne."

Silence.

King Bastien grimaced. His anemic hollow-eyed frown revealed the depth and seriousness of the decision he'd been called upon as monarch to make. Clearly, he favored Cellyn. Given the choice of the favorite child, Cellyn would clearly win the throne. The law, however, bound him to choose Casedren, a child for whom he seemed to have little regard.

Minister Gareth finally spoke up. "There is only one way to settle this, my liege."

Bastien nodded. "I suppose you are right, Gareth. I am hardly in the position to make such a choice. Given the task before us, we shall have to let the old wisdom prevail."

The old wisdom?

A slow chill crept into the back of Dani's mind. From her experience in the cultic world and her knowledge of the craft, she was fully aware that to refer to the old wisdom usually entailed the invocation of some slumbering entity believed to have a greater knowledge than those seeking answers. Knowing the origins of Casedren's people, could there be any doubt as to the entity to be consulted?

The devil himself would surely smile upon Cellyn's dark heart. And heartily approve his ascension.

Sure some bad shit was about to go down, she glanced to

Minister Gareth, their closest ally in the battle to help Casedren retain the throne. He did not seem at all unsettled by the king's decision.

Having decided his course, Bastien gestured in a ritual manner. "It pains me to see my sons pitted against each other, but I suppose it was inevitable this day should come," he finally said. "Casedren, I have always known you did not want the throne, yet you would act as duty compelled. Cellyn, your heart has been there from the beginning, but destiny made another choice for you. To follow the law, Casedren is my chosen. By the same rule, Cellyn has challenged my choice, calling into question fate's hand. In doing that he has effectively tied my hands and blinded my eyes. The choice, my sons, can no longer be my own."

As if to echo the king's word, a ragged threatening thunder rolled outside. The sky outside the crystal chamber, already overcast with leaden clouds, rolled and darkened. A storm was brewing, a menacing omen.

Dani couldn't help but flinch. She didn't like where this was leading. A single glance at Casedren was all it took to realize the ground had shifted under their feet, and not for the better. Casedren's brow was wrinkled in perplexed dismay. This was a development he clearly hadn't seen coming. The broadside escalated his clash with Cellyn onto an entirely different level. He could no longer assume the throne was his simply because he had adhered to constitutional law.

She mentally applied her palm to her forehead in despair. *Oh terrific.* Casedren's fate—and hers—now rested in the hands of some unknown entity.

Cellyn, it seemed, had played the better hand, holding all the winning cards close to his vest.

Minister Gareth bowed ceremonially. "What is your will?" he asked, voice close to breaking from the tension gripping the room and its occupants.

Stepping up to Casedren, King Bastien placed his hands on his son's shoulders. Cellyn's eyes followed his father's movements, his gaze unveiling naked hatred for both men. His lips moved as he whispered, "Check."

Dani clenched her fists and lowered her inner wall long enough to throw a taunt his way, like a kid tossing a water balloon. *But not mate.*

The moment she'd done it, she realized its ineffectiveness. Cellyn just sneered in acknowledgement and gloated over what he perceived to be the victory at his hand. His entire life had led to this moment and he clearly intended to savor his victory.

He knew this would happen, Dani reflected once her mental fortification had settled back into its place. *This is exactly what he wanted.* Whatever it was, Cellyn honestly believed Casedren would fail.

Cellyn had gambled. But had he truly won? That remained to be seen.

Suddenly weary under the weight of the office he'd borne so long, Bastien tried for a smile and found none. "My elder son, the first birthed from the womb of my beloved wife, Genessa," he proclaimed solemnly. "It is to you I must set the task, one you cannot fail if you are to rise to the Jadian throne."

"A task?" Casedren shook his head. "I don't understand."

King Bastien's gaze looked haunted as he spoke the words intended to seal his elder son's fate. "To seek and open the *Moir y'Divani.*"

12

The sacred chamber King Bastien led them into was guarded by heavy bronze doors. Walking inside, Dani was intensely aware of the windowless loom of the room around her. It took all her courage not to turn and run. Nothing about the place inspired confidence.

Lit by an illumination emerging from no apparent source, the room was bare save a platform located in its immediate center. An altar was been fashioned into the heart of the platform, one inseparable from the other. Though the light wasn't the brightest, it was adequate, allowing every corner of the room to be seen. Its atmosphere intimidated, the cold marble walls emanating a chill that penetrated to the bone. Beneath their feet the floor was just as chilly, a smooth white marble shot through with carmine veins, a color so richly scarlet the stone appeared to pulse with an unholy life all its own.

The platform could be reached only by a series of wide stone steps—five, perhaps six, forbidding steps that would take the seeker to the level of the altar.

King Bastien cast a baleful look at those steps. "This chamber has not been opened in many centuries," he intoned solemnly. "But always the *Moir y'Devani* waits."

Without explaining further, Bastien walked up the stairs, making a brief motion with his hands for Casedren and Dani to follow. Cellyn had not been allowed to accompany them, a relief in itself. Neither she nor Casedren needed the pressure his presence would have levered on an already-tense situation. Walking in the chamber has been like walking down an endless tunnel. They didn't yet know what waited for them at the end of the journey—and neither wanted to take the first step into the unknown.

Looking up at the altar, Dani froze. Her feet were literally rooted to the floor, leaving her unable to move an inch. Shaken by fine tremors, her mind was hovering over a narrow horizon between gut-twisting fear and absolute terror. She wasn't sure which was worse.

Full of dread and bitter conflict, she was tempted to run away, screaming. This was serious voodoo, hearkening toward a darker craft than she practiced as a witch. She doubted the entity they'd encounter up there would be easily appeased with a few candles and some incense.

Casedren glanced her way. One look at her face told him everything she needed to know.

He reached for her hand, his big warm fingers closing around her arctic ones. "Have courage," he whispered, attempting to pass to her a reassurance he hadn't mastered. His show of solidarity did little to chase away the fear shimmying up her spine. The little imp had settled down in a shadowy corner of her mind, gnawing away bravery and courage. Dread seeped in, threatening to drown her in fear.

They took one step, then another, following King Bastien to the top. The wide platform easily accommodated their presence. At least ten more people could have stood there without feeling crowded.

As glimpsed from below, an altar stood in the center of the platform, carved from the same marble fashioning the walls and floors. A spread of crimson silk covered its face. White candles spiraled up from gold candelabras, each positioned at a corner of the altar, representative of the four elements ready to answer a conjuror's will: earth, wind, fire and air.

Rising from the exact center of the altar was a statue of unusual fashioning. Two figures stood back to back, arms raised over their heads, hands spread in supplication for the great weight they must bear. An orb of pure clear crystal rested in the hands of the entities. The entities themselves were not difficult to identify. To the left stood a horned, tailed, cloven-footed being. To the right, an angel, its wings spread wide.

Good and evil. Back to back. Blind to each other, but hardly unaware. The air around the figures quivered.

Chillingly, the two statues, so unlike each other, reminded Dani of the twins. She knew who walked the side of light. She knew who walked in shadows. The orb was perfectly balanced.

Dani gasped as a prickling sense came and crawled up the back of her neck, like a spider scurrying softly across her skin. She felt rather than saw a strange mist hovering in the center of the crystal orb, strange distortions indicating a great energy trapped inside its icy center.

A huge book lay to the right of the suspended orb, what looked to be pages of parchment bound in a leather cover. Far from being decorated in an ornate way, the old grimoire was plain and well worn, clearly intended to be used by those who would dare invoke its secrets. A long slender dagger lay to the left of the orb, its hilt etched with symbols Dani didn't recognize—and doubted she wanted to. Its silver blade was dull, crusted with some rusty substance. Blood, no doubt. Many souls had probably fallen under the strike of the wicked stiletto.

Looking at the three items, a brief veil of darkness dropped in front of her eyes. Some slow vibration grabbed her from inside and began to shake her, a stirring of energy belonging neither to heaven nor hell, but something that encompassed the beginning and the end, and every second of time in between.

The shimmering inside her swirled faster and faster, threatening to pull her into a void she couldn't escape. The floor beneath her feet shook and cracked.

Just as Dani feared she'd be lost in the strange current of power surging through her, Casedren set his hand firmly on her shoulder. The sensations vanished in an instant, chased away by the reassuring weight of his hand on her skin. All went quiet. It were as if a door into another dimension had opened, then slammed shut, everything shifting back to normal in the span of seconds.

"Are you all right?" he asked, concern in his voice. "You turned deathly white."

Dani blinked quickly, taking a moment to focus her woozy mind. "I-I'm fine," she stammered, not really sure if she was. She pressed her hand to her forehead, anything to help still the thudding behind her temples. A headache loomed on the horizon of her mind, brewing a dark and dangerous ache. If she didn't lie down soon, she'd have a lulu of a migraine.

Casedren leaned close to her ear, whispering in a tone only she could hear. "I felt it, too."

Dani breathed a secret sigh of relief. At least she wasn't the only one feeling the power radiating from the orb. "Awesome," she murmured. And scary.

"You look now upon the *Moir y'Devani*," King Bastien said gravely. "What you see before you is the Eye of Divine Wisdom."

"What is it?" Casedren asked, clearly daunted to be in its presence. He looked tense and weary, having no more idea what was to happen than Dani did.

King Bastien extended a hand toward the altar, passing his

open palm briefly over the orb. The orb flared, sending out a spark. The candles guarding the edges of the altar sprang to brilliant life, flames chewing up the pristine wicks. Alternately deep ruby and sullen orange, the hot flames burned with brilliant intensity. The chilliness enveloping the chamber receded a bit.

Dani was impressed. She's already developed a fondness for the ease in which a simple thought physically manifested itself in this realm, as easy and natural as breathing. Her own abilities had advanced in leaps, practically overnight. In some sort of strange osmosis, she was soaking up the abilities of the Jadians. She'd never felt so energized.

"The *Moir y'Devani* is held only by the king," King Bastien said. "It is to be invoked only at a time when a monarch needs guidance from the powers that be. I am the only one who can invoke using this oracle of truth. This is a monarch's guiding light—and your challenge, my son."

Casedren glanced at the crystal orb. "I don't understand."

"When in doubt about the truth, the Eye can look into the heart and discern what is right and what is wrong. But it is not for me to invoke its power. That task lies to you, Casedren."

Casedren frowned, more confused then ever. "Me?"

Bastien nodded. "Yes, you, my son."

Dani swallowed, easily recalling the electrifying power seeping from the slumbering orb.

Casedren stepped closer to the altar. "These things, the book and the blade," he said with a wry little twist of his mouth. "What are their uses?"

Bastien laid a big hand on the grimoire. "This manuscript can guide you through the rituals of invoking the Eye. There are many ways it can be done. I hope you can find the one that works for you."

Casedren's brow wrinkled at the vague explanation. He looked to the dagger, none too reassuring in its presence on the altar. "And the blade?" A still, bitter smile had settled on his lips. Already suspecting its use, he knew for whom it was destined.

Bastien didn't reach for the dagger. "That," he said slowly, "is your fate should you fail in the task I have set for you. If you cannot open the Eye in forty-eight hours hence, you are expected to do the honorable—the noble—thing. Cellyn cannot ascend the throne with an elder brother still living."

A chill of disbelief spreading over her, Dani stared at the blade. Suddenly events had taken a turn for the worse. She hadn't felt good when entering the chamber. Now that feeling intensified tenfold and she wished they'd never set foot in this evil place. All the intrigue of this foreign world suddenly crashed down, falling on their heads like a ton of bricks.

Dani swallowed thickly. "Suicide?" she croaked. "You expect Casedren to take his own life?" A twinge settled deep inside her heart. The thought of his death dug a black hole in her soul, an ache so intense and gnawing that it stole her breath away.

King Bastien's face took on schooled neutrality. "Yes. It will be expected, by me and by the council. In this case, failure is not an option. If the Eye judges Casedren unfit to take the throne, he will also be judged unfit to live by our law." His strained, taut voice betrayed his doubt that Casedren would succeed in the task.

Eyes slipping shut, Casedren seemed shaken. "I had no idea it would come to this," he murmured.

Forgetting her inner wall of protection, Dani suddenly felt violently sick. It took a moment for her to realize Casedren's emotions were spilling over onto her, his feelings taking form in her body. His dread, his reluctance, the despairing horror dawning in his mind rolled into her skull. Casedren had assumed he'd acquire the throne despite Cellyn's disputing his suitability.

Big mistake.

Assume makes an ass out of you and me, Dani communicated through a spike of anger.

Sensing her displeasure, Casedren crept out of her mind. Her thought had hit him as sharply as a physical slap. He took a step away from her, indicating he would not invade her private space a second time.

Dani briefly closed her eyes, forcing the mental barrier back into place. Damn, this was tiring, always having to be on guard against things creeping into her head when she wasn't paying attention. No wonder Queen Genessa had fallen to an assassin's attack. What would it be like to live century after century, fighting off an invasion you couldn't even see?

The notion made her shiver.

King Bastien broke the silence between them with blunt words. "To be the firstborn son of a king is a heavy burden for any man to bear. Before your birth, your mother and I worked the spells to ensure the right child of the two would be born first when we found out she was to bear twins."

When Casedren's eyes opened again, determination dwelt in their depth. "Had I known Cellyn would strike so violently, I would have wished the little bastard strangled with his own birth cord." He scrubbed both hands over his face and glanced at the wicked dagger, granted indistinct life by the candle flames dancing above it. "Did he know this is where his challenge would take me?"

Between leveled, thick brows Bastien sent his son a look of naked frustration. "No doubt," he commented dryly. "His ambition has always been to become first son by law."

Casedren muttered some Jadian curse under his breath. Obscene, no doubt. "He needed only bide his time to make his challenge."

Dani didn't need to speak the language to understand the

images freely poring from his mind. Blocking them took a lot of effort, so vicious were his psychic vibrations.

The Jadian ruler looked at his son, unable to conceal the disapproval creeping into his gaze. "I warned you time and time again that your inattentiveness to duty would sink you, Casedren. But you gave in to other temptations. We were not meant to belong in the human world, and it never truly welcomed you as you would have wanted it to. Your responsibilities, your future, lay within Sedah. You have, I fear, thrown it away."

To his credit, Casedren didn't flinch under the verbal lashing. "I know, father. I know. The day of judgment is upon me and I am not ready to face it." The look on his face clearly stated he felt shamed by his negligence.

A strange prickle settled at the back of Dani's neck even as she listened. Somehow she had the feeling that failure was, of all things, most intolerable to the Jadian race. In this instance she doubted her instincts were misleading her. So far, everything she'd sensed had been spot on.

The weight of his command weighing heavily on his shoulders, Bastien sighed. "Sometimes our ability to sire only male children is a true curse upon our kind," he said quietly. "Had Cellyn been born female, we would not be having this conversation."

Casedren scoffed. "Yet, we are," he said in a strange, faraway voice.

Dani's guts tied into tighter knots. She swallowed hard, fighting back the crawl of sour acid rising in the back of her throat. One look at his pale face revealed his every thought. Blindsided by the challenge, he wasn't sure he could succeed at the quest. His lack of confidence wasn't exactly inspiring.

She wanted to reach out and comfort him, but trying to get into his mind now would be like trying to embrace a shadow. Casedren was mentally retreating from her, drawing away. He had every right to. She'd given him the heave-ho first. She sent a quick image his way, of her fingers touching his cheek. *Have courage!* she signaled.

The grim set line of Casedren's mouth softened a bit. A curious flare and a sensation of pressure passed between them, and Dani knew he'd accepted her mental touch. A responding pulse twitched deep inside her core.

Head cocking slightly, Bastien appeared to sense their silent communication. His accompanying smile offered approval. "This is your chance to prove yourself a man. Failure is not an option if you wish to parry Cellyn's thrust to your heart. Your brother intends to strike a fatal blow, take what by godly right belongs to you. You may think me harsh, my boy, but what I am doing is to your advantage. Use it wisely."

Having heard enough of the forbidding conversation, Dani felt compelled to address the one thing the two men had left unsaid. Desperate frustration gnawed her innards. "I hate to break in," she started to say, "but nobody's bothered to mention my role in this. I am the woman Casedren has sworn to be his legal consort." She looked from father to son. "If your son fails, what happens to me?"

Faint surprise and hesitation crossed Bastien's ruddy face. A brief stretch of the lips was all he offered. "As the throne goes to Cellyn, so does Casedren's consort. Under Jadian law and custom, you would be handed off to Cellyn." His tone, low and precise, indicated her fate would not be much better than Casedren's.

Caught by complete surprise, Dani's heart skipped a beat before dropping straight into the pit of her stomach. The thump behind her temples galloped into a double-time trot. "You're kidding me, right?"

Bastien winced at her inelegant phrasing. She had dared question a king out of turn and he didn't like it one bit. "No."

He spat out the single syllable word as if it had a bitter taste. The word was a rebuke, and a dismissal. He obviously prided himself on being ruthless and logical, and would brook no argument to the contrary.

Dani was too damn mad to care about the rules just this second. This was definitely something Casedren hadn't warned her could happen. He'd said nothing about Cellyn being able to step up and claim her—treating her the way one would a piece of jewelry or other inanimate object.

She glowered at Casedren's father. He clearly didn't care what her fate would be. All he cared about was settling the matter at hand between his warring sons. Cellyn was his favored son, something he'd made evident during the entire proceedings.

"Hell will freeze first," she fumed, "before that happens." She'd take the dagger first. And shove it right up into Cellyn's gut. Committing murder would be preferable to having such an arrogant bastard pawing her naked flesh.

Clearly catching her homicidal thought, King Bastien's brows shot up like twin rockets propelled into space. "In this case you might have no choice," he said stiffly. "If Casedren is unsuccessful, he loses you to Cellyn by default. As a secondhand choice, Cellyn would have the right to discard you as prime consort, keeping you only for his entertainment or amusement. As such, you would have no say as to whether to refuse his sexual advances. He would own you, completely."

Anger and frustration pulsed through her, intensified by the vibrations she honed in on coming from another source. Casedren's own feelings mirrored hers.

His eyes never wavered from his father's face. "That is unacceptable," he seethed. "In every way."

Talk about the rock and the proverbial hard place. Every sling and arrow of misfortune Cellyn could lob their way struck a direct blow. It was like standing on the deck of a sinking ship, tied in place and unable to swim as the water rose over their heads. One way or another, they were going under.

Settling her gaze on the crystal eye perched atop the symbols of good and evil, Dani glowered at the center of the crystal ball. Misty strings floated within the orb. Trapped behind a wall of glass, a great energy lived and seethed. This secret thing, sacred to Casedren's people, could change the course of many lives.

Frozen under the sweep of a tyrant's fury, she clenched her hands into fists. Her fingernails dug into her palms. She welcomed the tiny stabs of pain for the clarity they delivered to her swimming mind.

"Then this goddamned thing had better work its magick," she grated, "because I am not fucking that son of a bitch."

13

The rest of the day passed through Dani's mind in a blur. Following the meeting in his private chambers, King Bastien declared a brief moratorium on the time limit in which Casedren had to discover the Eye. The rest of the day, he declared, was to be spent acclimating Casedren's consort to the Jadian civilization.

Though she had no interest in such things, Dani trekked through the sights like one of the shell-shocked war wounded. Having no appreciation for their culture or arts, she might as well have been deaf and blind. Given other circumstances, she would have been thoroughly delighted with the sights. Their architecture was magnificent, a perfect blending of two very different eras already risen and fallen in her world.

As for the people themselves, Dani had never seen a finer species of citizens in her entire life. Jadian males were tall, lean and lithe. Their looks ranged from light and blond to dark and swarthy. Damn. She hadn't been around this many good-looking men since the Chippendales had taken over the strip club for a ladies' week engagement. These men were prime physical specimens, and any one of them could kick a human's ass all over the place. Their women, chosen from a wide gene pool of human females, were also striking. Stunning, luscious creatures—all too apparently chosen for beauty of face and figure.

Since the males outnumbered females, it wasn't unusual to see a woman circled by a cadre of adoring men, eager to serve her every whim and pleasure. The Jadians clearly worshipped the fairer sex. The women must have thought they'd died and gone to Shangri-La. Many of the women she saw were round and soft, their bellies full and ripe with pregnancy. Little boys abounded, but there wasn't a single little girl in sight. Once those youngsters grew into men, they too would be forced to seek mates outside their own realm.

It almost seemed like paradise achieved. These were a people not troubled by old age or disease. They were, literally, a super species. A fierce proud race determined to rise well above their origins.

Just like mankind.

The Jadians had obviously worked very hard through the centuries to become a civilized people, transparently adopting many human rites and customs as their own. Magick without substance or guidance produced nothing but pandemonium.

It would be a tragedy for all this to be destroyed under the hand of an uncaring king, Dani thought. King Bastien was right. Failure simply wasn't an option. Casedren must succeed in the quest set before him. She would help him, in every way. Whatever she could offer, she would gladly sacrifice to help him achieve his goal.

If Cellyn wins, everything will crumble.

Dani didn't want to think about it any more than she wanted to taste the lavish spread King Bastien had provided in her honor. Bad enough they should have to tour the day away. Even worse was the fact that duty compelled all of them into accepting the monarch's invitation to dine. The only thing she really wanted was to go back to her room and collapse. Time would start ticking away soon. Each minute would count in the desperate mission to open the Eye.

Glancing at the selection set out in front of her with great ceremony, she sighed. The first thing she'd learned about the Jadian diet was they were a people who did not consume meat. Of any kind. The platter overflowed with fruits and vegetables, both cooked and raw. Dark whole-grain bread, creamy wheels of cheese and red wine rounded out the menu. She blanched and her stomach turned over. Nauseatingly healthful.

The selections were elegantly laid out, served on the finest china she'd ever seen in her life. It was all too much, almost garish in its presentation.

Casedren reached beneath the table, setting his hand on her leg. He leaned close, attempting to keep their conversation private among the other diners. "Are you all right?"

Dani shook her head. Her burger-and-greasy-fries-loving heart could barely stand the medley. Yes, fruits and grains were good, if you were some kind of tree-hugging vegetarian freak. She hankered for a slab of pure beef, cooked until it was close to charcoal. Nothing better than meat slathered with BBQ sauce, then liberally applied to the fire. "I'm just not hungry."

Casedren barely touched his own plate. The challenge looming before them had clearly stolen away his appetite. "I understand."

Dani reached for the cut crystal goblet filled to the brim with a slightly tart vintage complementing the food. She took a long sip of the potent beverage. "I don't think you do." Not having eaten a morsel all day, she felt the alcohol go straight to her head. "I don't think you have any idea at all what I'm going through right now." She cut a glance down the table. Obviously the favored son, Cellyn sat closest to King Bastien.

Eyes narrowing, she tightened her grip on her glass. She sipped more wine, taking careful note that Casedren and Cellyn were fairly ignoring each other. It made for a tense and uncomfortable situation. Clearly, the evening couldn't end soon enough.

"Believe me when I say I had absolutely no idea—" Casedren started to say.

Dani swallowed more wine. "I don't know what to believe right now," she murmured under the rim of the glass. "I just know I don't want to be here right now."

Casedren shot a glance at his father, presiding over the head of the table. "He expects us to stay for entertainment," he said. "He has a fondness for Beethoven and wishes for us to hear a few selections."

She sniffed and emptied her glass. A steward quickly stepped forward with a carafe to refill it. "Isn't that nice? A demon with a taste for classical music." She clicked her tongue. "How sophisticated."

Her verbal jab struck home. "You are mocking me, I know." He sighed. "Perhaps rightfully so."

"Rightfully so," she echoed, attempting to tune him out and concentrate on her wine. She smiled gaily when Cellyn looked her way. He winked at her, damn him, with all the glee of a cat that's spotted a fat canary to stalk and eat.

Catching their interplay, Casedren grew desperate. "Please, do not be angry with me."

Ignoring his plea, she swallowed more wine. "Of course I'm pissed at you," she said when her glass came down. "You lied to me, misled me into believing this would be easy." Behind the wall she'd erected to shield herself, her thoughts seethed like a barrel of scorpions. Counselor Nash and Minister Gareth must have known Cellyn would pull out every weapon in his arsenal. They should have warned her rather than let her walk blindly into the unknown.

Her throat thickened, squeezing off her air. Surely she hadn't been sent in as some sort of sacrifice. No, that defied logic.

Nash wouldn't put her ass in the fire unless he knew for sure he could pull her back to safety.

But what if Gareth had somehow misled Nash? The devil was the master of lies and deceit. His progeny, however far removed, were probably no less practiced in the art of deception.

Casedren probed tentatively around the edges of her mind, seeking entry. She cut him off, firmly and immediately. At any other time, she'd have delighted in this newfound skill. Right now she detested it. She didn't want him rattling around in her skull. The evil dark thoughts she entertained would have blasted him dead on the spot.

Clearly not happy to be denied the chance to argue privately, he muttered a curse under his breath. "I did not lie," he said sotto voce in his own defense. "Because I did not know."

Dani sniffed, draining her second glass. "Right."

Casedren slid his hand atop hers. "Please do not do this," he murmured as the steward refilled her glass a third time.

With an unobtrusive grace, Dani slipped her hand out from under his. Recklessly, she emptied half the glass. Her head swam as the potent alcohol seeped into her bloodstream. "I'll do as I want, Casedren. Things surely can't get any worse."

Heels clicking sharply, Dani reeled toward the nearest stone bench. Pleading the need of a breath of fresh air, she'd managed to wrangle a few minutes to herself. Slipping through a set of doors leading into the king's private gardens, she'd set off in an unknown direction.

More than a little drunk, she plopped down into the welcome seat. She hadn't been lying when she said she could use a few minutes in the night air. The frigid chill caressed her numb face, biting into her cheeks and nose. Grass, flowers and trees, all was frozen into icy crispness. The sky overhead churned, a purple shaded haze creating a foggy, damp mist. The mist lent the gardens a strange appeal. Everything appeared to be wrapped in a soft layer of gauze, as if intended to be preserved just as it was, always and forever. Given her frame of mind, the night perfectly suited her gothic mood.

"Beautiful," she murmured. "Just beautiful."

A presence loomed behind her, unheard but felt. "I am glad you find the view so appealing." The voice, so strangely familiar, startled. Casedren had offered to accompany her, but she'd forbid him to do so.

Anger spiked. She hadn't even heard any steps on the cobblestone path. Jadians could slither very quietly when they wanted to move with speed and stealth. "I told you I needed a moment," she said sharply, without turning.

Her stalker settled on the seat beside her. "You said no such thing to me."

A nasty barb flying to the tip of her tongue, Dani turned to deliver it. The words died in her mouth. The man sitting beside her wasn't who she believed it to be. She gave herself a swift mental kick. Not only did they look alike, Casedren and Cellyn sounded identical, down to the soft drawl of their native accents.

Gathering her wits, Dani managed to lessen the sting behind her words. "I don't recall asking you, either."

"I wanted to come," he said bluntly. "To talk to you alone."

Her heart nearly stopped beating. "Why" She could feel him probing around the edges of her mind, but not attempting to enter. Giving her head a little shake, she tried to envision her wall, putting the bricks into place. She only got a few stacked up before the pile collapsed completely. The wine she'd consumed had left her wide open and vulnerable to attack.

Fear skated through her bowels on a sheet of ice. *Stupid, stupid, stupid,* she cursed her useless self.

Draping his arms over the back of the bench, Cellyn stretched out his legs. His posture reminded Dani of the night she'd danced for Casedren, the first time they'd made love. But while Casedren was tense with sexual hunger, Cellyn was looser, more relaxed. His lean, lanky form radiated confidence. The casual vibe he gave off indicated no threat whatsoever.

Fear evaporated. That stumped her. He wasn't acting in the least predatory.

Cellyn looked out into the gardens, the icy flora frozen in place, like some sort of magical fairyland. Dani had to admit there was a certain austere beauty to Sedah. Casedren had mentioned it was frozen because of Bastien's mourning for his slain queen. She couldn't imagine it any other way. The arctic chill felt ominously permanent.

"It is the scar, right?" He lifted a hand, tracing the ugly mark disfiguring one side of his face.

Dani wasn't following. "What?"

Cellyn shifted to face her. "The scar," he repeated. "It makes me look sinister, does it not?"

His question caught her off guard. Her nose crinkled in confusion. "I-I never thought much about it," she admitted.

He tipped his head to one side. "Casedren did it, you know."

Her brows rose. "Oh? I thought he'd never drawn a blade."

Cellyn laughed easily. "Not a blade. A push, actually." His gaze remained steady on her face. "We were wrestling, as boys are wont to do, and he pushed me." His hand passed over the damaged area. "I stumbled and hit the sharp corner of a table."

"I-I'm sorry."

Cellyn shrugged. "An accident, nothing more." He rubbed the scar with the tip of his index finger. "I have worn it since that time, though. My mother used to tell me it made me look mean." He laughed, a low easy sound pleasing to the ears.

Intrigued now, Dani studied his face through the filmy illumination of the night's mist. More in shadow than in light, his features were strong, well etched. Even with the scar, there was nothing displeasing about his looks.

"I think it adds character to your face," she offered.

He met her gaze and his mouth lifted into a smile. "Really?"

"Everyone here looks so damn perfect," she confessed without really knowing why. "You're not perfect, and that makes you stand out among the others.

Cellyn extended his hand. His fingers brushed her bare shoulder with the lightest touch. "Thank you. I enjoyed hearing that."

Dani stared at Casedren's twin and shook her head. He clearly possessed the same charm and charisma. In fact, sitting here beside him, he hardly appeared to be the terrible ogre she'd imagined him to be. Her body responded instantly. Her rapidly beating heart and unbidden rush of liquid desire attested to it.

Cellyn slid close, closing the narrow distance between their bodies. Like Casedren he practically dripped masculinity. But where Casedren's was confident, Cellyn's leaned toward control. "You are a beautiful woman yourself, Danicia." He caressed the curve of her unblemished cheek, tracing down the curve of her jaw. "I see why Casedren was so drawn to you."

The slightest pressures stroked her temples, seeping in around the edge of her brain. He didn't have to speak a single word. The images in his mind flashed through hers, of their bodies coming together in the most passionate of ways.

Her breath caught in her throat, confusion warring with the sexual need his touch ignited inside her soul. Her will suddenly wasn't her own.

Thoughts dimming, all she could think of was her need to be satisfied.

Either twin would do.

14

At the last vital minute, some alarm of self-preservation sounded in the back of Dani's mind. Making a grab for her brain, she shook her head. Displeasure stirred, weak but determined.

"I feel you inside . . . you're in my mind," she gritted through tightly clenched teeth. Hands closing into fists, she silently summoned the strength she'd need to ward him off.

Cellyn drew back. The psychic tentacles he'd sent out in pursuit withered away. "I would never slip into your thoughts without your permission." His lips quirked up in an insincere smile. "Unless you invited me."

The pressure against her temples receded, leaving a vicious void of nothingness in its wake.

Eyes narrowing, Dani pressed a hand to her forehead. That didn't help much. Her head felt like a bowling ball, heavy and awkwardly balanced on her shoulders. "Stop trying to seduce me."

Cellyn's hand came out, settling on hers. Embers of desire

flared in his eyes. His touch was hot, but his gaze even hotter. "No man could help trying with such beauty so near."

Dani regarded him the way one would a poisonous viper. "I bet you say that to all the women you want to fuck."

To her surprise, Cellyn threw back his head and laughed. "More than your beauty, I sense a great intelligence behind those snapping green eyes of yours. You are not one easily played for a fool."

Dani stared at him. The effects of the wine were beginning to fade a little, allowing a few of her brain cells to breathe sober air. She studied his face, so cruelly beautiful through the night's mists. "What do you want, really want, from me?"

Eyes settling on something in the distance, Cellyn rolled his broad shoulders in a shrug. "To try and convince you that your alliance toward my brother is misguided," he said bluntly.

"What would make you even think that was possible?" The question blundered past her lips before she'd given it a second thought.

Cellyn looked at her sharply. "Why would it not be?"

She blinked against the intensity shining behind his vibrant blue gaze. She would have sworn his eyes were glowing through the swirl of luminous mist enveloping them. Doubt flew in on ebony wings, perching on her shoulder. "I know what you are."

"Do you?" Cellyn drew back, giving her a little welcome space.

Dani wavered, without knowing why. Somehow he was backing her into a corner, and soon her back would be against the wall. Strangely, she couldn't think of a way to escape.

Now should have been the moment she got up and simply walked away. Deaf to the cries of self-preservation, she didn't.

"Yes. I do," she answered simply.

He slid his hands through his hair, cropped a little shorter and worn a little spikier than the style his brother preferred. It wasn't unattractive. "Of course you would think terrible things about me. I am sure my brother has told you in no uncertain terms that I would be the second coming of our forefather upon the face of this planet."

Dani's heart thudded dully in her chest. Well, at least he didn't beat around the bush. "I have entertained the vision myself," she allowed slowly.

Cellyn laughed low in his throat. He pinned her under a gaze, slicing through her like a laser beam. "And tell me, oh wise witch of the Wyr, was it through contact with him or contact with me that you came to entertain this vision?" A strange, almost vulnerable look flashed across his face. He quickly concealed it.

His question stalled the gears in her brain completely. What he asked totally had not occurred to her. "I-I'm not sure," she stammered. Her voice sounded low and strained.

Shifting his body even closer, Cellyn settled a hand under her chin, his long fingers curling around her neck, effectively bracketing her in his embrace. He leaned closer, giving her nostrils a hint of his unique musky scent. "I can answer that, and so can you," he whispered, his lips barely an inch from hers. "The being of destruction you saw was not me, but my own brother. Remember, he comes shielded in light, but his heart is a dark one."

In some strange, twisted way, Cellyn's words made sense. Was it possible he was telling the truth? Had Casedren somehow blinded her, misled her into believing Cellyn was the entity to be feared? Was it possible she had her thinking all twisted around so she believed she was on the side of the right brother—when Casedren wasn't the right one at all?

Thoroughly confused, Dani tried to draw back but useful motor skills had deserted her. Pressure built behind her eyes, seeping over her senses like hot, black tar. Her brain cells disintegrated under the attack.

Recognizing a full-out assault, she scurried to rebuild her

inner wall, managing to prop up a few bricks. They were too damn heavy to lift. Maybe bulletproof glass would work. Too bad she couldn't imagine it. She couldn't seem to form a single image inside her skull. All her necessary defenses had spiraled beyond her mental grasp. Open and vulnerable to attack, she couldn't resist Cellyn's invasion.

Though familiar with the ways of magick, she'd never encountered such an insidious force. Her limited experience was no match against a centuries-old being born to the practice. The takeover was quick and painless.

Her will was simply no match against his.

Dani's opened her mouth but couldn't speak. She realized what she'd meant to say wouldn't come out. "I-I, it's not true," she finally managed to stammered after a long minute had ticked by.

Cellyn leaned ever closer, almost close enough to press his lips against hers. "Do you really know what the truth is?"

Again a psi-pressure oozed around the edges of her brain, tendrils of his thoughts creeping in to mingle with hers. "I-I'm not sure."

Cellyn easily kicked away the remnants of her mental barrier. "Casedren likes the human world a lot. It makes sense he would want to possess it, call it his own personal playground."

The bottom dropped out of her world. It made perfect sense that Casedren would fear his brother's intervention in his ascension—especially if Cellyn's actions would derail his twin's destructive plans.

"I think you're right," she murmured in awe, embracing his logic.

Cellyn smirked. "I knew you would see things my way."

Dani nodded in mesmerized agreement. "I do. I think I really, really do."

Hand slipping lower, Cellyn's fingers traced the thin gold chain around her neck. A pendant hung between her breasts, drawing his attention to the low cut of her gown. "You wear the symbol of another god," he murmured. "But do you truly believe what it represents?"

Dani hesitated, her blood warming as his fingertips skimmed the silken curve of one breast. Her previous line of thinking had unexpectedly taken a turn to an entirely different subject.

Her brow wrinkled. Oddly, she couldn't recall just exactly what they had been talking about. The memory had been excised like a laser burning out cancer, neatly and painlessly.

"I—I'm not sure," she wavered. She gulped. "I mean, I believe in God's commandments."

Cellyn smirked and cocked a single brow. His fingers went lower, tracing her bodice. When she made no protest, he slipped in a finger to trace the hard tip of her nipple. "You mean as in 'Do unto others as you would have them do unto you'?" he murmured back.

Dani nodded as a slow stream of pleasure curled around her innards. Heat settled between her thighs, and simmered. "Uh, mmm. Yes, I think so."

Slipping her bodice lower to free her breast, Cellyn twisted the hard peak between thumb and forefinger. "Did you ever wonder why your god created so many wonderful sensations for man to enjoy, and then forbade them? All those *nots* after *thou shall*." He laughed softly, pinching a little harder. "Do you believe that is fair?"

Dani's tongue scraped dry lips. Feeling helplessly drawn to him, she couldn't resist. "No."

Cellyn leaned closer, giving her neck a warm, slow nibble. "We are men created by a being who gave us no limits such as that. We enjoy our carnal natures—" His lips briefly explored the curve of her collarbone. "As do our mates."

Shaking with pent-up desire, she caught her breath. "Do they?"

Cellyn offered a small, dark smile. "Oh yes. Very much."

Pressing her back against the bench, he swooped down on the aching peak, giving her nipple a long, slow kiss. His suckling touched every nerve ending in her body, igniting a blaze she couldn't easily ignore.

Lost in the spell he'd woven with ease around her senses, her fingers tangled in his thick hair, guiding him as he made love to her breast. "Oh, ah, yesss. . . ." Snared completely in his web, she had no choice but to respond. Her mind was completely bound in the invisible bonds of his magick.

Cellyn's experienced hand rummaged under her long skirt. Somehow he'd bunched it up around her knees, sliding one big warm hand between her thighs.

Dani gasped when his finger made contact with her clit, rubbing the tiny organ through the crotch of her underwear. A wild sensation swooped through the pit of her stomach, myriad tiny butterflies taking flight. It vaguely occurred to her she was having sex with the wrong brother, but the thought wavered and vanished like a mirage in the Sahara Desert. All she wanted was the satisfaction his touch promised. She'd do anything to ease the ache.

She blinked against the sweet blur hazing her vision. "My goodness," she panted. "That feels excellent." There was some wild excitement in being taken like this, and her senses responded. She was a female in heat and not one, but two, males were determined to conquer her.

Responding to her words, Cellyn pressed deeper, wiggling his fingers inside the flimsy cotton. His touch skimmed her dewy labia. "It is about to feel better," he promised, painting the tip of one erect nipple. "Much better."

Craving his entry, Dani spread her legs. "Please," she begged. "I can hardly wait." Her skin felt hot, as if stretched too tightly against her bones. Heart pounding in her chest, her blood pressure spiked. If she didn't come soon, she'd explode, detonate into tiny bits.

Penetration came quickly. Cellyn slid two fingers into her creamy little slit, pressing to the knuckle. His thumb flicked her clit. Her body lit up like a Fourth of July sparkler.

"How's that?" he breathed, teeth scraping the soft rise of her left breast. He pulled out of her slit, a slow teasing scrape of flesh against her most sensitive nerve endings. His glide back into her creaming sex impaled. His knuckles jarred her clit in the most delicious of ways.

Shivering in wild enchantment, Dani arched against the hard stone pressing against her back. She hovered on the edge of complete abandon, close to sinking into the long rolling waves of rising climax.

A man's rough voice broke through the enchantment. "I will thank you, brother, to unhand my consort."

Eyes snapping open, Dani's blurred vision settled on Casedren's looming figure. A quick glance followed his hand. Holding a dagger. Pressed against Cellyn's throat.

The blood slowly drained out of her face, leaving an icy chill in its wake. One moment she'd been floating toward the peak of ecstasy, the next instant she'd been dashed to the ground. How she'd come to be in this place at this time, she had no idea. Her mind was one big, blank void, unexpectedly wiped clean.

Confusion reigned. She'd blundered into dangerous waters and the undertow had pulled her down. Swimming for her life wasn't possible now. She'd already been dragged beneath the surface. "No," she murmured. "Don't."

Cellyn's fingers slipped out of her. Ignoring the blade in his twin's hand, he sprawled back against the bench. A chilling smile settled on his lips. "Oh, please. We both know you haven't got the courage or the nerve to actually use that thing."

The dagger in Casedren's hand hovered dangerously closer. "I would be within my right," he growled. "She was not willing."

Tossing off an insolent smile, Cellyn lifted his hand to his mouth, tasting the tips of his fingers. "I can assure you," he said, smacking his lips. "The lady was most willing. She sits there even now with her breast hanging out and her legs still spread." He laughed, a cruel mocking sound. "You are a fortunate man, indeed, finding such a lusty wench."

Sprawled half naked and very vulnerable, Dani belatedly pressed her legs together even as she crossed her arms across her exposed breast. Limp and spent, she shivered weakly. "I—I don't remember," she stammered stupidly.

Hitting his brother with a furious glare, Casedren quickly lunged in, pressing the tip of the dagger against Cellyn's throat. "I have never drawn a blade against a man in anger," he said quietly. "In this case, I could slit your throat and smile as I did so."

Ignoring the blade digging into his jugular, Cellyn laughed. "Smile away, brother," he taunted. His hand shot out, catching a handful of Dani's hair. He wrenched her head back. Still lost in a morass of confusion, she blinked up at Casedren stupidly. "In two days hence this beautiful little wench will belong to me. It is only right I should have a taste of her. A taste—" he gave her head a little shake, the way a puppy might menace a favorite toy "—I found most pleasing. I will enjoy having her again."

Casedren's blade flicked down, his blade slicing deep. "Again will never happen," he gritted.

Crying out in pain, Cellyn retaliated by flinging Dani forward. She tumbled off the bench, landing near Casedren's feet. Arms and legs a useless mass, she barely managed to lift her face off the stone scraping her cheek. A weak moan filtered from her lips. She felt shrunken, her sense of self stripped away.

Hand flying to his neck, Cellyn lunged to his feet, staggering away from the bench. His blue gaze snapped with anger. He threw a furious glare at Casedren. "Damn you, that hurt!"

Casedren stepped over her, shielding her from his twin.

"That was a warning," he smirked, calmly wiping the blade across his sleeve. "Next time, brother, it will be fatal."

From her skewed view on the ground, Dani saw Cellyn's hand come down. Blood dripped down his fingers, oozed down his throat. The cut wasn't deep enough to kill, just wound.

Cellyn bared his teeth. He made a slight gesture with his bloody hand. A shimmer of light surrounded his hand, surging out and shaping itself into the form of a long, heavy broadsword. "Next time, brother, I shall not be unarmed," he warned, his tone carefully controlled.

Dani scarcely remembered to breathe, her eyes widening. "He's going to kill you," she tried to warn Casedren. Her words came out an incoherent mumble. She couldn't seem to make her mouth or vocal cords work to her will.

Casedren quickly made a countermove. "Anytime," he rumbled. His right hand moved briefly behind his back. The sword glittering into existence more than equaled Cellyn's. "I am ready to take you on."

The air around them sizzled with tension. *Oh God*, she thought wildly. *They're going to kill each other!* Her mind connected briefly with Cellyn's. Lethal intent writhed behind his manner, eager to break free. An experienced soldier, he'd easily cut Casedren down into mincemeat.

Realizing Casedren would take the brunt of the damage, Dani tried to drag herself to her feet. "No," she mumbled weakly. "Stop it. Both of you." She strained and struggled, but couldn't move an inch. Her body remained stubbornly glued to the ground. Though the pressure behind her eyes had lessened, the pain throbbing inside the walls of her skull threatened to shut down her senses. It felt as if someone had shoved TNT into her eye sockets and lit the fuse. Explosion was imminent.

Nothing happened.

Cellyn unexpectedly stepped back, flinging his weapon

aside. It vanished before striking the ground. "We have no real cause to bicker," he soothed, spreading his arms wide and flashing a disarming smile. "After all, in two days the only one you will be turning your dagger on you, Casedren, is yourself. You've got a death sentence hanging over your head."

Casedren's jaw tightened. "You underestimate me," he snarled. "I have yet to fail."

Cellyn shrugged and took a step back. "You have never followed through on anything in your entire life. All I need do is bide my time." Turning on his heel, he disappeared down the cobblestone path. "The minutes are ticking away," he tossed over his shoulder without looking back.

Staring in his twin's wake, Casedren relaxed his shoulders. The dagger he held dropped from lax fingers. It clattered on the stone beneath his feet, a hollow, mocking ring.

"He's evil."

As if remembering her presence, Casedren turned toward Dani. Close to sobbing with relief, she still huddled on the ground. If either man had struck a blow toward her, she wouldn't have been able to defend herself. Strength had deserted her. She couldn't lift a hand to swat a gnat.

Casedren dropped to his knees. Arms sweeping around to embrace her, he swept her into his protective embrace. "I was a fool to let you wander off alone," he said, more to himself than to her.

Head lolling limply against his strong shoulder, Dani had no chance to respond. Numbness swept through her body as he lifted her off the ground, paralyzing her. Vertigo enveloped her, cocooning her mind in a suffocating void.

She couldn't react, not even to scream. Glimmers of light stabbed at her eyes, forcing her lids down. Grasping talons reached up from a black depth, dragging her far into a hellish pit from which there could be no escape, no salvation. Darkness stretched endlessly before her. Her struggle to cling to awareness failed. Her body was shutting down around her senses.

I've been hit with a death-spell came the vague, faraway thought. She was aware of nothing else except her inability to respond to what was happening to her.

Dani's equilibrium was short-circuiting, and her consciousness slipped through her fingers like tiny grains of sand.

A stygian malaise claimed her mind, and she knew only black peace.

15

Dani woke to pain. A lot of pain. Her head felt like a pumpkin drop-kicked through a goalpost and splattered on the field.

Moaning piteously, she pressed the heels of her hands against her eyes and rolled over onto her side, curling her body into a tight protective ball. Nausea rolled through her stomach, even as her bowels clenched around liquid acid.

She wanted to puke.

The pain spiked again, cutting through her skull like a buzz saw.

No, she wanted to die. Just die and get this hell over with.

A gentle hand settled on her shoulder.

Clenching her eyes tighter and tucking her arms against her chest, Dani moaned again. Her skin burned where the pressure had fallen, searing straight to the bone. She tried to shake the pressure off. "Please . . . you're hurting me."

The pressure persisted, then doubled, applying more force. Strong hands rolled her over onto her back. A warm palm slid under her head, lifting. A hard rim settled against her mouth.

The slosh of cool liquid against her lips urged them open. The stinging smell of mint tickled her nostrils.

"Drink this," a faraway voice urged. "It will take the pain away."

Hardly trusting the unseen source, Dani tried to turn her head. The liquid spilled over her chin, tracking in thin rivulets over her neck and chest.

"Please," the voice urged. "Drink." The cup pressed again, more insistently.

To stop the assault, Dani automatically opened her mouth and drank. A bitter-tasting brew, some foul nasty liquid, slid down her throat like lead pellets. She gagged, fighting to spit it up.

"Drink it," the voice urged. "That pain will go. I promise." Something in the gentle tone struck a chord deep inside. This was a source she could trust.

Fighting the rebellion rolling in her stomach, Dani clenched her eyes tighter and forced herself to swallow more of the medicine. As the last of the liquid disappeared down her throat, the rumble in her guts immediately abated. The pain receded to a tolerable level. Almost. Stubbornly persistent, the ache in her mind insisted on hovering behind her temples. Its tom-tom thump kept the parade marching.

The empty cup fell away from her lips. "You should feel better now."

Hoping her eyeballs wouldn't roll out of the sockets, Dani slowly cracked her lids open. Tiny little black lines danced in front of her vision. She blinked. A familiar face swam into focus.

"Casedren?" she croaked. Her gaze searched his face for signs of scarring. Yes, it was him. A sigh of relief broke from her lips.

Worry etched deeply around his eyes, Casedren smiled down

at her. "You are safe now," he said. "Cellyn cannot attack you here."

Mention of his twin's name sent a spike of fear through Dani's heart. Clawing at the bedding beneath her body, she fought to pull herself into a sitting position. The sudden move punished her, swiftly and severely. Dizziness enveloped her senses, her vision dimming. "That son of a bitch," she mumbled weakly, swooning backward. A pile of soft pillows caught her fall.

Sitting on the bed beside her, Casedren's hand settled across her abdomen, his touch a familiar and welcome weight. "It will take a few minutes for the potion to work." An angry frown worried his lips. "I am afraid Cellyn bedazzled you with an enchantment spell."

The black fuzzy lines persisted, annoying her to no end. "Feels like he hit me with a fucking sledgehammer," she slurred.

Her words broke Casedren's solemn manner. He treated her to a lazy smile. "The sledgehammer was most likely the wine on an empty stomach."

She lifted a shaking hand, pressing it against her forehead. Her pulse pounded in her temples, drumming hard. "Oh God. I've never felt this bad in my entire life. It feels like the flu crossed with malaria or some other nasty shit."

Casedren began to rub her abdomen in slow, steady circles, applying gentle pressure with his palm. "Just give the medicine a few more minutes to do its work," he soothed. "You will feel stronger as it enters your bloodstream."

Her stomach rumbled. "I could use some Alka-Seltzer," she mumbled. "And some Pepto."

He widened the circular motions on her belly. "That's just an empty stomach. You need some food."

Dani shook her head back and forth on the pillow like a stubborn child. "I'll puke what I eat," she insisted.

"Nothing heavy," Casedren insisted. His hand left her belly. Enoch, standing unnoticed nearby, handed over a small ceramic bowl. "Just some soup."

Dani blanched, pressing her lips together. "Let me die, please."

Casedren spooned up a portion, guiding it to her mouth. "Just try a bit. Come on, open up."

Dani reluctantly opened her mouth. A thick, warm liquid tasting of vegetables and herbs slid down her throat. The rich soup heated her insides, putting to rest the avalanche storming through her stomach. "That's good," she mumbled.

He spooned up another sip for her. "Good to see you eat. I wish you'd have had breakfast this morning."

Dani swallowed the delicious soup. "I hate eating in the morning. Besides, I was too nervous to eat." She reached for the bowl. "I think I can handle this."

Casedren handed it over. "Careful, now."

Ignoring the spoon he offered, Dani tipped the bowl to her mouth, gulping down slurp after slurp of the mouth-watering soup. Delicately seasoned, it was enough to fill her up without aggravating her touchy stomach.

Strength flooded through her, delivering a renewed sense of vigor and clarity. She almost felt like a new woman.

Dani lowered the empty bowl, smacking her lips. "God, that stuff is like nectar from heaven. It's scrumptious."

Casedren retrieved the empty bowl, handing it off to his manservant. "I am glad you find something decent about our food," he said, smiling. "I know it is hardly the two all-beef patties with special sauce, lettuce and cheese you have been thinking about since you got here."

Laying back against the pillows, a guilty grin crept across her face. "Am I that damn transparent?"

Casedren grinned. "Yes, you are."

Enoch offered a brief bow. "Anything else I can get for your lady, sire?"

Casedren shook his head. "No. That is all for now. You may leave us."

Enoch bowed deeply. "I am at your beck if you require me."

"Thank you. I believe we require nothing else. If we do, I am sure I can manage to provide it." Inclining his head in a royal nod, Casedren waved him away. "Your loyalty will be rewarded, my friend."

Taking up the tray of discarded dishes, Enoch walked straight toward the nearest wall. Just as he would have struck it face on, the wall began to glimmer, fading slightly but not entirely disappearing. Enoch easily slipped through the shimmering curtain of energy. Seconds later the wall reformed into solid stone.

Dani caught her breath, amazed at how easily the Magus manipulated the force within their dimension. She threw Casedren a glance. "That's impressive."

He reached out, smoothing a few wispy tendrils of hair off her damp forehead. His trembling hand and ragged breathing indicated how deeply worried he'd been for her. "It's just magick. Anyone can do it."

"Not me." She grimaced, rubbing her fingers against her aching eyes. Her eyeballs felt as if someone had loaded them up with millions of tiny pins. Tension.

He chuckled. "It takes practice, dear. But from what I've seen, you are doing a very good job learning to wield it yourself. I've been impressed, too, you know."

Letting her hand drop, she drew a deep shuddering breath, attempting to bring herself back to present reality. She didn't recognize the chamber around her, far different than the one she'd decorated.

Whether it was the same space or one entirely different, she didn't know. What she did know was everything had changed. The furnishings were heavy, old-fashioned things. Tapestries covered plain stone walls, and thick carpeting guarded bare feet against the chilly stone floor.

A crystal orb, the Eye, rested on a table across from the bed, perched on a velvety stand. The grimoire guiding the searcher in its use was spread open nearby. Casedren had obviously begun to study the spells committed to parchment by an unknown hand. What those pages might contain, Dani had no idea. Whatever magick lurked there was probably way beyond her comprehension.

A fire snapped heartily in the hearth. Aside from thick spiraling candles lit throughout the chamber, the fire was the only other source of light. Closed and intimate, the chamber was all very masculine and dark. Strangely, there were no windows or doors. It was as if someone had stuck them inside a box.

"Everything's changed."

He looked around. "This is a place I used to hide when I was a boy. Nobody knows of it but me and a few of my most trusted servants."

She accepted his explanation without comment. The windowless chamber felt safe, if a bit claustrophobic. One thing nagged. She had no idea if it was day or night. The gloom surrounding them held everything suspended in some sort of eternal midnight. "How long was I out?"

He shrugged. "A few hours. You will probably want to rest more. It is late, well after midnight."

His words jogged. "The deadline to open the Eye—" she began to say.

"Has begun," he finished calmly.

Guilt flayed. "You've lost time taking care of me."

"I have lost no time," he countered. "I have been studying the grimoire. The rituals appear fairly simple. Surely I can pull off any one I choose."

The mental whip came down a little harder. "I-I'm sorry," she stammered. "I didn't mean for this to happen."

Compassion flooded his vibrant blue eyes. "Of course you didn't. Cellyn saw a chance to strike at me and he did. It was my fault for letting you go off alone. I should have gone with you, or had a guard at your side, at the very least."

Her shoulders drooped. "I feel like a complete fool."

Casedren cleared his throat. "You were hardly at fault," he said, trying to reassure her. "Later, I will teach you a few meditations to better shield your thoughts from others. You have the right idea, but it is too exhausting to constantly concentrate on a mental picture. I can show you a way to shield your thoughts in a more natural manner, like breathing. With practice, it will come automatically."

Dani bit down on her lower lip. "I'd like that."

"You're a fast learner. You'll have the skill mastered in no time."

She wasn't so certain about that. At this point she really wasn't confident about anything she might accomplish. "I—I'm still not quiet sure what happened," she admitted, finally daring to approach the blurry images hovering in the corners of her skull. She didn't want to look at the gruesome things. The bits and pieces sticking out in plain view weren't pleasant. She winced. Like Cellyn's mouth at her breast and his fingers up her twat.

Clearly reading her thoughts, Casedren winced. "It is not your fault," he repeated patiently. "Cellyn got to you because—" His throat worked thickly. "You desired him, however fleeting the notion. All he needed was a small chink to enter your mind. You really had no will of your own once he assumed control."

Her cheeks heated. "I had no idea it would be that easy," she murmured in embarrassment.

Casedren's eyes snapped with anger even though he kept his voice level. "I am afraid it is difficult for most humans to resist mind-walkers. What human could imagine their thoughts being read and their mind so manipulated?"

Manipulated didn't begin to describe how Dani felt at the moment. Her jaw tightened. *Raped* might have been a better word.

Memories began to trickle back in like a dam springing a leak, slowly at first, then building as the pressure gave way and her mental defenses crumbled. She grabbed at the bits and pieces she recognized, slowly putting the sections of the puzzle into place until she'd formed a complete picture.

What she saw in her mind's eye twisted her guts into tight, vicious knots. It took all her self-control to keep the soup she'd drunk from coming back up. The fact she'd stupidly let herself blunder into Cellyn's path was enough to make her blood run cold.

What a stupid little fool.

More unwelcome images fell into place. Like the way she'd sighed when Cellyn had bared her breasts, twisting a nipple to deliver just the twinge to an already-demanding appetite for sex. By letting her anger with Casedren drive her actions, she'd placed herself directly in the hands of the enemy. Cellyn could have done a lot more damage had he taken the initiative. It was bad enough she'd allowed him to paw on her, easily reaffirming his claim she was no better than a common whore.

Oh God. How could I ever have found him attractive? Yes, Cellyn looked like Casedren. That was a given. But to be sexually aroused by him. . . . Worse still, she'd briefly enjoyed his controlling lovemaking.

Shame threatened to incinerate her. All she could do was beg Casedren's forgiveness and hope he accepted.

She wanted those terrible memories out of her mind. Now.

Lids dropping shut, Dani pictured herself sweeping the dreadful events into a box, then tossing it into a fiery hole. The box leapt back out, refusing to burn. *Go away,* she silently pleaded. *Just go away.* In this instance, it would have been more of a blessing not to remember.

Easily sensing her thoughts, Casedren stepped into her mind, helping her heave the box back into the fire. It stayed but still didn't burn. Unpleasant memories had a way of hanging around to point accusing fingers.

"Cellyn is well practiced in the arts, as all Magus are. As skilled as you are as a witch, your power does not even begin to compare to ours."

She rubbed her hands across her numb face. "You've got that right," she muttered. "I feel like I've run into the middle of a blazing house completely naked." A heavy sigh of frustration broke from her lips. "I've got no business being here. I'm more of a hindrance than a help."

Casedren's eyes, normally so gentle and placid, narrowed with anger. "You are not a hindrance, Danicia." His hand claimed her, fingers curling into a protective grip. "You do not know how badly I have needed someone to stand beside me. Most of the time I stayed out of Sedah not because I willfully shirked my duty, but because I was afraid to take it all on alone." Blurted out quickly, his confession prodded her interest.

"Really?" she asked.

He nodded. The candles lighting the chamber cast sad shadows on his blue gaze. "My mother always made it clear that Cellyn was her favorite child," he said slowly. "My father, too, seems to favor him. Always he's kept Cellyn close at hand, instructing him as to duty and honor." He shrugged, confusion briefly playing across his face. "My father has just always assumed I knew what to do and left me to myself. Most times I honestly believe they felt our birth orders were wrong."

Dani's fingers tightened around his. "Do you think your father really does want Cellyn to rise in your place?"

Casedren nodded again, slowly. "Yes, I think he does."

Her brow knitted. "Why?"

He hesitated, brushing his fingers over her hand, up the silken skin of her bare arm. The sensation caused the fine hairs on the back of her neck to rise. Unbidden, desire raised its head. She was coming back to life in more ways than one.

"I am not the first to be given the challenge to open the Eye of Divine Wisdom," he explained, barely managing to conceal a grimace. "Of the times it has been invoked . . ." He paused a moment to draw a breath, then rushed on. "Of the times the Eye has been called into judgment, most have failed its test. The dagger's blade is never wiped. Always it bears the blood of the fallen. I fear my blood will be the next it tastes."

Dani frowned at his defeated tone. "If you fail," she reminded him quietly, "I belong to Cellyn by default."

Pain filled his gaze. His hand rose, fingers skimming her cheek. "Had I known anything about that, I would not have made my claim on you—or any woman, for that matter. Despite Cellyn's dissatisfaction with being secondborn, I did not think for a minute my father would take his challenge seriously." His hand dropped. "I should have seen it coming, known that Cellyn would come up from behind. He has truly buried his blade right between my shoulder blades."

Despite the steadiness of Casedren's voice, his tone held defeat. The anger he'd displayed earlier against Cellyn had evaporated, leaving only confusion and depression in its wake.

He honestly thinks he's lost. That thought tossed her mental trolley off its track. If Casedren openly believed he'd lose to Cellyn, what about her? In death, he'd be getting out easily. She didn't have that luxury.

Dani gulped against the icy chill oozing down her spine. She would be Cellyn's fuck toy, something she suspected she wouldn't enjoy. Cellyn's sexual taste seemed to be as twisted as his ambitions. There was no doubt in her mind his favorite things included bondage and submission.

At the moment she wasn't feeling very submissive at all.

"You haven't lost yet, Casedren. While there's breath in us, there's hope."

He smiled weakly. "I am not exactly in a hopeful frame of mind at the moment."

A sudden blast of insight almost knocked her flat. Though their minds weren't joined, they were open to each other. So far, he'd been the one receiving all the impressions. Now, without, warning, some deep-seated piece of his psyche emerged.

As bright as the sun, as open as a book, he was there, and she clearly read his deepest fear. Beneath Casedren's kindness was a strength he refused to recognize. A savage beast lurked deep inside his civilized soul, one he feared he couldn't contain if ever it should escape its cage.

"You're not like Cellyn," she whispered softly.

He looked at her in disbelief. "What?"

She stared back at him. "You heard me, I know, so don't sit there pretending to be defeated when you're not."

"Are you serious?"

Ignoring the steady pounding of her heart, Dani forced herself to meet his gaze head on. "Yes, I am." A tremor shook her that had nothing to do with being a bewitched sex slave and everything to do with Casedren Teraketh. "When you drew your blade, Casedren, you drew it with the intention to commit murder. No kidding around, and no hesitation. You seriously intended to put Cellyn in his grave."

A small smile crept across his lips. "For you, I would have."

She cocked her head, searching his face.

"Why do you hide it?"

Casedren's gaze dropped. "I have always felt an unobtrusive

defense would be the most effective," he confessed. "It is a skill I have kept . . . concealed. I believe it is to my advantage to let Cellyn think I am a fool when it comes to handling a blade."

Dani eyed him with pure admiration. Smart move. Casedren obviously wasn't the slacker everyone believed him to be. "What else are you hiding up your sleeve?"

Relaxing for the first time since she'd regained consciousness, Casedren laughed, a low mellow sound of true pleasure. "Not much else, I am afraid."

He was wrong.

The one thing vividly standing out in her mind was Casedren's defense of her honor. He'd stepped up and threatened to kick the living shit out of Cellyn in no uncertain terms. What's more, Cellyn had believed his twin completely capable of following through with the threat.

Far from being a coward, Casedren had proven himself to be a crafty fighter. He knew how to pick his battles, bypassing those that would give him no gain, accepting those that would play his strengths to maximum advantage. Behind his self-controlled demeanor beat the heart of a man willing to take calculated risks. Neither irrational nor careless, he was careful. And careful men lived a lot longer than hot-blooded, hot-headed men full of swagger and bravado.

Dani reached out for his hand. "That's not true. I remember how you defended me." The only other man she knew who'd stand up and bash heads in without reservation was her brother, Brenden.

His eyes rose, gaze catching hers. "You truly think I compare to your brother?"

"Of course, you do." She tightened her grip on his hand, so much larger and stronger than hers. His fingers were cool and steady, betraying nothing of his own inner turmoil. She wished she felt as calm. "I wouldn't have a man who didn't."

"Thank you." He reached out, cupping her face. "That is a

compliment I shall always treasure." His fingers traced the curve of her cheek. "When you see him, please tell your brother I never meant to hurt you."

She pulled away. "What do you mean, when I see him?"

Casedren squared his shoulders in resolution. "I am sending you back to earth."

16

_____

Dismay at his words hit harder than a slap.

Feeling a chill spread over her skin, Dani sank back against the pillows. "No." She shook her head. "I'm not going any-where."

Leaving his place at her bedside, Casedren stood up. Frus-trated, he raked his hands through his hair. "Your passionate spirit is one of the things that drew me to you," he confessed. "But I can't let my folly endanger you any further. The only way to get you out of this is to send you back."

Dani grunted in disgust. "Sending me away is the wrong thing to do. It would look like you're afraid of failing."

Hands dropping to his side, he sighed. "I am not afraid of failing," he said quietly. "As I am of losing you."

The idea of being sent back to earth made her bowels knot. When she'd learned from King Bastien that Casedren's default would send her straight into Cellyn's unwelcome embrace, she'd been madder than hell, sure she'd been deceived. Then she'd gotten drunk and blundered right into Cellyn's path. It went without saying she'd dealt Casedren a stinging blow.

She swallowed, remembering the sudden chilling prickle of Casedren's shock when he'd come up on Cellyn making love to her. Even through the haze of Cellyn's sexual enchantment, she'd felt Casedren's pain and bewilderment. Part of him, she knew, blamed her, though he would never admit the words aloud.

As it was, Dani blamed herself. And she wanted to make amends. They'd both made grievous mistakes. That didn't mean the rift couldn't be repaired. They'd just have to work at it. Together.

"You haven't lost me," she said. "And you haven't failed. We still have time. I can work with you, help you with the spells. Whatever it takes, I'm willing to do."

Staring into the fire, Casedren shook his head. "That is a generous offer," he said slowly. "But I cannot take the risk. I promised your brother I would keep you safe. If nothing else, I am a man of my word. Sending you back is the only way to keep you safe."

Atremble with teeming nerves, he set to pacing the narrow chamber. Just as he would have hit a wall, it lengthened a little, giving him additional space to walk. His long male stride seemed to fill every inch of the chamber. Something about the rigid line of his spine said he intended to take care of things his way.

Stymied by his abrupt refusal, Dani glanced over his tall figure. Her gaze tracked the lines of his broad shoulders, his narrow waist, and solid legs. He'd discarded his heavy coat and vest, wearing only an open-necked white string tie shirt, breeches and boots. As he turned and walked past her, the intoxicating scent of male skin aroused her all over again.

Looking at him, her mouth suddenly went bone dry. His striking good looks never failed to steal away her breath. The silken fingers of lust reached in her core, tightening around her clit with an iron grip. A twinge settled between her thighs.

Thighs she wanted wrapped around his narrow waist as his cock pummeled her sex.

He's wrong. Sending her back would be a terrible move. Cellyn would sense weakness and exploit it to his advantage.

She had to convince Casedren she had to stay. She belonged at his side. She didn't know why she felt that way. She just did. She'd finally found the one man who set her senses on fire with a touch, a man she'd willingly followed not only to the ends of the earth, but beyond.

She wasn't a fool. She knew a good thing when she had it, however strange its origin.

Tired of being treated like a child, Dani whipped the covers off her body. Some kind of thin nightgown had replaced her gown. It clung to every sweaty curve, making it abundantly clear to anyone who cared to look that she wore nothing underneath. It was all she could do not to rip it off and spread her legs for him.

A vision unspooled across her mind's screen—Casedren, naked and aroused, laying on his back as she lowered herself onto his massive erection.

Dani swallowed, wetting dry lips. Trembling with pure need, she slipped out of bed.

Casedren caught her move, stopping dead in his tracks. "You should not be out of bed, my lady. Surely you need your rest."

Tired of his formality, Dani drew in a deep breath, then heaved it out. "The only thing I need is you," she answered in a voice quite unlike her own. Against her ears, this voice sounded husky with arousal.

Casedren looked at her in shock, clearly trying to decide what to make of her proposal. "You still want me?" he asked dumbly.

Duh! What a silly question. She couldn't remember wanting another man as badly as she wanted Casedren Teraketh. Need was slowly turning up the flame on desire, each passing moment intensifying the bittersweet ache. Her clit throbbed with the need to feel the stroke of his fingers and mouth.

Shuddering under the sensual assault, she nodded. "Desperately."

Hoping to entice him, she concentrated on opening her mind and letting every carnal image roam free. Waves of desire swirled, wafting on invisible currents to caress the empty air between them. As her craving floated between them, Dani imagined his hands ghosting over her bare skin, his mouth teasing hers with deep, consuming kisses.

Lost in the fantasy, her lids dropped shut and a low moan escaped from her throat. Her head dipped back, lips parting. *Oh God, Casedren,* she murmured through the psychic link. *I want you.* This time she wasn't the one being bespelled. She was doing the weaving, doing her best to cast a seductive charm.

Nothing happened.

Instead of rushing to her and crushing her against the hard planes of his aroused male body, the air around her remained frustratingly void of his presence. A pressure settled against her temples, gentle but insistent.

No, he insisted, shoving her out and shutting his mind. His voice took up where his thoughts left off, saying aloud, "Do not start what you cannot finish." His voice, though quiet, was strained.

Dani opened her eyes in time to see need flashed across his face, naked and raw. "I'm not the one who's holding back. You are."

Casedren quickly squelched his vulnerability with a shake of his head. He couldn't entirely conceal his emotions. His opalescent eyes simmered with sorrow and regret. "It would not be right to let you stay. My stupidity has put you in enough danger. Let me salvage it with some honor. Please."

The agony on his striking face made Dani swallow and wish she wasn't the one who'd delivered the blow. "I'm staying," she insisted. "With you."

Hands fisting at his sides, Casedren swallowed thickly. "Please, do not tempt me this way."

Fingers sliding through her hair, Dani skimmed the long tendrils off her shoulders. "I'm doing my best," she countered "to make you fuck me." If she had her say, she wasn't going anywhere anytime soon.

Boiling with frustrated desire, Casedren gritted his teeth, struggling to tear his eyes off her nearly nude body. His cock pressed against the front of his tight breeches.

He suddenly turned around. "No," he insisted, flinging the words over his shoulder. "It is too dangerous."

Desperate to convince him otherwise, the words rushed past her lips. "I'm willing to accept that."

He wasn't. "I refuse to endanger you any more than I already have. I have had enough of being a stupid, ham-fisted fool. It is time my head ruled my heart, instead of the other way around. Falling in love has totally destroyed me."

His words caught her like a punch to the solar plexus. "W-What did you say?" she stammered.

Realizing his slip, Casedren flung a glance her way. His body shook with hard, panting breaths. "I shall not say it again."

She wasn't willing to let it drop so easily. "You said you loved me. If that's really true, you would fight for me."

Casedren immediately pivoted on his heel. A line of confusion slashed between his blond brows. "What?"

Crossing her arms over her chest, Dani leveled her gaze, looking him straight in the eyes. "You heard me, magick boy. If you love me, you will fight for me. Think about it. Even if you send me away, what's to keep Cellyn from coming after me on earth?"

Backed into a corner, her otherworld lover cast frantically

around for a way out. His fine mouth pursed. "Counselor Nash and your brother will—" He didn't finish. Saying the L word to a female was like dangling a pound of chocolate in front of her during that time of the month. She would hang on with both hands and devour.

Dani gave him a sneer, just enough to hammer in her words. "It's not their job, buddy boy. It's yours. You took me as your consort, as the future wife who would stand beside you through thick and thin. Things get a little difficult and all of a sudden you're dropping me like a hot rock." She crossed her arms over her chest, ignoring the rasp against her sensitized nipples. "What the hell gives here?"

Clearly baffled, Casedren shook his head, looking at her with a mixture of wonder and delight. "I cannot believe you would want to stay," he murmured, more to himself than for her benefit.

Dani rolled her eyes. What did he think she'd been saying for the last five minutes? "Of course I want to stay. The only thing standing between me and your brother is you. Sending me back to earth makes about as much sense as hiding me under a rock."

Having lost the battle, Casedren waved the white flag. "You are right," he said with slow resignation. "No matter where I might send you, Cellyn would probably not hesitate to follow. He wants you, I know."

Fear mingled with disgust. Just imagining Cellyn, with his feral smile and glittering eyes, sent a shiver down her back. She remembered his touch, now as unpleasant as thousands of tiny ants crawling over her skin. "I know he wants me—and in the worst of ways. Somehow I get the idea he's a sadistic bastard when it comes to sex."

Casedren nodded slowly. "My brother enjoys bondage and the submission of his women."

She blanched. The idea of being tied down and forced to have sex with Cellyn made her blood run cold. "Thought so."

Casedren shrugged. "I guess this takes us back to square one. It is us against them."

She mimicked his move. "If that's the way it's gotta be, we just have to buck the odds and succeed."

His gaze followed her move, settling on her breasts. The hard points of her nipples peaked against the material, almost transparent in the glimmering firelight. "You are making it very hard for me to think about the Eye dressed like that."

Desire flashed back, stronger than ever. "Then I guess you'd better undress me."

That was all the invitation Casedren needed. Closing the distance between them, he grabbed the front of her nightie and ripped. The thin confection disintegrated, falling to her feet in a silky pool around her feet.

Totally naked, Dani grinned up at him. "Much better."

Casedren didn't give her a chance to say another word. Slipping his fingers through her blond tresses, he dipped her head back and claimed her lips with a kiss that said he was the only man who owned her, body and soul.

Dani's arms automatically circled his neck. Pressing against the ridges of his long, lean frame, she lifted up on tiptoes, eager to make the kiss last as long as possible. Her nipples scraped deliciously against his chest even as his cock surged against the soft nest of her belly. She pressed closer.

Casedren broke their kiss, lifting his head to treat her to a lazy smile. "We had better slow down," he warned. "Otherwise I will come all over myself."

Locking her fingers around his neck, Dani tried to drag his mouth back within reach of hers. He was too tall, damn it. When he stood up straight, her head barely reached his shoulder.

"I don't care," she murmured against his chest. "I just want to touch you."

Laughing low in his throat, he cocked a wicked brow. "Funny, that is the same thing I had in mind for you." His long reach slipped around behind her. Big warm palms settled on her rear, cupping her cheeks. He lifted her off her feet, easily settling her against his bulging erection.

Head spinning from the intense sensations his touch ignited, she felt liquid fire pour through her veins. Her heart thrashed in the hollow void of her chest, beating out a tempo of longing mingled with the relief that she'd been given a reprieve. She wouldn't be sent away.

Casedren wanted her and that's all that counted.

Dani locked her legs around his narrow waist. His strength amazed her. He lifted her with the effort he'd put behind lifting a child. Hardly any at all. "Looking forward to it," she murmured against his mouth.

He chuckled. "Oh, me, too." He set into motion, carrying her across the chamber. To her surprise he wasn't heading toward the bed.

Dani craned her head around. There weren't any doors to go through. "Where are we going."

Casedren continued walking. "I have a little ceremony in mind for you, my lady."

Her brow crinkled. "A ceremony?"

He nodded. "Yes, one I think you will find most enjoyable."

As he neared the wall Enoch had disappeared through, it wavered, thinning into a vaporous sheet.

Not expecting the rush of pure energy, Dani felt a shock jolting through her entire body, as if she'd grabbed on to a hot wire fence and couldn't let go. She scrambled to raise a mental shield against the onslaught. The energy snapped around her hard, without resistance or mercy. Like an angry giant, it wanted to snap her apart limb by limb.

Casedren stepped smoothly into her head. *Relax,* he urged. *It will not hurt you.*

Clenching her teeth, Dani swore silently. Closing her eyes, she pressed her forehead into the hollow between his shoulder and neck, fighting to drop the resistance of instinctive self-preservation. If he said it would not harm her, she would believe him.

Bolts of power simmered around their bodies, concentrating at the nape of her neck before crackling down her spine. Pressure pounded behind her temples, a sledgehammer demolishing her skull from the inside out. Her exposed skin felt hot and rubbery, gooey enough to slide off her bones.

Just as Dani was sure she couldn't take another single second, she felt Casedren shielding her from most of the vicious shocks. The pressure in her mind lessened. The magical shield's discharge faded, winking out into nothingness as quickly as it had attacked.

They passed through the wall with ease, vanishing.

17

Arriving, Casedren lowered Dani to her feet. Her senses tingled from the unexpected assault, and her legs all but collapsed under her weight. A strong hand steadied her before she fell.

"What the hell was that thing?" she gasped, still trembling.

"A spell-shield," Casedren explained. "To shield us not only from Cellyn's eyes but from his senses. Inside one, we can act and think freely without fear our thoughts will be invaded. It cannot come down for a second or he could sense us. One tiny crevice is all he needs to worm his way inside."

She nodded. This was something she should have known. She'd spelled up a few invisible barriers of protection in her time. This one, though, was leaps and bounds more powerful than anything she'd ever conjured. "I should have expected as much."

"You took it badly because it caught you by surprise. I am sorry I did not warn you. I assumed you knew."

She passed her hands over her face, rubbing away the strange numbness the shield's energy had inflicted. "I did," she said wryly. "I just had other things on my mind."

His gaze glimmered in a knowing way. "Ah."

"Thanks for stepping in. I owe you one."

He grinned. "Anything to help a lady out." His eyes skimmed her nude form from head to foot, and back again. "A naked lady, that is."

She eyed him back. "Speaking of me being naked, why aren't you?"

Casedren chuckled and turned her around. "I will be, very soon."

She stared at the chamber in front of her eyes. They were in a bathroom, but not like any water closet she'd ever seen. Instead of housing modern appliances, this was modeled on the style of a Roman bathhouse, with a few twists thrown in for good measure. Fashioned out of natural stone, the shower had been created to mimic the look and feel of an actual waterfall. The water poured onto a wide stone ledge, the runoff filling a deep, circular stone pool. Niches carved into the stone held an array of items useful for bathing—scented soaps and rich oils.

A flickering, golden radiance lit the room, emanating from a certain type of stone placed at regular intervals around the chamber. The low light bestowed an illusive, unreal quality of the chamber, adding to the illusion the waterfall was real.

"It's beautiful," she gasped. Whereas the chamber her wish-craft created had several modern touches, Casedren's preference still clearly favored a more ancient flavor. No matter. A shower was a shower, no matter the form.

"I am glad you like it."

"I do," she said, then wrinkled her nose. "But is this a hint I stink?"

He grinned, shaking his head. "Think of it as a reason to get my hands all over your delightful body."

Dani smirked back. "Like *you* need a reason."

Smile vanishing, Casedren suddenly grew serious. "Actually it is part of the purification ritual we need to undertake."

Her desire evaporated, replaced with dead seriousness.

Thinking back to the orb and accompanying grimoire, Dani nodded. She understood the concept of cleansing and preparing oneself to undertake ritual spell casting. "Do you know what to do?"

Casedren studied her face. "While there are some parts I do not understand due to my lack of knowledge with the old language, I have picked up the base concepts for invoking the Eye. The text instructs that the physical self must be cleansed, then cleared of negative energy to clarify the Eye's ability to see." He sighed. "At least, that is how I read it."

Uh-oh. Not a good sign at all. She frowned and cocked her head, looking up at him. "Then you're not sure?"

Casedren shrugged helplessly. "The language the manuscript is written in was abandoned at least a millennia before my birth. The *Quarayan* dialect is close to being a dead language nowadays. As a schoolboy I had some instruction, but only enough to give me a working knowledge. The rest is guesswork."

Dani's mouth quirked down. She understood his pain. Her mastery of Latin, the language most Wyr spells were cast in, stood on shaky ground. Guessing wasn't good when magick was concerned. One wrong word, one wrong gesture, and everything could go *kerflooey!*

Brenden is living proof of that, she thought, but quickly squelched that line of thinking, hoping he hadn't picked it up. "Well, at least you fellows have English down fairly well," she said, digging around for something to compliment him about.

Casedren grinned. "We actually do not speak your language—at least not a lot of it."

"That's ridiculous. I understand you perfectly."

"I am actually speaking my language, the common *Madnhar*

dialect," he explained. "It is a spell-language allowing you to understand it in the tongue you are accustomed to speaking. Because you are more perceptive than the average human, your ears perceive a slight accent to my speech." He chuckled. "And you thought I was someone hailing from your own ancestral lineage."

Yeah. That was true. She'd have sworn on her grandmother's grave Casedren had an Irish or light Scottish accent. Now she understood she heard him that way. "Must be nice to be able to be understood wherever you go."

He chuckled. "You forget our women come from all over the human world. There are many languages in the human repertoire of communication. It is easier to have a spell-language than to try to learn them all. Your people, believe it or not, even have a term for it."

Her brows rose. "We do?"

His gaze narrowed slyly. "Ever heard a man called a 'silver-tongued devil'?"

"Every girl on the planet knows that one." Dani laughed. "No wonder you guys are such irresistible sweet-talkers."

Blushing a bit, Casedren cleared his throat. "We try, my lady. We definitely try."

Speaking of trying. Her mind circled around to the task at hand. "So while I was blissfully unconscious, did you have enough time to read up on how we should proceed with the discharge of negative energy?"

"Actually, I did." He quoted, "'To look into a heart that is true, the Eye must see not one, but two.' It clearly takes more than a single person to adequately neutralize harmful vibrations that can muddy the Eye's ability to open."

"Sex magick," she murmured.

The smile crossing his lips held a hint of carnal wickedness. "Exactly."

Dani mulled the idea. Liked it. A lot. She'd always wanted

to dabble in that aspect of witchcraft but had never found a partner she could dare to be so open and intimate with. The practice of sex magick required absolute trust between both participants. If one faltered, the end result would inevitably fail.

She plucked at his white shirt, hinting. "I think you're a little overdressed." She flashed a wicked grin.

He glanced down. "Indeed, I am." A pass of his palm across his body and all his clothes faded away. "Better?"

"Much better." She loved the look of his naked body, particularly the cock nestled in its thatch of tight blond curls.

Naked, he led her around the pool, guiding her onto the ledge directly under the waterfall.

A shock of icy cold water cascaded down over her body, sending dozens of tiny shivers across her bare skin. Eyes snapping wide open, Dani clenched her teeth against the torrent. She definitely hadn't been expecting this!

"Oh, that's icy!" she grated out. "The water's cold." She backed into the crevasse behind the falls, thankful to be out of the arctic blast. Talk about dousing desire!

Braced against its insistent beat, Casedren smiled at her through the torrent. "Invigorating," he corrected. "That will wake you up."

She rubbed her arms. "It'll freeze me to death."

Casedren made a quick motion with his hand. In less than a second, the water turned from desperately frigid to steamy heat.

"Better?"

Dani stuck out an experimental hand. Ah, the water was a comfortably warm temperature now—not too hot, but definitely not too damn cold. She stepped back under the stream. "Much."

"Glad you think so."

"I do." She reached for her neck, rubbing at the twinge between her shoulder blades. The ache from sleeping at an odd angle had made itself welcome deep in her muscles. Not to mention all the tension from recent events. Every time she got stressed, it went straight to her neck and shoulders. "That's just what I need, some nice soothing heat." Closing her eyes, she stood, soaking in the drenching warmth.

Casedren stepped behind her, his hands brushing hers away. "Let me." Strong fingers delved, immediately finding the source of the pain.

Head dropping onto her chest, Dani let herself go limp. "Oh, bless you."

His talented fingers massaged the tendons in her neck, working out the knot of pain. Conquering it, his fingers pressed in the curves under her shoulder blades, sorting through the little aches bundled under the bones.

She sighed, submerging herself in the pleasure of his touch combined with the cascade of water over her naked skin. The water sluiced over her curves in thin rivulets, caressing every inch. "That feels so damn good."

Casedren dropped a light kiss on her damp shoulder. "I'm glad you're enjoying it." His hands trekked down her back, thumbs working the little nooks and crannies around her spine. By the time he reached the end, he'd worked out every tiny kink.

Lulled and thoroughly relaxed under his touch, Dani leaned back into the hard plane of his body. Pressed so close against him she believed she felt the steady rhythm of his heart beating, not in his upper left chest, where a human's heart lay, but lower. The pulse against the small of her back was echoed in his cock, taut and pressing against the crease of her ass.

She smiled. "Feels like someone's a little hard," she teased. "Must be the warm water."

Casedren's arms circled her body, and his fingers plucked at the tips of her erect nipples. "Must be the beautiful naked woman in my arms." He rolled his hips, working his erection between the crack of her ass. The surge of lust conjured by his body trampled through her mind, burning her senses up with the intensity behind his need.

Dani caught her breath as his hands, skillful as those of a master violinist, sought out the pleasure points of her body, one hand stroking and squeezing a breast, even as his other slipped over the smooth plane of her belly and eased into the folds concealing her sex.

She trembled in pleasure when his index finger curled up, the tip burrowing into the sensitive bundles of nerves between her thighs. Whimpering in surrender, she let herself fall into the abyss of arousal that deepened with every slow, creamy stroke against her clit. At the same time he rolled and tugged her left nipple.

Climax struck without warning, rapture unwrapping inside her core, uncoiling wave after wave of sensuous heat.

Dani shuddered against his solid body, her senses rolling under the hot, glorious wave of rapture pouring straight into her veins. The water pounding against her naked skin enhanced the lustrous vibrations of pleasure.

Limp and spent, her legs were close to turning to noodles when Casedren bent and swept her into his arms. With a single smooth glide, he carried her down the wide stone steps into the pool. Warmth enveloped her all over again when he lowered her into its depth.

When she sat, the water came to the depth of her shoulders. "Wow," she murmured through her daze, spreading her arms and leaning back against the side for support. "That was . . ." Words temporarily escaped her numb mind. To make her point, she lifted her rear and scissored her legs through the water, opening them wide so the silky water caressed the insides of her thighs. "Wow."

Casedren watched her move with pure appreciation. "Yes," he agreed with a smile. "Wow."

Arching her back against the stone, Dani stretched, enjoying the feel of submersion. "Oh God, I think I've died and gone to heaven. Talk about disbursing negative energy." She cocked a grin his way. "I could do that all over again. A lot of times."

His serious gaze lightened. "I assure you we will be doing exactly that."

Languorously stretching her legs, Dani let her head loll back against the rim of the pool. "Mmm. Sounds good." The ceiling overhead looked a million miles away, part of the illusion lending artificial height to the waterfall.

Settling across from her, Casedren reached for her foot. Strong fingers worked the front of her foot, his thumbs digging into her arch. "According to what I can understand of the text, the energy of the female partner is most important to the ritual. Her needs must be satisfied."

Dani almost purred at the sensation of his strong fingers working her instep, heel and ankle. Tossing back her head to clear away the tendrils of damp hair clinging to her face, she smiled at him. The long golden strands persisted in snaking down her shoulders, slipping down to tickle the tips of her nipples. Arousal rose all over again. She couldn't seem to get enough sex from this beautiful man. "I can honestly say you're doing a great job," she complimented.

Casedren switched feet. His capable fingers ferreted out every pressure point on her foot, carefully kneading her stress away. "I do not wish to fail," he said quietly. "I want to be able to face my father as a success."

She nodded. "I can understand that."

He continued massaging, working around her ankle and the lower part of her calf. "But it is not because I want to follow my father. But I do want you, as my wife. And I will do anything to make that happen. Anything I have to."

His unexpected words touched her deeply. Since the night he'd first walked into the club, she'd felt a connection with the silent stranger who watched her dance. She'd always hoped he'd say something, but he never did, always slipping away before she left the stage. Even then, she'd felt the connection behind his simmering blue gaze. Her sixth sense had always told her he'd keep coming back. At the time, she just didn't know in what capacity.

She'd just held her breath, waiting and hoping.

She had no regrets about having sex with him that fateful night he'd paid for a private session. The silent anticipation building between them had to be satisfied in any way possible. Even if she'd never seen him again after that night, she wouldn't have regretted her decision to let passion rule her head.

Closing her eyes, she let her head loll back against the rim of the pool. True, she'd had her share of lovers, each experience giving her a little more of an idea what she might seek in a permanent mate. She supposed she'd built up the image of a dream-lover in her mind, imagining what the perfect man might be. Mentally ticking off each of the things she considered important, she wasn't surprised to find the circle led back to Casedren. The few days they'd been together already felt like a lifetime. One look from him was all it took to turn her insides into a quivering mass of jelly.

An achy little pain twanged her heartstrings. It also felt like a lifetime wouldn't be enough time. *I could stay here forever.*

The massage moved from the sides of her foot to her toes, working the space between each with experienced fingers. His touch felt wickedly sensual. "I hope you can," he answered quietly.

Forcing heavy eyelids open, Dani raised her head, belatedly remembering how easily his kind could step into the human mind, effortlessly entering and picking up thought waves the way humans would pick up pretty shells on a beach. "That's hard to get used to, someone who knows what you're thinking."

Kneading up her calf to the crook of her knee, Casedren shrugged. "How can you think twice about an ability you are born with? Mind-walking is the most intimate thing we can share. When you open your mind to another, it means you completely trust them."

Enjoying the massage, Dani flexed her toes. "But it's also something you block from one another."

"Yes." Casedren sighed like a man who knew the downside. "Once you open your mind up to another, you are vulnerable on every level—mentally, physically and emotionally. Not everyone you invite in is operating with pure motives."

She snorted and slapped the water. "Like your brother."

"Like my brother," he agreed. "And so there are ways to safeguard the mind against an outsider walking in at their leisure."

Dani nodded. "Which you said you would teach me."

His fingers continued to work their magic as he spoke, moving down the firm curve of her calf and back to her ankle, then her arch. "When—if—time allows, I will," he promised.

Another sigh escaped her lips as his gentle touch hit a particularly sensitive spot on her instep. The way he treated her was sensual and intimate, with seduction being the crucial goal. She'd already figured the rituals would involve a lot of sex, but she appreciated the way he was taking his time to help her relax and not trying to hurry the process.

Nevertheless his words brought home the fact that they were under a severe time limit. No telling how much of their forty-eight hours had already slipped away.

"So when do we get started opening the Eye?" she asked.

Casedren easily singled out the salacious images forming in her mind. His slow, uncomplicated grin shifted Dani's heart from a normal rhythm into overdrive. The signals of intense arousal hit every part of her body, tightening her nipples into rosy little buds and turning up the heat simmering between her thighs. What he had done earlier, she knew, had been only a little taste of the sexual delights yet to happen.

His vivid gaze sparked like flint striking stone. "Oh, we've only just begun to get started."

A smile twitched at Dani's lips. Heavy awareness pulsed through her body. In this case, one orgasm wasn't going to be enough to discharge her tension.

She'd need . . . *several.*

18

A few changes had taken place in the bedroom during their absence. The bed had vanished, making way for a new, more intimate arrangement. A large fur blanket was spread in front of the hearth. An array of thick pillows were scattered on top for extra comfort. The soft strains of a classical sonata filled the air. Soft and subtle, it perfectly set a calm, romantic mood. A wicker basket sat nearby, along with a silver carafe nestled in a bucket of ice.

A vague sense of uneasiness rippled through her. Each step put them a little closer to the Eye. Still, there was no reason to let him know nerves still gnawed at her guts. "Nice," she murmured. "Very romantic."

Unselfconsciously naked, Casedren reached for her hand. "Thank you." He led her toward the fireplace. "I thought you might be a little hungry, so I asked Enoch to arrange something special for you."

Throat tightening, a thousand words tangled around the lump forming there. Warmth and a startling sense of comfort embraced her. How sweet of him to think of her, try to ease her

transition into rituals she'd never dared to think about partici-
pating in. Sex magick was the most intimate form of conjuration. Trust in one's partner was an implicit part of making any
ritual work.

Silently following her every thought, his knowing gaze met
hers. "You know I would not hurt you."

Heart pounding in her chest, she nodded and sat on the fur
throw, enjoying the feel of the soft hair tickling her bare skin.
Gathering her composure, she glanced up at him. "I know. It's
going to be fine."

He settled down beside her. Dani's breath stalled in her
lungs as the fire caught the fine blond hair on his chest, giving
his skin a golden sheen. An unearthly, otherworld glow. Not
for the first time it occurred to her that though Casedren
looked human, he wasn't human at all.

Lucifer was God's most beautiful angel, she remembered
him say. Whatever his heritage, she couldn't deny that Casedren belonged to a most striking race of beings. The back of her
neck prickled when he reached for the picnic basket. His muscles rippled beneath taut flesh. There was no denying the sinew
in his arms, or the generous size of his penis, impressive even
when flaccid.

Trying not to stare at this beautiful creature, Dani deliberately cut her gaze to the fire, feeling a hot flush burn her cheeks.
The knowledge of physical ecstasy they'd shared—and would
share again—was in the forefront of her mind. Every time she
looked at Casedren, she couldn't help but think about sex.
Even though he'd just given her a mind-blowing orgasm, she
wanted more. Another and another, kindling for the flames
he'd lit so easily inside her soul.

He sat the basket down and flipped the lid open. "I hope
you are hungry."

Dani's attention flickered away from carnal appetite to
physical appetite. Her stomach rumbled with interest, remind-

ing her she hadn't eaten a solid meal in quite a while. "Actually, I'm starving," she admitted. The broth had definitely worn off.

"Good." He flashed a satisfied smile. "I think we have managed to do a little better on the food situation."

The music playing in the background changed to another melody, one she found vaguely recognizable. It played at a subtle volume, just at the reach of hearing. What its source might be, she couldn't guess. Sedah didn't seem to have any device remotely resembling modern technology as she knew it.

"Beethoven?" she asked.

Pleased she'd noticed, Casedren nodded. "Yes. One of my favorites. Perfect for seduction." There was a naughty half grin behind his gaze.

Dani laughed and made a face. "Brings back memories of all those hours at the piano. My parents insisted." She stuck out her tongue. "I studied about a year before begging to be switched to dance classes instead."

He cut her a mischievous grin. "Where you learned to make love to metal poles for the benefit of horny males."

Hand flying to her mouth, Dani felt her face flame. "Uh, actually, no." She tried to laugh but didn't quite manage. Her dancing was already a sore point with her brother. Had her parented been alive, they would have definitely registered disapproval. "My parents would shit bricks if they knew all that good money they spent on dance lessons was pretty much wasted."

He leaned closer. "I do not consider it time wasted at all."

Dani shook her head. "Most men don't. I studied ballet, actually, not strip teasing. I thought I would be a great prima ballerina, except I got too damn tall and filled out in all the wrong places. I just haven't got that tiny, perfect little body."

He cast her an admiring look. "I would disagree most vigorously with that assessment. You have a gorgeous body."

"Thanks. I've always felt that my tits were a little heavy."

His gaze glinted with a hint of lechery. "I've held them, and I can assure you they feel just fine."

She glanced down at her chest, briefly giving her girls a little cupping to test the theory. "You're a man," she huffed. "All titties are wonderful to you."

He considered. "I suppose that is true."

She shook a finger at him in mock anger. "And shame on you for hanging out in nudie bars anyway. That's no way for a future king to act."

Casedren shrugged. "Can I help it if my future queen was a stripper?"

Dani considered. "Well, think of it this way. Maybe I wouldn't have been as alluring sitting in front of a piano banging out show tunes." She rolled her eyes. "God, I hated those lessons. *Bo-ring!*"

He chuckled. "I am not surprised. You did not appear to enjoy the music earlier in the evening."

She shook her head, lifting her hands and wriggling her slender fingers. "Don't get me wrong, I appreciate the music of dead old men. They were the rock stars of their time." She sighed. "As for playing, I can make my way through a few short pieces, but forget playing a full sonata. I learned to sorta appreciate the music, but I really love modern rock the most. If it has a catchy beat and some lyrics I can halfway understand, I'm good. You?"

He crinkled his nose. "I admit to having little taste for what you call modern rock. It seems so grating on the ears."

She gave him a friendly poke to the ribs. "Seems to me you liked it just fine, smart-ass. Especially when I was bumping and grinding to the beat."

Casedren responded with a good-natured wince, followed by a quick wink. "It was actually the bumping and grinding I enjoyed most. I was so busy looking at you I barely heard the

music." He reached into the basket. Two glasses came out. Lifting the carafe, he poured two generous helpings. "I have to admit you can do things with a pole that are obscenely amazing."

"I can do even more amazing things with my lips," she countered.

He offered her a glass. "Of that I have no doubt."

Dani accepted his offering. "Just so you know I'd still fuck you even if you weren't a prince."

Casedren sighed. "Alas, that status may soon be yanked out from under my feet."

"That hasn't happened yet," she countered.

Gaze turning pensive, Casedren sipped his wine. "What if I cannot meet my father's challenge?"

She regarded her own glass, keeping in mind to take it easy this time. "I wouldn't worry about it until it's time to worry."

Lifting a hand, his fingertips rubbed briefly at his temples. Despite trying to keep the conversation light, he clearly had a lot on his mind. "Easy to say. Not so easy to do."

A smile tugged at her lips. "I have complete confidence in you."

His blue eyes glimmered with curiosity, and his hand dropped. "Is that so?" He looked genuinely pleased at the compliment. He obviously hadn't gotten many in his life.

Blood thrummed through her veins. "It isn't every day I get picked up by the sexiest man in the underworld." The words sounded oafish the second they came out of her mouth, but she meant them.

His lids fluttered closed, a look of both longing and despair shadowing his masculine features. "Oh, you flatter me. Tell me another story, please."

Just looking at him caused a flip-flopping sensation in her gut and a delicious twinge of need between her thighs.

She drew a breath, stifling a groan with a mouthful of wine.

Cool down. "It's true. You're one of the most gorgeous and fascinating men I've ever met in my entire life." She raised her glass in a toast. "I'm truly honored you chose me."

Casedren eyed her with an air of quiet certainty. "Would you believe me if I told you I knew from the time I was a young boy there would be only one woman I would ever want to marry?"

Dani snorted in disbelief. "Oh please! Now you're the one telling stories."

He held up a hand, hushing her. "No, honestly, I am not." He reached out, lightly brushing the curve of her cheek with the tip of his finger. "In my world, a child's astrological mate-chart is drawn up at birth. In this chart, it details the dates and times that potential compatible female souls will also be born— even if it is to be several centuries into the future. Many of us have more than one choice."

Her eyebrows shot up. "So is this your way of telling me you've had a lot of women in your time?"

Casedren's gaze never wavered. "Absolutely not. In my heart, I knew there was only one woman for me. So I waited, and waited some more, spending more than half my life alone. And then a young girl afar cast a spell, wrapping herself around my heart. It was then I knew my wait had not been wasted."

Dani tilted her head to one side. For all she knew he was making the entire story up to amuse her. "My grandmother always swore that spell would bring me the man of my dreams." She tried to sound casual but her voice came out deeper, more heated, than she'd expected. The fire crackled, casting a delicious glow over her naked skin. The glow in her inner core grew warmer. She took another swallow of wine to cool her need.

Casedren's gaze met hers, crinkling around the edges. He brushed the wisps of hair off her forehead before tracing the curve between her shoulder and neck with a feathery touch. "Do you think it did?"

Dani let out the breath she'd been holding. What she felt for Casedren Teraketh was more than instant attraction or the need to fulfill an inner lust. They belonged together and she knew that as surely as she knew she needed oxygen to breathe. She'd never felt that kind of conviction in her entire life. It was more than a little bit daunting.

"I'm pretty sure it did." She clucked her tongue. "Though I might be a bit delusional thinking that."

Surprised, he arched a single brow. "Oh?"

Her stomach rumbled and she laughed. "I'm starving, and wine on an empty stomach will make a woman say crazy things. You'd better feed me so I can think straight."

Casedren shook his head. "Ah, I see. It is not me you want, but the bounty I have here."

She nodded. "Exactly."

He reached for the basket. "I will have you know that Enoch had to cross an entire dimension to acquire these delights for you."

That piqued her interest. "Oh? Is that so? Must be something hard to get if you had to go all the way to earth to get it."

"Something we do not have here," he confirmed. "I could not fail to notice you seemed less than pleased with our vegetarian diet."

"Given all you big brawny men, I'd have imagined a more carnivorous diet. You know, ripping a piece of meat off the shank of a cow with your bare teeth."

"Although we have livestock, it is not for slaughter. What the animals provide helps maintain our diets. We certainly do not have the right to take their lives in order to devour their carcasses."

"I suppose there are those, ah, persons who live by that philosophy even on earth, too," she said, trying to be diplomatic. She supposed she would eat whatever he served, however terrible and healthful it might prove to be. No reason to admit she'd prefer a nice meat-laden pizza with extra sauce.

She watched him dig into the basket, unwrapping one delicacy after another, all carefully done up in white wax paper. The spread he laid out was magnificent—a baguette of French bread with various cold cuts and cheeses and slices of choice fruits with chocolate and caramel sauce for dipping.

He looked over the food. "I think this might be more to your liking."

Dani agreed. "Oh my God. You got meat. Real, honest-to-God food."

Casedren passed out napkins and plastic utensils. His lips parted into a mischievous grin. "Shall we eat?"

She grinned back. "Gladly."

The bread was presliced, allowing them to easily build their subs. Condiments were even included, and Dani chose turkey and Swiss with mayo while Casedren went for the roast beef with American cheese and tons of mustard.

"I'm surprised to see you eat meat." She bit into her sandwich. The bread was crusty, chewy and fresh. It tasted wonderful with the wine to wash it down.

Casedren looked a little embarrassed. "I admit, living among your people has changed my tastes more than a little."

Dani reached for her wineglass. "When in Rome, eat as the Romans, eh?" She took a deep drink of wine. It created a warm glow in her belly

He picked a piece of meat out of his sandwich, nibbling on it. "Exactly."

She stuffed down another bite. "You didn't have to go through all this trouble for me."

Casedren swallowed a bite of his food. "No trouble. We do

have access to your world any time we want, remember? Besides, I want you to feel comfortable here."

Sandwich devoured, Dani wiped her fingers and mouth with a napkin. The much-needed meal had definitely hit the spot. She felt a little less shaky, her mind a little clearer. "That reminds me what I wanted to ask you. Your world mirrors earth a lot, so why isn't it as advanced?"

Casedren thought a moment before answering. "Sedah is powered by the sole natural resource we have at hand, a psi-level energy shaped by the will of the conjurer. Some things we can duplicate within reason. Others we cannot, because electrical or mechanical things simply will not function here. For example, I can wear a watch on earth. Here, it will not run a single minute. Anything mechanical shuts down."

Dani thought about her iPod and inwardly cringed. "How do you people live?"

Casedren shrugged. "Quite well, actually." He reached for the chocolate sauce, pulling the lid off the small plastic container. "Ready for dessert?"

Dani patted her stomach. "I'm stuffed, but anything with chocolate definitely gets my attention."

He reached for a ripe strawberry, dipping it into the dark sauce until it was coated to the stem. "This definitely adds to the flavor of the fruit." He held it out for her to taste.

Dani leaned forward and opened her mouth wide. Casedren placed the berry inside. She closed her eyes, chewing slowly to savor all the flavors. "It's fabulous."

His eyes never left her lips and Dani's insides heated up all over again. "I am glad you enjoyed it." There was a deep rumble behind his words. The intensity in his gaze sent a shiver down her spine, renewing her need and anticipation all over again.

She licked her lips and grinned. "I could use another."

He dipped in another berry. This time he teased her by outlining her lips in the chocolate before letting her taste it.

She laughed. "Goodness, you missed."

Casedren leaned forward. "I didn't miss." His tongue expertly traced her top lip, swiping away the confection, the beginning of a deliciously sweet kiss.

Dani couldn't resist, letting momentum take over. His lips were firm, gentle. He tasted of yeasty bread and the spicy mustard he'd slathered on his meat, not altogether unpleasant. But beneath his gentleness she felt an extra tug of longing.

His? Or her own?

She wasn't sure. Maybe a little bit of both.

Breaking their kiss, Casedren reached for her hand. Spreading open her fingers, he traced her palm. His touch was electric. "I think we should prepare for the ritual." His voice lowered a dangerous, seductive octave. "Are you sure you want to do this?" Gaze never veering away from hers, he lifted her hand to his mouth. His lips closed over her index finger, tongue teasing the sensitive pad.

Mesmerized, Dani couldn't pull her hand away. As she looked into the electric energy alive in his eyes, any doubts she'd had about accompanying him to Sedah melted away. Her whole body tingled, nipples swelling into tight peaks that longed for his lips to suckle them. She groaned and shifted her body. The insides of her thighs boiled with liquid heat. "How should we do that?"

Casedren caressed the curve under her chin. "Like this." He lowered his head, brushing his lips over hers.

All her fears and doubts melted. She felt herself being swept away, caught up in the fantasy Casedren wove so deftly around her.

19

Pulling her closer, Casedren deepened their kiss, his tongue leading hers in an exquisite dance.

Pressing against him, Dani relished the feel of his muscular body against hers. They seemed to fit together perfectly. It felt right, natural. His hand moved lower, coming to rest on her breast. The sensation sent blood pounding through her temples. "I've never worked sex magick before," she breathed.

"Me, either."

She laughed. "I've been wanting to, but never found anyone to cast the rituals with."

Eyes dancing with delight, he whispered, "I hope I am not just anyone." He gave her a slow lingering kiss that sent a thrill clear to the tips of her toes.

Dani eyed the naked man. Broad shoulders, flat stomach and a narrow waist met her hungry gaze. He was flawless, right down to the erection jutting up against his ridged abdomen. "I don't cross a dimension just to be with anyone."

Big hands claimed her. "I do not ask just any woman to

come with me." Easing her back onto a soft pillow, he nuzzled her neck, his hot moist breath tickling her skin. He traced slow circles around the hard little bead of one nipple, even as he grasped an earlobe gently between his teeth and tugged.

The erotic sensation traveled through her stomach, straight down into her crotch. She clenched her legs tightly together, trying to alleviate the ache in her clit. The waves of longing crashing through her body only intensified the sweetest of pains. Her body arched, begging for more of his touch.

With his thumb and forefinger, Casedren rolled and tugged at the erect nubbin. His head dipped, tongue flicking the hard tip.

Dani let out of whoosh of breath as the world tilted on its axis. Her vision blurred when he began to suckle the sensitized tip. All rational thoughts fled her mind. Blood pounded at her temples, blurring everything but sensation. All she wanted to do was feel, enjoy the sensations of pure unadulterated pleasure. The heated sensation of his mouth felt more than good. It felt oh-so right. She was aware of only the slow circles going around the sensitive pink areola.

Without a second thought, she moved her own hands toward his body, feeling for and then finding his erection. Fingers wrapping around his vein-covered shaft, she gently jacked up and down its length, enjoying the surge of sheer power radiating from his cock. He was all man.

Casedren's mouth recaptured hers, the tongue tangling beginning all over again. Dani closed her eyes, imagining his body on top of hers, his thighs between her spread legs as he positioned his body to enter her. There would be no hesitation. His thrust inside her womanly depths would be swift and sure.

Casedren groaned against her mouth. "Harder, please. It is not made out of glass."

Enjoying the feel of his aroused heat, Dani laughed low in her throat. "Any harder and I'll pull it off."

He treated her to a sexy grin. His eyes danced with delight. "Let's not get too excited."

She tossed him a naughty grin. "Excited is just the way I like you. In fact, there's something I'm just dying to try." She wriggled out of his hold and reached over his body for the container of chocolate.

Realizing her intent, his erection bobbed with renewed interest. "Oh, you naughty little girl."

Dani brandished the chocolate. "On your back, please. I'd like to finish my dessert."

Casedren rolled over, tucking his hands behind his head. "I think I am going to enjoy dessert more than you are." His cock bobbed, arching up against the plane of his flat belly.

In one smooth move, Dani straddled his legs. "I wouldn't be so sure about that." Her fingers wrapped around his shaft, turning the expression on his face from one of amusement to that of pure pleasure. Peeking into his mind, she sensed him mentally losing his grip on self-control.

Casedren groaned low in his throat, flexing his hips in an upward motion. "I am fairly sure I am getting the better bargain."

Dani tossed a wicked grin. "We'll see." Dipping a finger into the chocolate, she spread it across the crown of his penis like frosting on cake. "Mmm . . . looks good enough to eat." Bending over, she licked away the sweet treat.

Casedren moaned in vulnerable delight. "That feels so damn good," he gritted out through clenched teeth.

Dani added more, then licked the chocolate away before swirling her tongue around the ridges of his flushed crown. His cock pulsed with every flick and lick she delivered.

Catching his breath, Casedren moaned long and loud.

She lifted her head. "Feel good?"

"Um, ohhhh . . ." The ability to speak coherently seemed to have deserted him.

Dani continued to please him, delivering tiny little nips and slow licks all over the veined ridges of his cock. Reaching the end, she started upward, repeating the whole delicious torture all over again. She ended back at the top of his cock, giving a long, suckling pull.

Throat working, Casedren swallowed hard and licked dry lips. "You are a goddess. I worship at the altar of your glorious mouth."

Dani cupped his balls, giving them a friendly little tweak. She felt them drawing up as the blistering pressure of climax built inside him. She scraped the tip with her teeth. "I'm the one who's doing the worshipping, of your absolutely perfect cock." She rolled her tongue against its sensitive head before opening her mouth and engulfing him all the way to the root.

Just when she had him on the edge of total release, Casedren fisted a hand in her hair, lifting her lips off his straining cock.

"What—" she started to say.

Casedren lifted up, rolling her onto her back in one easy motion. "The only way I am going to come is inside of you." Letting loose of her hair, he eased himself over her until he lay half on top of her. His erection pressed against her thigh like a branding iron sizzling against vulnerable skin. Dipping his head, he nibbled lightly at the soft flesh between her neck and shoulder.

Turned on by his rough handling, a soft moan of pleasure escaped Dani's lips. Her hands settled on his shoulder, fingers digging deep. Hot muscle pulsed beneath her palms. She hadn't meant for things to get out of hand so quickly, but the tempest of desire twisting inside him refused to be easily harnessed.

She tightened her hold, wanting to feel her heat merge with his. "I want you inside me." A violent shiver ran down her spine, all the way to the tips of her toes. With every whiff of his fire-warm skin, her clit pulsed harder.

"Not so fast. First I need to administer a little payback."

"Payback?" she squeaked. "What are you going to do?"

Casedren's gaze subtly darkened with wicked intent. "You are about to find out." With a soft growl, he brought his mouth down on hers, hungry and demanding more. At the same time his palm slid down over her flat belly and over her mound to the crux between her thighs. The glide of his fingers against her most sensitive flesh sent red-hot darts of flame through her every nerve ending.

Dani gasped, writhing, frantic to ease the ache building inside her. "Oh my . . . That feels wonderful."

Need twisted brutally inside her. Hardly aware of the action, she spread her legs wider, offering him full access. Her hips bucked upward even as she heard his name escape her lips.

Casedren sensed her need, easing a finger inside her creaming sex. Strong vaginal muscles, warm and moist, gripped him.

The smoldering embers of arousal were threatening to turn into an incinerating firestorm. "More," she urged, her breath shallow and fast, rasping her bruised lips. He'd ravaged her mouth, taking everything and giving nothing. "Give me more." The single profound ache shimmered inside her, like wax melting under hot flames.

A second thick finger joined the first, filling her a little further. He increased the tempo even as his thumb expertly worked her clit. The sensations of his solid digits against her softness made her crave for something harder . . . longer . . . thrusting . . . driving her over the edge into pure pleasure.

Caught on the edge of a scream, Dani's entire body shuddered. Muscles deep inside clenched. She cried out, moaning like a bitch in heat as her cunt squeezed his fingers and held them.

Casedren's compelling gaze locked on her. "I love to hear you whimper."

"Damn you," she shot between clenched teeth. "Don't stop

now." She began to move her hips in time to his fingers as he thrust deeper. With every gliding motion, he went farther inside. The tremors began in small waves and continued until they grasped her firmly in the heated convulsions of orgasm. Madness engulfed her, and she wasn't going to be satisfied until she felt his cock ramming into her. More than that, she wanted him to lose control as she had, lead him to the glorious abyss of sheer pleasure.

Casedren suddenly pulled his hand away. He spread juice-stained fingers across her mouth. She tasted her own sweet cream mingling with her womanly fragrance an instant before his lips claimed hers. "Chocolate is good," he murmured against her mouth. "But this is better."

Dani sighed aloud. "Much better." Her carnal ache was so bad she'd do anything to ease the pulsing, pounding waves of longing rolling through her veins.

Casedren's hands slid down her stomach to her hips. Lifting her off the fur throw, he turned her over. Settling on his knees between her spread legs, he tucked a pillow under her to elevate her height. His big warm palms settled on the curves of her rear. "You have a most delectable ass," he complimented, giving both cheeks a little squeeze.

Sprawled flat, Dani pushed up and managed to brace some of her weight on her elbows. "Thank you." She glanced over her shoulder and offered a challenge. "Oh, I hope this is kinky."

One side of his mouth curved in an upward arc. He gave a devilish laugh. "As much as imagination and a willing woman will allow." Gripping his penis in one hand, he stroked it a couple of times, then pressed the swollen purple crown against her clit.

Dani trembled with pleasure as he stroked the little nub, sliding his cock easily between her silky labia but not entering her depths. She shuddered, remembering all over again how powerful desire could be. Her whole body ached to melt into his, but he was tormenting her, savoring the feel of her as though his only purpose were to pleasure her.

Restraint broke with an audible crack. To urge him on, she made a soft little sound of need.

Immediately, Casedren responded. He thrust hard. The head of his penis was smooth, but with every push she felt the ridges creating a rasping sensation that was almost unbearable. His cock filled her, an iron bar throbbing with heat, stretching and possessing her as no other had. The shock of his entry stole her breath and she gasped in surprise. Each time he took her felt more incredible than the last. Downy inner muscles automatically clenched his length with the frantic, mindless urge of mating.

Chuckling in delight, he pulled back, holding her hips. "You're so damn tight." His voice came out strangled with need.

Dazed and overwhelmed, she whimpered and pressed her ass back against him in invitation. She loved being stuffed full of hard cock. "Mmm, glad you approve."

Giving a low, sexy chuckle, Casedren eased back in, making sure she felt every delicious inch. "Oh, I approve in every way." Outstretched arms supporting his weight, he lowered his body over hers like a blanket, slowly stroking in and out of her silken depth. "What about you? Do you enjoy my cock?" To emphasize his words, he ground his hips harder against hers.

Jarred to the bone by his punishing stroke, Dani dug her fingers into the fur. "Oh, God, yes. . . . This is too good." Her clit was swollen, poking between her lips, rubbing against him even as his balls slapped against her ass.

Gaining some leverage with her knees, she pushed back to meet his thrusts. She added her own hip action, bucking back against his hips to increase the friction between their bodies. A blossoming frisson of sensation coiled through her, an ache she welcomed.

Casedren slipped one hand beneath her body, squeezing, teasing the taut nipple he found an erect peak. "I want all of you, Danicia. Everything you are willing to give, I will take."

Dazed by his thrusts, Dani couldn't think of a suitable reply. Her entire body quivered. "Take everything," she whimpered. His every caress seared, burning its way to the bone. Each stroke was like a burst of sweet fire, delivering luminous rapture. Her internal temperature shot into the feverish range. She couldn't get enough of him.

She shuddered violently, her lips pressed together as she struggled to make the sensations last just a moment longer. Her back arched in fierce response when he slowed his rhythm. A new game began. Just when she was about to go over the edge, he slowed his pace, sending her into a spiral of need that had her begging shamelessly for completion. He was in control and determined to keep it. He wasn't going to let it end until he'd wrung every ounce of pleasure out of her body.

"Damn you," she moaned in a husky voice. "You're tormenting me." With every gliding motion, he speared deeper, claiming her in a way no other lover ever had before. It was as if her body had been created to be conquered by this man.

Getting her knees under her, she lifted her hips into a new position, allowing him a more penetrating access to the depths of her feminine core. Long blond hair tumbled into her face.

Casedren delivered a light nip, his breath singing the back of her neck. "Who is the tease now?"

It was no use to try to continue to speak coherently. Words failed her, but her emotions definitely did not. The feelings overwhelming her were sending rational thoughts right out of her head. All she wanted to do was concentrate on, and enjoy, the incredible vibrations his touch produced. Somehow, this man had drawn her into the center of a whirlpool so deep and fast that she barely had time to breathe before disappearing under another crashing wave of desire.

Sensing her unspoken need for release, Casedren let the tension between them build anew, beginning a rhythm unlike any she'd ever before experienced. Their bodies were coming together, parting and rejoining through thrusts that were harder, faster and more intense than the ones before. All she could do was let him have his way and hang on for the ride.

Bracing her palms against the rug, Dani tossed her head back and screamed out at the mind-bending pleasure hovering just out of her reach. He took her with deep, spiking thrusts that made contact with every raw nerve in her body, sending the coil of orgasm straight up her spine, all the way to the nape of her neck. If only he'd thrust deeper—*one . . . more . . . time . . .* — she might be able to reach the peak of an absolute and perfect completion.

Driving home one last time, Casedren pressed his hips against hers. Buried to the balls, he groaned as his orgasm detonated with a brutal magnificence. His cock surged, releasing a torrent of warm semen into her waiting womb.

His peak simultaneously triggered hers. Something animalistic and primal broke free inside her. Climax arrived like a blast of mortar fire. Liquid heat seared her senses in a red-hot wave of punishing bliss. Barely able to catch her breath, she toppled over the edge of rapture. Climax rose inside her, streaming up and out of her core like molten lava disgorged from the peak of an active volcano. Pouring down the mountain, it devoured everything in its path.

Releasing control at the last possible second, she shattered. Pleasure crashed through her, the beauty of it fracturing her senses. Shuddering from head to foot, she closed her eyes against the starburst of sensation, grabbing one of the glittering streamers and riding it all the way to the end of the universe.

Pressing her ass against Casedren's hips to keep him inside her a bit longer, Dani wanted the moment to last forever as the mingled sensations flowed together through the psychic link they'd unconsciously slipped into. She'd never known how powerful a moment like this could be when shared by two minds. It was awesome, frightening and fabulous all at once. Stripped naked in more ways than one, she'd not only been taken, not only claimed.

She'd been possessed.

Completely.

20

Shaken from the inside out, Dani collapsed in a boneless heap. Heart raging against her ribs, exhaustion stormed through her. Casedren was spread on top of her, his breath shimming across her left ear, his own collapse as absolute as hers. Hot and sweaty, their skin adhered together, his chest pressing against her back. His penis still filled her sex, half flaccid in the aftermath of shuddering climax. The intoxicating scent of sexual musk permeated the air around them.

Shifting restlessly, Casedren groaned softly against the nape of her neck. "That was amazing," he whispered.

Feeling limp as an overcooked piece of pasta, Dani moaned and stirred under him. "Incredible." Her head swam from the intensity of their lovemaking. She felt dazed and feeble, totally unable to lift a hand to swat a fly. With a belly full of good food and a body sated by incredible sex, all she wanted to do was drift off to sleep. She didn't even need a blanket. Casedren was doing the job just fine.

Lifting his weight off her just a little, Casedren moved his hips in a circular motion, slowly pumping against hers. A little growl of physical need rumbled deep in his throat. He definitely wasn't finished. "My lady," he murmured. "I want you all over again."

She definitely felt him, too. Undercurrents of lust rippled down her spine, tying tight knots insider her core. Damn. She couldn't seem to get enough. Neither could he.

Spreading her legs and lifting her hips, she sucked in a breath while tightening her abdominal muscles, which in turn flexed muscles deep inside her core. Her internal grip tightened around his shaft in the most delicious way. Praise be to the dance instructor who'd taught her that move.

Casedren pulled in a quick, hard breath. "I feel you rippling around me." Delight rasped his voice. To return the favor, he flexed his powerful torso, grinding his hips against hers with more intensity. Pulsing with renewed strength, his cock nestled deeper.

Hands curling around his corded forearms, Dani sucked in her own surprised breath. Somehow the slight, gentler movement renewed all the earlier sensations, triggering her third orgasm.

Shuddering beneath his weight, Dani dug her nails into his skin. Heat swamped her senses. Closing her eyes, a low, soft moan eddied over her lips. Instead of washing her away with a violent tide, pleasure lapped at her senses like long, lazy waves eddying up on a beach.

The minutes ticked by, lost in the swirl of an all-encompassing passion.

Reveling in the exquisite sensations of total gratification, Dani let her lids drift shut, committing every nuance of the moment to memory. Nothing this perfect lasted forever, and she wanted to remember it for the rest of her life. It didn't take a wiser head to warn her that rapture like this was fleeting. King Bastien's challenge to his son still loomed over their heads.

Fail, and Casedren would lose the Jadian throne. Fail, and she'd be handed off to his twin, a man clearly walking the line between psycho and sadist.

Utterly spent, Casedren rolled off her. Tucking a pillow beneath his head, he stretched out. A moment later Dani felt him drag his fingers down her spine, then over the curve of her ass. "I thought you said you'd worry when it was time to worry," he murmured.

Lifting her head, Dani turned to look at him. Blond locks tumbled into her face, obscuring the view. Annoyed, she swiped her hair out of her eyes. "I'm not worried." *Yet.* "I'm just thinking."

His frown was grim. "That you really do not want to be my brother's fuck toy." His mouth twisted wryly. Saying the words was obviously distasteful.

That's exactly what she'd been thinking.

A vague sense of uneasiness ripped through her. His words chilled her, but she didn't let herself react. It was strange, not saying a word but having another person totally aware of everything going on inside her mind. In several ways it was an unwelcome invasion. Some things needed to be kept private. She really needed to get him to teach her how to keep her mind masked without conscious effort.

She swallowed down the lump rising in her throat. "No, I don't."

Casedren spread his palm out over her rear, his big hand claiming one exposed cheek. Lightly stubbled with hair, the line of his jaw was taut with apprehension. "No matter what happens, I promise you, here and now, that I will not allow that to happen."

Staring into his eyes, Dani clearly discerned what was on his mind. The images came as clear and bright as television signals. The thought of her making love to another man bothered the hell out of him—especially if that man was his own twin. His surge of jealously at the possibility seared through her mind.

Feeling as though she'd intruded on a very private moment, Dani averted her eyes. His thoughts indicated desperation, just as his gaze brewed jealously. Though he hadn't said it aloud, seeing her in his brother's arms had wounded him, deeply and profoundly.

Though she didn't want to know these things, Dani couldn't help picking up the sublevel psychic vibrations emanating from within his mind. For some reason, he seemed unable to close his mind to her—just as she was unable to avoid picking up his thoughts. It was like being tied to the tracks in front of an oncoming train. There was no way to stop it.

Buried in a far corner of his mind, Casedren suspected she would in fact prefer Cellyn as her lover. Far from putting it out of his mind, the memory had burrowed into his brain like a thorn, festering a bitter poison.

Don't think that way, she signaled, attempting to take advantage of their silent connection. All she could do was open her mind and hope he understood she wasn't concealing anything from him. The impulses she'd felt under Cellyn's touch were falsely induced. Under his spell, she couldn't help the responses of her body any more than she could stop breathing oxygen and survive.

Casedren's hand abruptly lifted, leaving a terrible cold spot in its place. The level of tension abruptly ratcheted up a notch. She heard the release of breath he'd been holding. "I not only saw how you reacted to his touch," he said quietly, "I felt your enjoyment."

His accusation struck like a breath stealing punch. The slam hit her in the heart, almost shattering it. His sudden leap to attack stunned.

For a moment she didn't know how to respond, letting instinct overrule common sense. Her temper raised its head, coiling tight. The way he talked made it sound like she'd slip out of his bed and into Cellyn's without blinking twice.

Fury swept over her with such force that the words tangled on her tongue. "You really think so?" Her hand ached to connect with his face. "That I really want to be with your brother?"

Face brewing anger, he shrugged. "Admit it. You are attracted to him. Your lips may deny it, but your body said another thing."

Confused as to why he would try and bait her, Dani bit down on her bottom lip. Belatedly, she realized he'd made love to her so fiercely not only out of desire, but to erase his brother's touch on her skin.

Looking into the depths of his eyes, she saw not anger, but something deeper and more profound. He wasn't simply jealous. No, this was much worse. Casedren truly had feelings for her, deep unalterable feelings welling up from a place inside his soul he couldn't question or control.

Suppressing a tremble, she shot him a hard look. "Of course, I'm attracted to him," she said quietly. "He looks like you, and I happen to be attracted to *you*." She shook her head. "As for wanting to fuck him because of that, I don't. Your brother took advantage of a woman who'd had too much to drink. That doesn't make him any kind of a hero. It makes him a rapist."

Casedren didn't look convinced. His thoughts were still negative. Dark. Attempting to spare her, he immediately shut his mind with brutal precision, abruptly and effectively shoving her out. The closing was like the slamming of a heavy metal door, loud and clanging through her skull in an endless echo.

Staring directly at him, Dani saw the shimmer of nerves beneath the surface of his calm. His skin practically crackled with pent-up tension. Through the last few days, his every nerve had been stripped bare and exposed. His entire world had been knocked out of orbit when his father set before him a challenge few men succeeded in conquering. One of the reasons he had not yet attempted to work with the Eye was because its purpose befuddled him. He had no sure way to solve its mystery.

She narrowed her eyes. "Instead of fearing it, why don't we simply begin working the rituals?"

Letting out a shuddery breath, Casedren allowed his gaze to reconnect with hers. "I have never worked rituals such as this," he admitted after a long hesitation.

Realizing her skin had suddenly turned icy, Dani sat up and extended her hands toward the snapping flames. "I haven't either," she said over her shoulder. "We'll just be learning together."

Casedren stirred behind her. Sitting up, he scooted closer, pulling her between his legs and folding her in his embrace. One of his hands found hers. Their fingers linked. The air between them shifted and thickened. Her pulse spiked. "What did I do to deserve a woman like you?" he whispered into her hair.

Leaning into the hard planes of his body, Dani settled her head on his shoulder. "You have good taste," she teased.

He suppressed a shiver. "No one has ever accused me of being a wise man."

One side of her mouth curved upward. "No one knows you like I do," she murmured. Her feelings for him were burrowing in, becoming a deep and irrevocable part of her being.

For several long minutes, the only sounds came from the crackling flames in the hearth and the soft, steady breathing of two bodies.

She would have sighed with contentment if the situation facing them hadn't been so dire. God. Three days ago, her life had been absolutely normal. Meeting an underworld prince was like tripping and falling down the rabbit's hole. She'd come in blind, deaf and dumb, unready and unarmed for what she faced. All she had right now was Casedren.

He had to be enough.

When the silence became unbearable, Casedren dropped a light kiss on her temple. "Would you think less of me if I told you I was afraid?"

Shaking her head, Dani glanced up at him. "At least you're honest. I would think less of you if you were swaggering around here, saying how you'd knock your brother on his ass."

He laughed with true amusement. "I probably should knock my brother on his ass."

"I hope you do. Someday."

Drawing a deep breath, Casedren squeezed her tighter. "No matter what happens, I will not go down without a fight. I am not totally without resources. I have men who would take up their swords against my father and brother if necessary."

Dani literally froze in shock at the idea. A man with a death sentence hanging over his head had nothing to lose. Casedren wasn't stupid. He surely knew that action would ignite a civil war in Sedah faster than a match hitting gasoline. It didn't take a genius to figure out that an all-out conflict among the Jadians would inevitably spill over into earth.

Swallowing thickly, she licked dry lips. "No," she said, surprised by the single word that popped out of her mouth.

His body immediately stiffened. "No?" he echoed, surprised. Frustration snarled through the single word.

Stomach roiling, Dani felt nauseated when she considered Casedren's nature shifting to match Cellyn's. He wasn't that kind of a man. "Whatever you do, you have to play this fairly, honestly and with all integrity. To do anything less would take you to Cellyn's level. You're not like him, Casedren. I don't want you to think you have to be."

"Stooping to Cellyn's level might save both our lives," he said dryly. The low rumble in his voice punctuated his words with an ominous foreshadowing that raised goose bumps on her skin.

The thought of violence made her guts twist. With his sons at each other's throats, King Bastien might have no choice but to choose the one he favored most. Given what she'd witnessed, there was no doubt which twin he'd select.

Dani broke out of his hold. Shaken, her breath rattled tremulously as she rose to her feet. "In that case, I might as well be with Cellyn." She clenched her fists until her nails dug painfully into her palms. "One despot is impossible to separate from another."

Casedren's brows shot straight up. "Do you know what you are saying? What you are risking?"

Dani looked at him. Oddly, strangely, her vision began to tunnel, going black around the edges. Everything around her suddenly felt distanced, very far away and muted around the edges. She gasped and blinked, feeling a strange pressure begin to build inside her brain. Before she could blink a second time images flashed through her mind, a montage too fast and too blurry to make real sense of.

Dark things swirled through her mind like an all-consuming tornado, thoughts she made no attempt to hide from him. She broadcast everything to Casedren as it poured through her mind like boiling lava—fire, death and destruction all rolled into one horrifying beast.

Just as she was beginning to bring everything into focus, everything went black, her mind clicking on and off the way an electrical appliance would during a lightning storm. The last thing she remembered before the vision spun away into oblivion was a disembodied voice expressing a single, succinct warning: *Hold steady.*

To her utter astonishment, an answer arrived, rolling over her lips with ease. "You have to play this out the way your father arranged, Casedren," she choked out, not really sure where the words were coming from. Her mind vaguely processed that she wasn't in total control of her own mind. At the moment absolute, paralyzing shock was a good description of her condition.

Awareness gradually seeped back in. What had seemed like an eternity had, in reality, lasted only seconds.

An oracle, she thought dimly. *Something's trying to channel through me.* Where the manipulation might be coming from, though, she couldn't begin to guess. All she knew was that the man in the room with her wasn't the source.

Casedren clearly picked up her notion. A scowl crossed his face, one he quickly erased. "Who is speaking through you, Dani?" he asked suspiciously. "Be it friend or foe."

Hands shaking, Dani pressed her palms to her head and screwed her eyes shut as tightly as possible. The blood beating in her temples built a pressure threatening to rip right through her veins. "Friend," she murmured vaguely, her voice sounding so muted and very far away even to her ears.

"Are you sure?"

She nodded. "I think we're being warned that the future I'm seeing is soon to come if you attempt to take up arms against Cellyn. Do that and it will hasten the inevitable end that much faster."

He frowned. "How can we know it is not the opposite? That if I do not take up arms, the end of time will arrive that much faster?"

Dani shook her head vehemently. "There will be a time when you have to make the decision to take his life," she choked out. "But that time has yet to show itself."

Staring at her narrowly, Casedren slowly nodded his understanding. Hard knowledge permeated his gaze. "So you believe you have been warned that we must pick our next battle carefully?"

Totally wrung out from the explosion of motion inside her skull, Dani let her hands drop. They hung limp and useless at her sides. "I-I think so." Aware time was against them, she shook her head. "I really don't know for sure." At the moment she felt like they were nothing more than mice, cornered by a stalking cat. Scurry the wrong way and they'd lose more than their freedom.

21

_____

Casedren sensed her grim thought. "Perhaps there is something that does know," he said quietly. His suggestion slammed into her gut like a well-aimed bullet.

Dani cut her glance to the table across the room. The Eye was perched on its stand. Even from a distance she saw the tangle of light writhing in its crystal core, ribbons of color swirling together, binding and untying in a sensual dance easily reminding her of the lovemaking between a man and a woman.

She clenched shaking hands. "The Eye of Divine Wisdom," she murmured.

Casedren climbed to his feet, moving in that languid, elegant way that reminded Dani of a jungle cat stalking through its territory. He seemed just as comfortable naked as he did clothed from head to foot. The sheer presence of the man overwhelmed, stealing her breath as easily as a thief snatched a valuable trinket. It was amazing how such a simple move could beckon immediate interest in her body. She wasn't sure what forces mixed up the chemistry brewing between them. Sometime you just looked at a person and knew he was *the one*.

Knees going to jelly, Dani caught her breath. Fear drizzled away. Voyeuristic tendencies blossomed inside her as she watched him stretch his long limbs, cramped from sitting. A thrill of sexual awareness knotted around her heart. She had to admit she preferred him naked.

The dazzling man beside her smiled and shifted his position, walking toward the waiting orb of light. "No more avoiding the inevitable," he said over his shoulder.

Dani didn't move. She preferred to watch him walk, mouth watering at the dimples that formed on his delectable ass. *Oh God.* All she wanted to do was drop to her knees and take a nice big bite out of one of his curved cheeks.

Catching her thought, Casedren turned and shot a wink her way. "I am sure that can be arranged."

Tossing tawny locks off her shoulders, Dani grinned back. "Oh, you don't know half the things I've got in mind for you."

He grinned. "Actually, I do." He gestured for her to join him. "But at the moment I require you for other things."

Drawing back her shoulder and stiffening her spine, Dani manned up, walking toward the table with a nonchalance she could fake but didn't feel. Closer, she saw the manuscript was opened to a series of passages, one Casedren had obviously studied closely as she'd slept. The text scrawled across the parchment was faded, hard to read by the sharpest eyes. What it might say she hadn't the slightest clue. A series of crudely sketched drawings accompanied the text. Despite their lack of finesse, there was no doubt as to their meaning.

Feeling her cheeks heat, she glanced up at Casedren. "You didn't tell me you were reading the *Kama Sutra*."

He eyed the drawings. A slow grin blossomed across his face. "I have to admit these spells make the practice of ritual magick more alluring, would you not agree?"

She grinned at the innuendo implied in his words, his eyes

glinting with a hint of male lust. "Looks kind of complicated," she admitted, hesitant to take up the sexually charged gauntlet he'd presented. Rule number one of witchcraft: Never fuck around with what you don't understand. She'd fucked once and gotten her brother turned into a vampire.

Casedren looked at her intently. "I do not think we have any choice," he said. "While I admit I do not understand the entire purpose behind these rituals, I will say they seem to be the key to opening the Eye."

Dani reached out, sliding the tips of her fingers over the illustration on one page. A little crackle jumped between her skin and the arid parchment. She jerked back with a squeal. "Holy hell!" She rubbed thumb and fingers together to restore the feeling to her numb digits. "The fucking thing zapped me good."

Casedren's brows rose innocently. "Must mean it likes you."

Her gaze narrowed. "If shocking the shit out of me makes it friendly, I don't think I want anything more to do with it." She glared at the grimoire. "Do that again and I'll toss you in the fucking fire," she grumbled.

The old manuscript responded with a quick riffling of pages, flipping one to another in rapid succession. Another ritual was revealed when the pages finally stopped turning.

Casedren looked at her. "I think it is trying to tell us something."

Violently started by the explosion of motion from an inanimate object, Dani agreed. "I guess this is the one we're supposed to work with."

Casedren studied the page, reading through the complicated graphs and glyphs outlined there. "Wow."

Dani understood nothing. "Wow, as in good?" she asked. "Or wow as in bad?"

He smirked and her heart skipped a beat at the flash of white teeth. He slipped a hand around her waist, and one big palm settled on her hip. Tugging her close, his eyes settled on her lips like he contemplated kissing her. "Good wow, I hope."

Riding the wave of rising desire, Dani tipped her head, lifting her chin and offering her lips. "So what do we do?"

His head dipped, lips brushing hers. Their breaths mingled, humid heat caressing her mouth. "We could do what I want to," he murmured.

"What's that?" she murmured back.

His mouth brushed her enticingly. "Toss the damn Eye against the wall and just take you again."

Dani's hand lifted, palm pressing against his chest. Her thumb flicked over the nub of one flat nipple. "Do that and we'll definitely be in trouble."

His tongue snaked out, tracing her top lip. "It would be the best trouble of my life."

She thumbed his nipple again. "You'll think that when you're slashing your wrists," she said reasonably.

The import of what she'd said snapped Casedren back to attention. He pulled back abruptly. "Good point."

Dani winced. The idea of her lover having to commit suicide to preserve some twisted sense of honor among his people held no appeal whatsoever. "Your honor is the last thing they'll be considering. I'm sure arrangements can be made to hurry you along—" She shivered. "If you get my drift."

He nodded. "Indeed, I do. No doubt my brother would volunteer to help me out." His tone was grim with certainty.

"No doubt," she echoed, reinforcing her words with a little mental push. Men had a way of procrastinating. She didn't know why that was. It had to be some rogue gene dominant in the male sex. Given the choice of sex versus threat of death, they'd choose sex. Even if sex would lead to their demise.

Casedren threw up his hands. "All right. I will get started." He turned, surveying the entire area. As the dimensions could change at any given time, it was difficult to know what he was looking for.

He lifted a hand, making a quick practiced gesture. "First we need some room." Every object in the chamber slowly faded, blinking out and disappearing completely within a second. All that remained were four walls and the fireplace, the sole source of light in the chamber now.

"Nice," she complimented. "Smooth move."

"Thank you." Eyeing the space, Casedren stepped into its exact center. "First we need a circle of protection."

Dani nodded agreement. Within a consecrated circle, the conjurer could transcend the physical world, taking mind and body to a deeper and higher level of consciousness. The circle also acted as a barrier of protection from unwanted entities. From within a circle, the conjurer could invoke or summon any demonic or angelic being desired for their bidding. In this case, they had no idea what they'd be summoning. Be it good, evil or indifferent, there was no guessing what they might encounter until the Eye actually opened and revealed itself.

Positioned just so, Casedren extended his arms, fingers spread and palms down. Closing his eyes and centering his concentration, he began to murmur a series of strange words in a steady, melodic voice.

Before the last word had faded a series of embers jumped from the fire, settling about six feet away from him. Flaring up into orange-red flames, the animated fire proceeded to burn a series of patterns into the stone floor, eating through the marble like acid ate through flesh. One set of flames drew a complete and round circle, even as another set went in a different direction, etching out the shape of a pentagram.

As the flames completed their work and flickered out, Dani

gasped. If the head of the pentagram pointed northward, it represented the conjurer's supplication toward the will of good and light. If the pentagram were turned horns up, it represented the conjuror's intent to summon evil forces.

Unsure of the direction in a totally alien world, Dani looked to Casedren to provide the answer. Given the origins of his kind, it was entirely possible they'd be summoning a force she'd rather not be messing with.

The air around her suddenly thinned, like some invisible force was sucking away all the breathable oxygen. A vision of her lover transforming into a giant serpent flashed across her mind's screen. Clamping her eyes shut, she thrust the vision out of her head, recoiling violently at the thought.

Circle and pentagram complete, Casedren turned his palms upward. "We are in supplication." He lifted one blond brow. "You thought otherwise?"

Relief drizzled back in, along with a much-needed breath of air. "I guess it depends on your point of view," she admitted, more than a little relieved. She made a mental note to brick off a bit of her brain so not as to offend him when thoughts like that jumped to the forefront. All access was like all porn, all the time. Eventually all the sensitive parts would be chafed, dry and painful to endure. The idea of having to guard her mind didn't appeal in the least. Only a creator of wicked intentions would bestow such a curse on his progeny.

"You find it hard to trust my kind," he said quietly. "Your mind—and your heart—are still very much against us."

She smiled weakly. "What can I say? Must be the Wyr in me."

Hurt shadowed his gaze. "We are a people capable of controlling our own destiny," he reminded her gently. "Despite our origins, we choose who to serve—and who to summon.

Being born into darkness does not mean we cannot be drawn toward the light."

"I'm sorry." She drew a breath, plucking the seeds of doubt from her mind and tossing them away. Now wasn't the time to undermine his methods. As it stood, his knowledge of ritual magick outran hers by miles. She felt like the tortoise to his hare, hardly equipped to keep racing. "Let's keep going."

He nodded. "Of course."

Still positioned in the center of the circle and pentagram he'd created, Casedren again spread his palms toward the floor. More strange words slipped past his lips, words driven by a strange melodic shift in his tone. More embers jumped to his command, taking positions in the five spaces where the points of the pentagram made contact with the circle surrounding it. Flaming high and hot, a series of strange symbols were burned into the stone. When the flames winked out, Dani didn't recognize the symbols, though she knew why they'd been placed there.

Symbols of protection.

Casedren turned his penetrating gaze on her. "The circle is complete."

Dani gasped, immediately noticing that his light blue irises had taken on another color, a deep almost reddish-purple tint. With his golden hair and pale skin, he truly looked like some angelic being down from heaven.

His fiery gaze raked up and down her nude body, sending an involuntary shiver racing up her spine. "There is nothing to fear."

Fighting to steady the wild thump of her heart, Dani raised her chin. "What do I do?"

"Bring the orb. As the female, you are its bearer, and the vessel through which I will channel my energy."

The panic she'd successfully managed to hold at bay suddenly tightened into a death grip around her senses. "I-I'm not sure I can," she stammered, not really able to give voice to her protest.

"It will take two of us to work the ritual of the Eye, Dani. I cannot do it alone. Without you, it is pointless to continue." He slowly extended a hand. "Please, join me."

22

Clamping down on her mistrust and doubts about rituals she had no familiarity with, Dani slowly walked toward the waiting orb. The colors swirling in its icy heart grew brighter as she approached, dancing with mesmerizing animation.

She reached out, cupping her palms around the cool crystal and lifting the orb from its stand. Its weight surprised her. Instead of being heavy and solid, like objects fashioned out of crystal usually were, the orb was light, almost weightless. She had the sense that if she were to let go, the Eye would hover without dropping.

"My goodness!" she exclaimed with delight. "It's light as air." Uncertainty draining away, she tightened her grip. A series of light vibrations resonated from the orb, shimmying through her hands and up her arms. The strange quivering soothed and relaxed. Tension drained out of her neck, shoulders and spine. The orb was communicating with her, assuring her it would do no harm.

Smiling down at the mysterious object, Dani believed it.

Turning toward Casedren, she walked toward the circle of

protection he'd created, stopping at its edge. She didn't enter. At least she knew what to do at this point, careful not to violate the sacred space Casedren had created around himself. The creator must grant entry.

"Oh, noble man of perfect mercy and grace," she said slowly, careful to keep each word clear. "Please grant me entry into your sacred space." She offered a brief bow of respect.

Smiling his approval, Casedren pressed his palms together, the tips of his fingers touching his chin, and returned to her bow. "Oh, noble lady of perfect mercy and grace," he said. "You are welcome inside this place."

Careful not to step on any of the symbols etched on the floor, Dani entered the circle, joining him in its center. The moment she stepped past the circle she felt an almost electric crackle flex over her naked shin like an invisible shield. She caught her breath in surprise. The sensation was like grabbing on to a hot wire fence and holding on.

She tightened her grip on the orb. "Wow, that's awesome." The sensation wasn't painful, but very intense.

Casedren reached out, settling one big, warm palm against her cheek. "Thank you."

Heat began pooling between her legs. "We can do this," she said, her voice trembling more than a little.

They stood in the heart of the pentagram, a not inconsiderable space given the size of the room and the circumference Casedren had worked in.

"What next?"

He stepped back and spread his arms, palms down. "We activate the protective forces. Even though this chamber has been sealed from all outsiders, I am taking no chances."

"Good idea," she agreed. "We'll do whatever it takes."

He raised a mischievous brow. "This ritual takes a lot of whatever," he said, voice husky with innuendo.

She grinned back into his magnetic eyes. The orb in her hands pulsed, perfectly synchronizing itself with the beat of her heart. It was like holding a living, breathing thing. It was also incredibly erotic, sending all kinds of little shivers directly to her boiling core. "Let's get to it then."

Casedren slowly rotated his hands, turning his palms up. He spoke in a low soft tone, not exactly sung but intoned in a rhythmic cadence. Outside the circle, shadows drifted in from far corners, enveloping the room from all sides.

Dani blinked in surprise. Everything seemed to have gone completely out of focus outside the circle. A strange, soft luminous light hazed the air in the heart of the pentagram, softening the lines of Casedren's masculine body even as it blurred reality. The whole circle took on an unreal, ethereal quality. It was like slipping through the cracks of sanity and entering an unreal, insane universe on the other side of reality. The energy surging around them all but knocked her over.

His simmering gaze dropped to hers. His lips were finely sculpted, sensuously shaped. More than ever he looked like the otherworld being he really was. Skin flushing hot, her breathing accelerated even more. Heat scorched her tender lips.

With a grace defying gravity, Casedren sank to his knees. The level of his head came to just below the curve of her breasts. His arms came up, warm palms settling on her hips. Leaning forward, hot breath tickled. "For your energy to be at its strongest," he murmured against her bare skin, "you must be aroused to the point of climax." He gently nibbled a ticklish spot on her abdomen. "But try not to climax or we will lose the momentum."

Breath drizzling out of her lungs, Dani felt a bubble of sensual anticipation begin to inflate inside her chest. "That's going to be damned hard," she gritted out. "Especially the way you're touching me now."

Casedren didn't answer. His mouth, hard and hungry, nibbled an erotic trail across the flat plane of her belly. His hands circled her body, cupping and squeezing the curves of her rear.

Dani's hands tightened around the orb. The more aroused she became, the brighter the lights inside swirled. "I think we're on the right track," she breathed out. "This thing's humming right along."

"I hope you are, too," Casedren murmured, running his fingers down her crack before delving in deeper. He burrowed the tip of one finger toward her anus, stroking slowly to stimulate the sensitive nerve endings.

A fine tremble enveloped Dani's entire body. The violent desire to toss the orb and make love to him right then and there shuddered through her. His touch ignited every nerve.

Her gaze dropped to the top of his head, to the thick silky hair looking like so much spun gold. His skin glowed in the filtered illumination around them. The memory of his lovemaking swirled through her mind with the power of a one-ton truck. Her hands ached to stroke the hard plane of his back, feel hot muscles pulsing beneath her touch as he rammed his generous cock straight into her sex.

Licking dry lips, Dani gulped as Casedren worked the tip of a finger inside her anus. A thrill of pure appreciation swept through her. "Oh my God," she moaned. "That feels so good."

Casedren shifted, one hand sweeping along her inner thigh. A low groan settled deep in her chest when his fingers almost made contact with her aching clit. "It is about to feel better," he promised.

Dani's breath vanished when he swept the tip of one finger through her dewy labia. The motion of the soft pad of his finger making contact with the tiny hooded organ sent a shudder all the way to her toes. She gasped at the sensation, swamped by the pleasure fluttering in her core like thousands of butterflies taking flight.

Casedren moved his finger in a slow circular motion. His mouth worked the hollow beneath her breastbone, delivering slow, wet licks. His other hand worked from behind, the tip of his finger slowly penetrating tight muscles from behind.

In danger of losing complete control, Dani fought against the sensations spinning around and through her body like a silky web, wrapping her tighter and tighter in the grip of absolute liquid bliss. Her self-control began to drizzle away, especially when his finger abandoned her clit. A second later, he worked two fingers into her creaming sex. His touch filled her, front and back. Sexual shocks tore through her senses.

Whimpering low in surrender, Dani let herself slip into the pool of surrender, giving herself to the slow, seductive arousal he pulled from her with every long stroke. Barely able to see straight, she unconsciously swiveled her hips, trying to get him to penetrate her deeper. Dying for more, she couldn't get enough of him. Lust rolled off her in thick waves, crashing through her body the way the ribbons of light filling the orb smashed against the crystal, fighting to break free of their confines.

Climax barreled in.

Dani inhaled on a gasp, holding her breath until she was sure she'd pass out. "I-I'm close," she finally managed to spit out. "You'd better stop or I'll come right now."

His finger slipped out. "Try to hold on. Just a little longer."

She forcibly calmed her pulse. "I—okay. I'm all right."

Casedren nibbled a little kiss onto her abdomen. "You are doing fine." Settling back on his knees, he began to guide her down onto his lap.

Knees close to collapse, Dani sank gratefully into his embrace. She couldn't fail to notice his cock strained, arching up against his cobbled abdomen. His strong hands used just the right amount of gentle pressure to guide her. He groaned as she settled in, aiming the tip of his penis directly at her core.

Casedren speared her with one deep thrust, bringing their bodies together in a single expert motion.

Dani groaned under her breath, automatically lifting her arms so that the orb was balanced directly over their heads. Her legs, back and shoulders ached as if she'd been digging and tossing boulders. His cock, ridged and rock solid, filled every inch. The power he wielded permeated her. His essence flowed over her and through her, seeping into her blood and bones like a powerful narcotic. It was completely unlike anything she'd ever experienced before in ritual magick. It was forbidden, primitive and animalistic, stripping her bare and laying her out for sacrifice. The psychic link between them concealed nothing.

She loved it. It felt wonderful to be claimed and over-powered by so much male energy.

Casedren braced one hand against her back to keep her in place. His lips traced the straining cords of her neck. "Try to blank your mind and think of nothing."

"Hard to do," she breathed, "when you're stuffed full of cock." Every time his hand rubbed along her spine or his lips caressed her neck, a new sizzle traveled beneath her skin.

The carnal energy between them took on new proportions when Casedren's free hand slipped between their bodies to cup her left breast. He pinched and rolled, tugging glittering rib-bons of pleasure from the sensitive bead. She gasped, com-pletely out of breath.

His touch branded and possessed. "Concentrate on the orb as I make love to you," he whispered. "Hold off your climax as long as possible and center your thoughts of the Eye."

Shuddering, she tugged in a much-needed breath. She tight-ened her upper thighs around his, desperate to take him deeper inside. "I'll try," she promised, almost too dazed to think of anything else aside from the way her soft curves melded per-fectly into the hard planes of his body, shimmering together like steel heated to a molten temperature.

Casedren's hips moved against hers. One palm slid to the small of her back, urging her closer even as he speared himself deeper inside her

Lids dropping shut in delicious anguish, Dani concentrated on tugging her mind away from her aching liquid core. The swollen nipple he manipulated transmitted gut-throbbing signals. She moaned, her entire body undulating softly against his. Her skin felt like liquid silver, flowing and simmering beneath his touch. The hand behind her skimmed to the crevice of her rear, passing quickly back into its depth. He slowly eased one finger into her anus. Straining with pleasure, she clenched hard.

Casedren began to speak long words, parts of a spell rising and falling with a sonorous rhythm. He simultaneously added the thrust of his hips as a subtle counterpart.

The sexual tension grew, pulsing through their bodies with a force and friction that bordered on painful.

Dani opened her eyes. The orb above her head glowed, almost transparent. The light inside its core was so fierce she saw the bones in her fingers outlined. Jagged flecks of color danced.

At that exact moment, Casedren surged up into her, demanding all, taking everything. Her body trembled at the intense assault as he pounded out the tempo of his spell with one body jarring thrust after another.

What happened next caught her by surprise.

Energy snapped the air apart, crashing around them with bone-shattering force. The orb in her hands flared into a blinding radiance. The relentless sweep of a space-tearing force bore her straight into an abyss of pure, unadulterated energy. Fused body, mind and soul, Casedren followed her over the edge.

In the same instant, Dani felt the climax of their lovemaking pour through her veins, the power of her release picking her up and flinging her straight into the center of the mind-crushing blow Casedren's spell had unleashed.

Dani opened her mouth, one long last scream tearing out of

her throat. Shredded down to atoms, she desperately reached for the individual self trickling through her fingers like so many grains of sand. Transformed into something far beyond human, the energy of the Eye poured into her just as Casedren reached the peak or orgasm. Releasing a strangled bellow, his body convulsed beneath hers. He drove into her a final time, forcing every ounce of his body's energy into hers. Hot semen jetted from his twitching cock, filling her womb with fiery heat all over again.

His climax shattered everything.

At the moment Dani began to grasp the intelligence behind the Eye, the energy reversed, rolling out of her as the force ebbed away, retreating beyond her reach as quickly as it had arrived. The connection with the Eye faltered, fell away, disintegrating like a spider's web hit by a hurricane force wind.

Realizing they had lost the momentum propelling the spell forward, Casedren cursed. She didn't care. Orgasm ruptured inside her, a shower of iridescent sparks scorching her veins from the inside out. The orb slipped from her grasp, rolling off the tips of her fingers and plunging to the ground with alarming speed. The fragile thing shattered, spitting out sparks as it showered them with a billion tiny shards of glass.

Driven by a rush of inexplicable terror, Dani yelped. She felt flying bits of glass go right through her as they rocketed by on their way to infinity. The luminous mists filling the circle of protection went insane around them, pulling and tearing at her skin as if to punish her for failing. A surreal burst of fireworks detonated inside her skull.

She screamed and everything went black.

23

Failure was a bitter pill to swallow. Not only had they failed to open the Eye, they'd gone one better, totally destroying the orb. Whether by accident or intention, neither knew. The hours remaining loomed ahead like a huge black tunnel leading nowhere. If there was a light at its end, it was probably the oncoming train. Collision was inevitable.

Hands pressed to her aching temples, Dani lay on the bed. Her memory of the recent event was shredded and blurry. She remembered very little of the ritual itself. All she recalled was gazing into a light so clear that it took her breath away. For a moment, a very brief second, she'd made contact with . . . *something.* A presence so pure and wonderful she didn't even possess the ability to begin to describe it. It was that damn awesome.

She did know the peak had occurred when Casedren had climaxed, sending his energy directly into her body. The awareness of being crammed so completely with another person's essence had damn near sent her to the edge of no return. Her nerves still sparked from the furious sensations she'd experienced. Even now, his touch scorched. She was so very aware of him she heard not only the sound of his breath–already preternaturally quiet–entering and leaving his lungs but also felt the pulse of blood through his veins.

Lowering her hands and opening her eyes, Dani looked toward Casedren. He'd dressed completely, abandoning the intimacy of nudity for the impersonal distance of clothing. She wore nothing, still naked and ready for his touch.

One look was all it took to steal her breath away all over again. She drank in the sight of him like a woman denied water for months. His build was just perfect, slender yet muscular. She felt herself go all wet and sticky at the thought of his sleek hips descending between her spread legs.

By the look of things, Casedren wouldn't be touching her any time soon. He stood in front of the hearth, hand resting heavily on the mantel as he regarded the crackling flames within.

Restored to its former state, the chamber held no sign of witchery, save for the old grimoire resting on the table, now closed. The stand holding the Eye was made all the more starker because of the orb's absence. It appeared as though they had done nothing, accomplished nothing. Still, time had ticked away, their two days ticking down to mere hours. Soon they would stand before King Bastien and be forced to admit defeat.

Neither of them looked forward to that.

Since the incident, Casedren had separated himself from her, both physically and emotionally. His mind, however, remained wide open, brooding dark and terrible things. He worried not for himself but for her. The idea that she'd wind up in the hands of his brother ate him up inside like acid. He couldn't tolerate the idea. Because he loved her.

Casedren loved her.

His notion whirled through her own mind, driven by gale

force winds. They'd known each other less than four days and he was deeply and madly in love with her.

Try as she may to creep out of his head and stay within the confines of her own mind, Dani found it increasingly difficult. What the hell was she supposed to feel in response to something so private and profound?

She sighed heavily. The truth was she loved him, too. If anyone asked, she'd have to admit she was mad about the man, head over heels in love.

Too bad their whole world was about to be yanked out from under their feet.

The directness behind her thought reached Casedren. Lifting his head, he turned away from the fire. "We never stood a chance to begin with," he said quietly. "Not only did Cellyn outsmart me, he outmaneuvered me. Worse, I let him do it." A pang of remorse hit him, cutting directly into her. "I am truly sorry I dragged you into this, Danicia. You deserved a better man."

Dani swallowed the knot forming in her throat. "You are the better man," she barely managed to whisper.

He shook his head. "My brother is a very charismatic man. I cannot deny that. He is also a dynamic leader, very capable of rallying huge numbers of men who want to believe in him. The Jadians are a powerful people, feeling chained and suppressed by the bonds of a civility absolutely foreign to our true natures. I am all too aware that many want to return to the old ways, when our demonic natures ruled our actions. Cellyn thirsts for that power. He will take the cup and drink down the souls of the innocent he is capable of slaughtering without regret or remorse." He clenched his hands into tight fists. "And I bear unto my death the guilt that I was unable to stop him."

His words tore at her heart with steel-tipped claws. Dani swiped angrily at her cheeks, upset he'd given in so easily. "You honestly believe it's over, then?"

Casedren threw up his hands in surrender. "I failed to open the Eye. As close as we got—and it was very damn close—we still failed. In less than two hours' time, I will have to look my father in the face and concede my defeat." Despite the heat of the fire he stood beside, he visibly shuddered. "I would rather take that dagger to my heart now than have to do that."

"I'll take it, too," she said quietly.

Her words elicited an instant response. His gaze snapping to hers, his eyes were hard and sparking. "That's not going to happen," he countered savagely. His tone ripped through her like the serrated edge of a knife.

Dani smiled at his quick leap to defend her life. "You think I'd adjust to being with your brother?" she asked quietly. "I'd rather die first."

Casedren crossed to where she sat on the bed, taking a place beside her and capturing her hands. "I have one final recourse left, one which I intend to use without hesitation." He drew a quick breath. "My final request as man facing death will be that you do not fall into Cellyn's hands."

She stared at him, incredulous. "You think it will be so easy?" she asked, not really sure how she felt about his confession. On one hand she was relieved there might be a way out for her. On the other, she felt she'd be tossing him away like trash if she actually allowed him to do as he planned.

A fierce certainty crossed his face. "Among our kind, a man's dying wish is carried out if reasonable and possible." He leaned forward, his voice deadly serious. "In the event my father refuses, I have made arrangements with my guards for them to take you to your brother, protect you even if it means giving their own lives."

Dani shook her head adamantly. Her heart skipped a beat, then shifted into overdrive. "We've already discussed trying to run," she started to say.

Casedren hushed her with a single finger across the lips. "I know Cellyn will come after you," he countered. "But you must go back to your brother, and Counselor Nash. Warn them what is coming." His grip tightened on her hands. "Live to die another day, Dani. Do what I could not."

Hearing the urgency in his words and feeling it through his touch, Dani stared up at him in shock. The directness of his words knocked her completely off balance. "Is that really what you want?"

Letting go of her hands, he nodded and sighed. "Yes. Through these last few hours it has become perfectly clear to me. We fight a current too strong to conquer. What is to come was predicted eons ago. I once believed prophecy could be rewritten, but the stars—and the gods—seem to be against us. What you cannot turn away from, you must prepare for. You have seen what is to come. You will be the one to lead them."

His reasonable tone screeched through her senses like fingernails down a chalkboard. "I don't believe that," she said bluntly.

He answered immediately. "Do you see any other way or recourse? Tell me so, please, and I will listen."

Dani glared angrily at him, refusing to believe what he'd told her. In her heart, and in her soul, she knew he was right.

Lids dropping shut, she fortified herself against the searing pain cutting through her. *Now we must prepare.*

Her need to stop Cellyn coalesced into a tight knot of resolve. "You're right," she whispered. "We've known all along." Though she acknowledged the truth, her heart wept openly now. For his loss. For her loss. For their loss of the life they could never have together. The future, grim and dark, held no place for them to be together. They each had a different path to walk, though each led to the same, inevitable conclusion. Casedren's sacrifice wouldn't prevent, only prepare.

Casedren reached out, cupping her cheek in one warm palm. "Please, do not mourn my loss." A gentle, calm smile curved his lips. He'd accepted the inevitable, prepared himself. There was no fear in him, only regret and resignation. His downfall had been of his own making and he accepted it, completely and without anger. "In this case, the world loses nothing more than a weak and foolish man."

Attempting to tuck her anger away, Dani opened her eyes. The anger wasn't worth holding on to. Later, she'd need such a brutal emotion. But not now. Not when too precious few hours remained to them.

Her gut knotting painfully, she covered his hand with hers, pressing his warmth even harder into her skin. "Don't talk like you're already dead."

A soft smile curved his mouth. "I wish I had been second-born now."

"Me, too," she murmured, suddenly feeling exhaustion creeping around the edge of her senses. She felt as wrung out as a nasty old dishrag hung out to dry. "Things might have gone an entirely different way for us."

He leaned closer, his warm mouth brushing hers. "You should rest a while."

Dani shook her head. "Make love to me," she whispered. "One more time." She tried to pull him down onto the bed with her.

Casedren gently untangled himself. "You must forgive me that I am not in the mood." His smooth deep voiced caressed, attempting to soothe his rejection.

He settled onto the bed, stretching out his long, endless legs. Rolling onto his side, he drew her against him so their bodies were spooned together. Snuggling a kiss into her hair, his hand sneaked under her arm. One big hand cupped her breast. He drew slow circles around the distended bead. "Just rest," he murmured. "Try to dream good things."

Reluctantly, Dani gave in to his decision and let the matter drop. She had a feeling no matter how much she argued, he wouldn't change his mind. That matter was settled. Casedren knew what he wanted to do, and would do it come hell or high water. Unfortunately, hell would be coming first. Whether right or wrong, she had to support his decision fully. To do less would be a betrayal not only to his manhood but his heart.

She pressed back against his powerful body, enjoying the feel of his strength and solidity. She felt protected.

Nevertheless, unbidden tremors rippled under her skin. She was far from the mind of dreaming good things but said nothing. Lids heavy with exhaustion, she needed rest—even if she preferred to hold out for the desire his touch ignited.

She yawned and stretched with the lazy contentment of a kitten. *I really ought to let him get some rest.* The thought spun away before she finished it, her mind instead trekking toward the remembered sensations of his mouth on her skin, of the delight he wove with his tongue, fingers and cock.

The sound of his steady breathing lulled her. Inhaling his musky, exotic scent she reluctantly closed her eyes. She wanted to rest, just a minute, no more than two.

24

A jolt to her senses brought Dani instantly awake. Vision blurred with confusion, she blinked, trying to clear her senses. All she saw when she opened her eyes was a fuzzy mess of blond locks falling over her face. Neither would her hands follow her command to respond. They couldn't.

Confused as to why she would be paralyzed, Dani painfully rolled her head back on her shoulders. Her hair fell away from her face, clearing her vision. Heart making an instant leap, all the oxygen drizzled out of her lungs.

Her arms were tied above her head. The tight rope wrapped around her wrists chafed, biting uncomfortably into her skin. Feet barely touching the ground, her ankles were similarly tied, her legs spread apart. Cold realization crept in like a cockroach through a crack.

She'd been strung up like a side of beef.

Panicking, Dani swung her head around, trying to figure out where she was. The blank walls of the chamber were familiar enough, but nothing else. Everything, including the hearth, was gone. Nothing remained.

She turned her head to the left, visually searching for the source of the strange glow surrounding her nude body. The answer chilled her blood.

The circle and pentagram Casedren had cast were back in place. Their lines glowed with a weird, unearthly radiance, but it wasn't the same. The symbols that Casedren had carved into the five edge spaces had changed, no longer representing protection, but something else. Something darker. Something evil. Flames danced around the circle, almost seeming to have the form of bodies writing together in the throes of sadistic love-making.

Dani hung in the exact center, and the view to her eyes indicated the pentagram was now in the horns-up position. The changes in the chamber pressed in from all sides, seeming strangely distorted, surreal even.

Gulping hard, she licked dry lips. *Aw, damn.* She groaned faintly under her breath. This was trouble. Big trouble. Alarm leaped through her like a wild tiger released from captivity.

It didn't take long in arriving, either.

The shadows in one dark corner quickened, shimmering and thickening. A serpent, long and thick, slithered out of its mass.

Fear blossomed inside her chest, driving her heart straight into her rib cage. Dani knew the identity of the snake. She fisted her hands until her fingernails bit deeply into her palms. Pain shot through her wrists and arms, nailing in the realization that this event far outstripped any nightmare she'd ever had before.

It all felt real. Much too real. "What do you want?" she snarled.

Course unwavering, the snake slithered closer, entering the glowing circle. Its thick body rose from the floor, coil after coil draping around her body as it circled her. Its heavy weight clung, squeezing tightly. Its skin rasped unpleasantly against hers, dry and scratchy.

Dani stared in total, riveted shock. *Oh. My. God.* She winced, feeling the squeeze around her legs, hips and chest. Her sensitive nipples felt like they were being rubbed by a Brillo pad. "If this is your way of turning me on," she spat, "it isn't working."

Arcing around, the serpent's face hovered in front of her face. Wide jaws cranked open, revealing a set of deadly sharp fangs. Its tongue rolled out, flicking the tip of her nose. "You desired me once," it said, impossibly speaking out loud. "I am sure I can arouse you again."

Glaring at the beastly thing, Dani gritted her teeth in disgust. "Never."

The serpent suddenly shifted. Before Dani could blink an eye, Cellyn stood in front of her. Naked, he hadn't come unarmed. He clutched a dagger in one hard. Sharp and deadly, its silver blade glittered with menace.

But this monster wasn't the Cellyn she knew. His hair had changed color. It was now black as a raven's wing, highlighted with luminous strands of crimson. His eyes, too, glowed like embers in a volcano's heart.

The change in his looks caught Dani by surprise. Then she realized. This man wasn't Cellyn, but an apparition when dream-walking. He clearly had no compunction whatsoever about practicing the blackest of magick, arts hearkening back to the dark heart of his creator. The beast inside him stood before her, unveiling the terrible truth behind ancient prophecy.

The beast was poised to rise to power, ready to devour everything in his path.

Dani closed her eyes, praying reverently. This couldn't be happening. Somehow Cellyn had found a weak spot in Casedren's hiding place, wriggling his way in like a worm. Asleep, she had no defense against him. He could do with her as he wished, at his leisure.

It took only seconds for her to put the pieces together, but by then it was too late. Cellyn had control of her mind, and that gave him control of her body.

Dani tried to withdraw into herself. "Impossible," she murmured, attempting to defocus her attention off his terrible face.

Cellyn wouldn't let her go so easily. He loomed over her, a dark, dangerous presence. "Hardly impossible since I am here."

She gazed at him through narrow eyes. If looks could kill, that fucker should be dead on the floor. No such luck. "It's just a dream," she snapped defensively. "It's not happening."

Laughing shortly and without humor, he raised the dagger, flicking at her left breast with its sharp tip. "When someone else has control of your mind, it is very real."

Dani gasped at the shard of pain he delivered. A tiny droplet of blood oozed from her nipple. "You can't be here," she said through gritted teeth. "I didn't let you in."

Cellyn raised an amused brow. He regarded her with a sinister and hungry smile. "Oh, you didn't let me in. Casedren is the culprit in this case—or rather, one of his attendants is." He smirked and lowered his voice to a confidential tone. "His servants are not so faithful when torture is applied to persuade co-operation. Enoch, ah, he always was the weak link in Casedren's armor. All I had to do was mind-walk right through him to find your hideaway. Of course, my brother would think himself safe enough to lower his defenses. Both of you went right to sleep, minds wide open with not even a spell to lock the mental gates against the hound."

Dani glared at her captor. "I don't believe you."

Cellyn dragged the tip of the dagger over the swell of her breast, then upward toward the hollow of her throat. "Oh, you had better believe me when I say Casedren is too weak to protect you." He dug the tip in a little. "I, on the other hand, have the will strong enough to keep you in line. There is a lot of passion—and a lot of power—coursing through your veins. Your

Wyr bloodline has given you the potential to be a very powerful witch."

Dani refused to wince against the threat he inflicted. Let him plunge the damn thing through her throat for all she cared. "A power I'll use against you every way I can," she threatened.

Cellyn grinned, the intent behind his smile entirely sociopathic. The dagger inched higher, up her chin toward the curve of her bottom lip. "A power I will shape to suit myself," he chuckled. "Your body, your mind, your soul will be mine to command."

Ice settled at the back of Dani's neck, traveling down her spine. She writhed against the bonds holding her arms and legs immobile. "I'll die before I'll serve your cause, you sick fuck."

Cellyn's expression contorted into something between glee and lust. The dagger fell away. Stepping closer, his free hand cupped her mound. He worked a finger between her nether lips, forcing his middle finger into her depth. His lips hovered just inches from hers. "Back at the beginning of time, your creator and mine made a little pact, you see. For ceasing our attack against heaven, earth was promised as our domain." The implications behind his words slammed into her gut like a sledgehammer.

Dani felt his invasion of her sex all the way through. She gritted her teeth, determined not to fall to his touch a second time. To take her, he'd have to rape her, a specter no woman welcomed. She felt ill at the thought of his cock making penetration.

Glaring at him through narrow eyes, she forced a sneer. "That's not true." Her muscles strained as she fought to escape. The ropes around her wrists and ankles dug into her skin, biting hard and deep. She tried to clamp her legs together, but the ropes around her ankles made the move impossible.

"Oh, but it is so very true." Cellyn stabbed his finger deeper, harder. "All of mankind was laid out before us, a feast to feed our hunger for blood, flesh and bone. Imagine it. All those souls ripe for the plucking."

Her pulse roared through her head. A moan slipped past numb lips. "No," she moaned. "I won't let it happen."

"It is happening, and you will be the first to be taken," he murmured against her lips. His breath was blistering, fetid. "This night will happen again and again as I train you to be the perfect consort to serve a dark god."

The chamber around her began to shift, contorting into strange and new shapes. The floor disappeared beneath her feet even as she felt herself falling onto a cold, hard surface. It took her a moment to comprehend she was laying flat on her back in the heart of the pentagram. Spread-eagled, her arms and legs were still tightly bound, the rope melting into the stone to hold her in place.

Cellyn knelt between her spread legs. Lifting the dagger over her, he plunged it straight in a deadly downward arc.

Dani winced, steeling herself against the inevitable. The sliver blade sank into floor, easily melding into the stone.

Hands settling on her knees, he slid his palms upward. His skin was warm and dry, like cardboard. "Later," he murmured, "I will teach you to enjoy true pain." His gaze skimmed the length of her nude body. He smiled. "Your skin is perfect, just waiting for the cut of a blade to scar it. Then you will truly belong to me." Lust glinted inside his fiery gaze. His cock arced up toward his lean abdomen, hard and ready to plunder.

Dani arched her back, struggling harder against her bonds. "No," she insisted. "This isn't happening. It isn't real."

Cellyn's hands moved higher. Her breasts disappeared under his palms. He squeezed.

Dani's insides twisted with disgust as he fondled her. Biting back a wave of nausea, she moaned. Her entire body clenched under his touch. "Don't," she pleaded.

He rubbed his fingers in circles around her distended nipples. "Nice," he guttered, claiming and twisting the sensitive beads. "I'm going to enjoy fucking you."

Arching her body, Dani struggled vainly to escape his disgusting touch. Her wrists twisted against the ropes, slick with the blood and sweat of her struggle. "You bastard," she snarled. "I'll never serve you."

Cellyn chuckled, running his palms down her sides. His strong grip settled on her hips, lifting her off the stone floor and angling her body upward. "You will do more than serve. A god needs sons . . . many sons." He forced himself inside her, his cock stabbing like a steel-tipped icicle.

The slide of flesh on heated flesh freed a cry from Dani's throat. His erection filled her, the unwelcome penetration sending a spear of ice straight up her spine. Her body was damp and hot. Chest rising and falling, her lungs dragged in breath after breath of heated male skin, a gut-turning combination of sewer and sulfur. She gagged, barely able to tolerate the horrible odor. This was the smell of evil, a tainted and dreadful evil.

Cellyn lowered himself over her, supporting his weight on outstretched arms. His hips rubbed against hers like sandpaper on concrete. Gaze glittering with savage amusement, his cock invaded, plundered and conquered.

The ice filling her insides was so intense Dani nearly lost consciousness. Wrenching her head to one side, she clenched her eyes shut. Here, inside her own head, there was no escape, no salvation. As long as Cellyn manipulated her mind, her body was his to use as he wanted. Her sanity was a fragile thing, a barrier he was determined to completely break down, shatter into tiny pieces.

Attempting to shut herself down, feel nothing, recall nothing, Dani had the sense of Cellyn leaning down. Hot, nasty breath scorched her ear. "You are mine now," he rumbled. "Casedren has lost." Underscoring his words, his cock surged.

Boiling hot semen poured into her womb, the seed of the demon spawned beast planted deep.

Dani's scream of terror ripped through the chamber, echoing through the empty vastness inside her skull.

A terrible sound tore into the silence around them. A bell rang out, resonant and far away, marking the end of the final hour she and Casedren would ever spend together.

Time's up, she thought dimly, fading away.

25

King Bastien silently regarded the small group filling his private chamber. He did not look pleased. Minister Gareth stood to the left of his king, equally stoic. He made no attempt to hide his distaste for the entire matter. In his mind, he'd made a choice between the twins. However, the declaration that could make one man a king or send another to his death wasn't his to finalize.

Standing beside Casedren, Dani concentrated on keeping her mental lock firmly in its place. She wanted no invaders in her mind, creeping around, doing as they wished. She certainly didn't want to share her thoughts with anyone, not even Casedren. She wasn't the only one guarding their thoughts. Every mind in the chamber was sealed tightly, allowing no access. Whatever those present held in their minds, they kept private.

Not that all the mental walls around her mattered. She didn't have to be a mind reader to know how everyone felt. Nervous tension practically crackled in the air, so thick she could have reached out and grabbed a handful.

Bastien broke the heavy silence. "It appears we are all in our place," he observed.

"The hour of judgment has arrived," Minister Gareth filled in. "Prince Casedren, do you agree to accept your father's word as his final wish?"

Pale but composed, Casedren's face was a mask. The dark circles ringing his eyes and the downward arc of his mouth revealed a deeply worried man. "I do."

Minister Gareth looked to Cellyn. "And you, Prince Cellyn, do also agree you shall abide by your father's final word?"

Cellyn gave his head a cocky toss before throwing out an arrogant smile. "I always have," he said confidently.

Dani cut a glance toward the man she hated. Again clothed in his military finery, he stood separate from herself and Casedren. Though his face was impassive, the slight curve at the corner of his mouth and the eager glint in his eye revealed his pleasure in the entire situation. He was firmly convinced he would soon step into Casedren's place.

Dani's guts tied into painful knots at the sight of him. Her skin felt damp and hot, suddenly too tight to be stretched over her bones. He'd gotten to her in the worst of ways, and he knew it. What's more, he had enjoyed it, thoroughly and completely.

Feeling the intensity behind her gaze, Cellyn settled his unblinking stare on her. Raking her from head to foot, his eyes glittered with predatory menace, holding no goodwill.

Dani began to feel nauseated. Damn the bastard for standing there so smug and confident. Right now all she wanted to do was slap that sneer off his face. It took every ounce of restraint she had not to reach up and scratch his evil eyes right out of their sockets. She wished him dead, deeply and absolutely.

Her entire body clenched at the memory of his phantom invasion. What he had done to her last night had been more of a violation than if he had physically held her down and assaulted her. He'd forced himself into the one place she couldn't escape, imprinting his presence on the walls of her skull like a branding iron. More than that, he let her remember every terrible thing he'd done—and intended to do again.

Dani hadn't told Casedren about Cellyn's invasion. She couldn't. Not when he was already under so much pressure. It would be pointless. She'd deal with it, on her own.

Forcing herself to turn away from a presence that sickened her, Dani looked toward Casedren. Shoulders pulled back, his hands were clasped behind his back. As still as he stood, he might as well have been a statue. She couldn't even detect a hint of breath entering his lungs.

King Bastien addressed Casedren. "My son, to you I gave a task, to open the *Moir y'Divani*, the Eye of Divine Wisdom. To open the Eye is to know the truth of one's self. Its gaze is all knowing, its vision into the soul absolute." He paused, drawing a deep breath. "Tell me now, if you will—were you able to open the Eye?"

Casedren swallowed painfully. Clearing his throat, he spoke only a single word. "No."

King's Bastien's brows rose. "No?" he repeated, more for his own benefit than theirs.

Minister Gareth looked stricken by some invisible force. He made a quick gesture with his hands, a cross between despair and dismay. If ever a man looked worried, he did.

Cellyn chuckled, clearly amused. It didn't take a lot of imagination to know he was mentally seating himself on his father's throne.

Bastien frowned. "Then you were unable to complete the task?"

Casedren slowly nodded. "Forgive me, father, but I have failed." He sighed heavily, the sole indicator of the burden he carried. "As you suspected and as my own brother has accused me, I am unfit to rule Sedah. The Eye has borne out that truth." He offered a slight bow in supplication. "I am prepared to step aside in favor of Cellyn."

Hearing his words, Dani's heart wrenched painfully in her chest, aching to the core this magnificent man she called lover should be reduced to such a humble state. Confidence shattered, she knew he doubted himself immensely. Doubt led to weakness, and weakness led to failure. And failure led to death.

"And these are your final words?" Minister Gareth asked quietly.

Casedren shook his head. "I have only a single request to make."

King Bastien spread a hand, indicating his willingness to listen. "I will hear you out."

Casedren reached for Dani's hand, drawing her closer to his side. His touch, though cool, was smooth and dry. Her own clasp was less pleasant, clammy and sweaty. He squeezed her fingers gently, sending a silent signal. "I ask that Lady Danicia Wallace, my chosen consort, be returned to her people," he said quietly. "She is innocent of all wrongdoing, having entered into an engagement under the auspices of deception on my part. Despite our custom, she should not be made to suffer because I lied."

Except Casedren couldn't promise she'd be safe in days to come. All he could do was hope that his final appeal would buy her a little time to warn her people of the threat to come. Even if she were allowed to return to earth today, there was no doubt in her mind that Cellyn would come after her.

Dani shivered against the thought. He'd made his intentions perfectly clear last night.

Bastien nodded. "Is this your wish?" he asked Dani. "To be returned to your world?"

Realizing there was no way she could leave Casedren to face death alone, Dani made a sudden, impulsive decision. She wanted to stand right beside her lover, even if it meant sharing his fate. She cared too much about him to be selfish, sacrificing his hide to save hers. Even if she made it back to earth, she'd never be safe. Once Cellyn assumed the throne, he'd come after her with a vengeance—and all the power of hell at his beck.

She wouldn't stand a chance and she knew it. Counselor Nash had already warned that the Wyr were too outnumbered to engage in any further combat with the Jadians. It wasn't true that the meek would inherit the earth. Her world had already been signed away in a pact made countless millennia ago. Man's own creator had betrayed him, handing over the earth to the reign of a beast given foul birth inside heaven's own gates.

I'll die beside Casedren, she decided then and there. In life they had belonged together. So it would be in death.

Dani shook her head resolutely. "My wish is to stay with my lord and liege," she stated with more calm than she felt inside. "Whatever he is to face, he will not face it alone. The blade that is to be his end shall also be my own."

Casedren looked at her, a mixture of betrayal and stunned puzzlement mingling in his eyes. Realizing the implications of what she'd done, he rushed to undo her spur-of-the-moment damage. "What she says are the words of a confused woman," he hurried to explain. "She believes I love her when, in fact, I do not."

Dani's chest tightened, but she managed to squeeze out a rebuttal. "Whether or not he loves me isn't important. I love him, with all my heart. And I will go where my heart leads me." She didn't know why she'd made the choice, and she certainly couldn't question it now that she'd made her feelings known to all concerned. All that mattered was she'd chosen to stand at Casedren's side forever—even if their forever was whittled down to hours.

Shaking his head in dismay, Casedren settled his hands on

her shoulder. "Why?" he asked, desolation in his voice. "Why do this now when we had already agreed you should go?"

Dani tipped her head back, looking into his eyes. Such strong emotion swam within the depths of his blue gaze she couldn't doubt for a second he truly did love her. She opened her mind, silently reaching out to him. A connection was made, silent emotions passing between them. An awareness and, finally, and understanding. Their relationship was inviolable. They were in this together, for better or worse.

King Bastien stared at them keenly. Dani wasn't sure, but she thought she saw his expression softening, until she would have sworn tears glistened in the old man's eyes.

Leaving his seat, Bastien walked toward them. Stopping a few feet away, he did something no one in the chamber expected.

He bowed to Casedren.

Everyone psychically gasped, stunned by his move.

King Bastien straightened. Stepping up to his son, he placed his hands on his shoulders. "You are most fit to be king, Casedren."

As if disbelieving his ears, Casedren shook his head automatically. "I am?"

Bastien's eyes crinkled at the corners when he smiled. "You have shown humility in the face of opposition. You have shown you can admit a failure and accept its consequence. And—"his voice took on a tremble he simply couldn't control "—you have chosen a consort fit to be queen. Not only must you have a wife who will temper your anger with forgiveness, a wife who will council peace in times of war, you have chosen a consort who is capable of standing beside her husband in times of defeat."

There were no words to describe the expression on Casedren's face or the relief of such a terrible burden lifting off his soul. Even Minister Gareth looked stunned. Coming like a shot out of nowhere, no one had expected such a revelation.

"Are you saying my failure *is* my success?" Casedren asked, voice strangely toneless, as if he expected the whole thing to be an elaborate hoax.

King Bastien grinned in the face of his eldest son's dismay. "My son, your queen is the key to your strength as king. Her love is the light you seek when you look into her eyes. Your queen is *Moir y'Divani.*"

Dani started. "I'm the Eye?"

King Bastien nodded.

"But what about the orb, the grimoire," Casedren spluttered. "The rituals we were to work—"

A knowing glint filled Bastien's eyes. "You took much pleasure in them, did you not?" A quick wink followed. "There is no better way for a man and woman to learn each other's bodies than to try a few of those positions." He chuckled. "I imagine you two generated quite a bit of energy."

Casedren blushed to the roots of his hair. Dani felt her own cheeks heat. They hadn't needed that damn book to give them any ideas. They managed to think of enough ways to have sex all by themselves.

Bidding his son to raise his hand, Bastien asked Dani for hers. The old man placed their hands together, hers atop Casedren's. "Do you love this woman?" he asked his son.

Casedren nodded. "Completely."

Bastien looked at Dani. "And do you love my son?"

Licking dry lips, she nodded. "Absolutely." A little tingle of exultation shimmied down her spine. They had truly discovered the secret behind the Eye.

King Bastien placed his hand atop hers. "Then I do declare, absolutely and without reservation, that Casedren, my first-born son, shall be heir to the Jadian realm." He tightened his grip. "You have chosen wisely, my boy."

Minister Gareth chimed in his congratulations. "Long may you reign."

Cellyn stood a few feet away, a voiceless, angry presence. The look on his face was one of dismay blurred by fury. He couldn't comprehend that he'd lost. "No," he murmured. Barely audible. "It cannot be so."

No one noticed.

Still too stunned to realize what had happened, Casedren spluttered. "But the orb," he insisted. "We shattered it on the first try."

Hand dropping away, Bastien shrugged. "Oh, that old thing." He made a dismissive gesture. "I have a dozen others to replace it."

"A hoax?" Face a pale, corpselike mask, Cellyn exploded. His words disintegrated into an animalistic snarl. "This cannot be. The throne was to be mine!"

Bastien turned, unruffled by his second son's outburst. "My word makes it so," he said in a carefully controlled voice. "You think you have hidden your true self from my eyes, but I see right through you as only a father can. There was never a day you were worthy of my choice, Cellyn. Never."

Cellyn quickly drew his sword, the blade ominously scraping the leather hilt from which it was drawn. "A worthy man is one who finds opportunity in defeat." Before anyone had time to act, he speared his blade straight into King Bastien's gut, twisting it viciously in a sideward arc. Razor sharp steel sliced through vulnerable flesh. "A true king takes what he wants." He laughed inhumanly.

Guts spilling, Bastien toppled to the floor, dead. A stream of blood pooled on the carpeting beneath his body.

Horrified, Dani gaped at the body of the slain monarch. Looking at the mutilation, her blood ran cold. Without blinking, Cellyn had just cut his father down where he stood, giving the old man no chance to raise a hand in his own defense. She stared at the dead man until she thought her eyes would roll out of their sockets. She'd never witnessed death so up close and personal.

Forcing her gaze away from the dead man, she looked at Cellyn. The entity visiting her last night had returned, this time in the flesh. The tips of Cellyn's hair began to take on a dark cast, as though soaking up the evil coursing through his veins. His gaze snapped, eyes glowing like coals straight from the heart of hell.

A quick series of images soared through her mind on crimson-tipped wings. *He's going to kill us all.* "Oh my God."

Gaze raging with hate, Cellyn turned his blade toward Casedren. "The old fool was easy to dispose of," he spat violently. "You will be even easier, brother."

Casedren reacted instantly. Shoving Dani into Minister Gareth's embrace, he planted his big body between his brother and the unarmed. Muttering a few strange words, he made a quick grasping gesture with his right hand. His fingers closed around empty air. No hilt slapped against his palm.

Cellyn's mouth quirked up in a mocking grin. "Did you honestly think I would let you draw a weapon on me a second time?"

Casedren stared at his brother, stunned. "How?" he demanded, close to choking in shock. Narrowing his eyes, he glared suspiciously at his brother.

Cellyn raised his brows and stared back belligerently. "Last night when I was doing a little illicit mind-walking, I made a trek through your head, shutting down a few neural pathways inside your brain." He flicked the tip of his blade toward his twin's face. "You have no magick at your beck."

Casedren dodged the blade aimed at his eye. "I need no spells to defeat you."

Cellyn laughed. "Think again." Passing a hand in front of

his body, he shifted into serpent form. Slithering like greased lightning, he shot around Casedren, curling up around Minister Gareth's body and crushing the poor man to death.

Gareth died, a weak whimper of surprise escaping his slack lips.

As she saw him die, grief swept over Dani in a crushing wave. Head spinning, she could barely think to breathe. Knees close to collapse under her weight, her entire body felt numb. Her mind went blank except for the overwhelming realization that Casedren wouldn't live long enough to claim the throne.

It was far too late to stop Cellyn now.

Cellyn shifted, tossing Gareth's corpse beside that of the monarch he'd served so faithfully. His hand shot out, fingers curling like steel cords around Dani's wrist.

Dani bit back a scream, straining to pull free of Cellyn's hold. "Let go of me!" She turned her body, twisting violently.

Cellyn's grip held like superglue. He pulled her closer to his lean body, bringing the blade to her throat. The intent on his mind slammed into hers. *I will not hesitate to kill you.*

Feeling the bite of cold metal against her neck, Dani instantly stilled. A rush of icy air whooshed into her lungs. *Please let me die quickly,* she prayed, imagining his blade slicing through her jugular.

Casedren held his hand out in appeasement. "Cellyn, do not harm her. You know I would step aside willingly to save her life." The desperation in his voice chilled Dani's blood. He would sacrifice himself this instant to save her.

"That is hardly good enough," Cellyn threw back.

Dani's body felt strangely rigid, every tendon locked in place. She could literally smell the odor of hate and obsession emanating off Cellyn's skin. "Don't do it," she cried.

Cellyn tightened his steely grip. "Once she is gone, the little bit of backbone you have will crumble, brother." He laughed, pressing smoldering lips to Dani's cheek. "She is going to die, very painfully and very slowly. And there is nothing you can do to stop me."

His threat ended there and Dani heard no more.

Coming from nowhere, some unseen force smacked her right between the eyes. An intense burst of pure energy ripped through her skull and her brain exploded into a million tiny pieces. Feeling her legs crumble, she sank down, lower and lower still as everything around her vanished.

26

The world around Dani was white. Dead white. Sky, ground, air, a misty haze churned, covering everything, revealing nothing. Confused, she looked around, trying to get a grasp on her whereabouts. The air was thin, hard to breathe.

Her pulse pounded until she felt light-headed.

"Am I dead?" Spoken aloud, her question echoed around her, endlessly, without ceasing.

A new presence intruded on her senses.

The mist began to churn. Cellyn slipped neatly between the veils, materializing in front of her. "Oh, you are not dead yet."

Seeing him, Dani started violently. Nerves close to failing her, her body trembled uncontrollably. Her heart had to be pounding at least a hundred beats a second. The tension all but choked her. "Where am I?"

Cellyn slashed his blade through the mist. "Everywhere," he said. "And nowhere."

Dani caught her breath, waiting for the blade to slam into her gut or slice across her throat. "I-I don't understand."

Blade pointed at her, Cellyn circled around her. "Your mind

is still too immature to see the spellbinder's continuum for what it really is. All you see is a lot of fog because you haven't learned to form it, shape it to your will."

A quiver ran the length of her. "Why did you bring me here?"

He stopped, smiled. "Because I wanted to play."

Aware of his idea of play, Dani flinched. The lump jamming her throat felt like lead. "Play what?" she whispered, almost afraid to ask the question. Whatever he had in mind, it wasn't going to be something she would enjoy.

Cellyn flicked his blade, catching her cheek. "A game we have."

Fire invaded her face. Blood welled from the cruel slice, oozing down her cheek with a warm trickle. Swiping her hand across the wound, she took a quick step back. "You don't have to do this," she wavered. "I'm no threat to you."

He flicked the blade across the back of her hand, splitting her skin open. "Oh, but I do. I love this game too much to stop now. Among my kind, it is known as the thousand cuts." A nasty chuckle slipped between his lips. "I am going to enjoy taking you apart, piece by piece while you are still alive to feel every inch of your skin being peeled away."

Her fear so thick it made her light-headed, Dani didn't smile back. Anybody who knew anything about witchcraft had heard of the thousand cuts, a torture ritual so sadistic it had been outlawed since the times of Torquemada.

She shook her head, fighting to deny the reality of the whole situation. Whether Cellyn was again in her mind or if they were indeed inside the spellbinder's continuum, she couldn't be sure. She did know one thing: if she believed it, it was real.

Dani held out her hands in a defensive gesture, taking a slice across one palm. Pain blazed up her arm, whip hot. "What am I supposed to do?" she asked stupidly.

Cellyn grinned. Amusement snapped inside his demented gaze. "Run," he said bluntly.

She stared at him in disbelief. "What?"

He advanced and the blade came down a fourth time, slicing through her skirt and nipping her thigh. "The quicker I catch you, the sooner you are going to die."

Dani got the idea. She didn't have to be told twice.

She ran. Like hell.

She tore through the grasping mist, speeding forward, heedless of the fact she didn't have an idea where she was going or where she'd wind up. The long skirts of her gown tangled around her legs, making it damn near impossible to get any speed. She cursed the ridiculous thing, tearing at her waist and bodice to loosen the ties crisscrossing her body. Without missing a step, she grabbed a handful of the velvet material, wrenching it up past her shoulders and over her head with mighty effort. It didn't matter that she was running blindly. Her only goal was to keep ahead of Cellyn for as long as possible.

Leaving the damn dress by the wayside, she pounded on, grateful the heels of her boots weren't too terribly high. She could run in them and that was a definite plus. Stripping off the dress had left her clothed in little more than a thin chemise and pair of panties. She didn't care. It was enough.

As to why he'd given her a head start was obvious. It would be too easy to pounce on her, kill her right off. Like every sick psychopath, Cellyn wanted to drag the game out, raise her fear past terror level as he stalked her. No matter where she ran, she wouldn't get far. Cellyn wanted to make her suffer. Suffer for giving his brother what he could not rightly earn himself, by virtue or action.

Lungs and muscles burning from hard exertion, she forced herself to run faster. There had to be a way out. There just had to be. None of this made any sense. Reality had taken on a surreal quality, like a nightmare within a nightmare. She couldn't figure out where one ended and the other began. It was all too crazy to be believed but too real to be ignored.

A great whirling vortex loomed ahead, crackling with color.

Recognizing a wormhole, Dani sprinted toward it. Giving no thought or hesitation, she leaped into its center.

The core of the wormhole closed around her like a velvet fist, smothering her in its blinding grip. Fighting its crushing strength, Dani swam through its viscous hold, praying it would take her somewhere familiar.

She fell out of nowhere so hard her body spasmed painfully as she landed on her back against something solid and unforgiving. Her head smacked, too, sending a pattern of purplish stars shooting behind her eyes.

Heavy rumbling tires whizzed by. A horn honked. An angry voice shouted. "Get outta the street, you stupid bitch."

Rolling over, Dani pushed herself painfully to her knees. Agony detonated through her limbs. Her knees and palms felt scraped raw. She grimly ignored it, forcing herself to lift her head, focus blurry eyes.

Another car whizzed by, followed by another.

Dani struggled to get a grip on her fuzzy brain. Familiar things began to materialize. Recognition slammed in. She had landed smack in the middle of a busy city street. She looked around, her searching gaze met by an unfamiliar landscape of buildings, people and automobiles.

A pair of legs clad in knee-high boots appeared in front of her. The tip of a blade pressed into her forehead. "You are not trying hard enough," a too familiar voice chided.

Clamping her jaws together, Dani rose to her knees. Cellyn stood in front of her. How the hell could she ever escape someone who was one step ahead at every turn?

"Fuck you," she snarled.

The blade disappeared. Cellyn's hand shot out, catching her

squarely. His palm smashed and her face exploded. "You will," he chuckled through a nasty little grin. "But you will not enjoy it."

Tasting blood courtesy of her fat lip, Dani snarled. "I'll die before I do that again." Somehow she had a talent for attracting maniacs. Being nabbed by Auguste Maximillian was a cakewalk compared to Cellyn Teraketh's reign of terror. Auguste had only worshipped at the altar of evil, hoping it would grant him power. Cellyn *was* that evil—and he had a lot of power to back it up. Having Satan rooted in the ground beneath the family tree undeniably gave him an advantage. The acorn definitely hadn't fallen far.

Her mind latched on to the fact no one in this bizarre world was stopping to help. Many people gaped, but no one came to her aid.

What's the matter with everyone, she thought dimly. Or maybe these people were just jaded to the sight of some dude with a sword in his hand beating up a half-naked woman.

Cellyn easily read her mind. "Oh, they can see you," he chuckled. He spread his arms and stepped into the path of an oncoming vehicle. It sped right through him without stopping. "But they cannot see me." His warped grin widened. "I thought it would be more interesting this way, letting people see you sliced to pieces right before their eyes." He laughed. "A little mind fuck can be nice."

The intent behind Cellyn's distorted plan finally dawned on her. He was going to turn her death into a show, a grand warning of what was to come once he tore through the barriers separating Sedah from earth. Human beings wouldn't stand a chance.

Forcing a snarl, Dani hardened her resolve. She wasn't going to die in the street like a dog.

She took off running, dodging through the traffic and hitting the sidewalk at top speed. People screamed and scrambled out of her path.

Dani ignored them, grimly focused on getting somewhere that wasn't anywhere near Cellyn. In the back of her mind she knew the effort to be a fruitless one, energy spent on nothing more than a few more precious minutes of survival. But they were her minutes, damn it, and she wanted them. Adrenaline cut a path through her heart, giving her a fresh burst of strength.

She slammed into a heavy glass door, pushing it open and running inside. Her heels skidded on the smooth tile floor.

Dani fell down, landing squarely on her butt. She looked around. Stunned faces looked back. It took only seconds to assimilate her surroundings. She was in a bank.

Two armed security guards scurried her way. "Hey, you!"

Dani breathed a sigh of relief. If only she could convince them of the danger, get them to contact Brenden, she'd be okay.

Assessing her bloody, scraped body, one of the guards bent over her. "Are you okay, miss?"

Those were the last words he spoke.

Cellyn stepped out of the veils, slicing the man's head off with an expert slash of his sword. The man's head suddenly wasn't attached to his neck. His lifeless body dropped like a stone right beside her.

Dismay swept through her like a flash flood. "No!" she screamed. She heard panic in her voice but didn't care. If ever there was a time to panic, this was definitely it. A thick pool of blood streamed from the stump left by the absence of his head. She stared in stunned disbelief at the growing pool of shiny crimson. Damn it. She didn't want to die like that. Moving like a crab, she scrambled away.

The second guard had no time to react. His fate came quickly, and just as gruesomely. Two dead men in less than a minute, slain by an unseen assailant.

People freaked around her, scrambling to get out. Panicked

tellers hit the emergency buttons. There was a thunderous explosion of motion as people scrambled to save themselves. A faraway alarm shrilled as customers and employees stampeded toward emergency exits. No one was going to hang around and watch some strange woman die by the hand of a sword swinging out of nowhere. The bank's security tapes were going to make for gruesome viewing.

Cellyn's laughter reverberated around her. "I love scaring the hell out of human beings," he chortled.

Determined her head wouldn't be the next to go, Dani powered to her feet, backing away from the reach of his blade. "Why are you doing this?"

Cellyn closed the distance between them. "Because I can." His evil red gaze dug into hers. His pupils were dilated—big, empty black holes of nothing. His nostrils flared as though he breathed fire. "And because human beings need to be reminded they are not the superior race in this universe." He lifted a hand, muttering a quick spell. The alarm around them went dead silent. A viscous black mist crawled out of the cracks, sealing them inside the bank.

Realizing what he'd done, her blood ran cold. Just as she couldn't get out, no one could get in. He'd separated her from the outside world.

He chuckled, amused by his own cleverness. "They can watch, but they can offer no help." He stalked toward her, closing the distance. "Shall we continue our game?"

Dani turned to run, not really sure how far she could get before Cellyn swung that deadly blade again. Feet rooted to the ground, she sprawled face down. Her hands caught her weight before she smashed face first into the floor. Pushed from behind by an invisible hand, she was stunned by the violence of the impact. Pain flashed brutally through her left wrist. She felt the bone crack and would have cried out, but there was no air in her lungs. Wobbly and anxious, she mentally racked up her injuries.

Trying to gather her wits, she heard the sound of herself breathing. The click of his heels behind her on the ceramic tile. She felt as if the lobby were pressing down on her, shrinking, growing smaller with every step he took.

Dani rolled over just as Cellyn stepped over her, heavy boots planted on both sides of her body. Her gaze rose up toward his endless legs, moving higher over his powerful torso, his whipcord-strong arms. The sword he wielded with a master precision.

A shriek echoed inside her head. *Oh shit.* Bowels going liquid, she slowly fell apart inside. He was going to hurt her. Bad.

Cellyn regarded her the way he'd consider an ant he intended to crush under his heel. "All this running and screaming is getting boring," he announced, pointing the blade at her gut. "Let's play."

Nerves coiling tighter, Dani shifted uncomfortably. "What are you going to do?" she breathed.

Cellyn's blistering gaze fluttered over her. Pushing the blade into her chemise, he jerked it upward, cutting the thin material in half. Using the tip, he jerked the material away from her left breast, baring it. He circled the hard peak of her nipple. "I could take you right here, right now, if I wanted."

Dani's skin crawled as his gaze swept over her. Unable to endure the thought of further sexual contact, she flinched at the excitement in his gaze. Sexual heat simmered around him. Pressing her lips together, she turned her head, saying nothing. She wasn't going to give him the satisfaction of taunting her anymore. She didn't even want to begin to imagine what might be simmering inside his sick-puppy psyche.

The idea flashed through her mind that she'd lost. Whatever Cellyn chose to do, she couldn't stop it.

There was only one way out. One honorable way out.

She eyed the blade. If she sat up quickly, she could ram the thing home, force it right through her heart. It wouldn't be the prettiest death; it wouldn't be the neatest. But it was the only option left open.

Cellyn easily picked up her idea. Amusement sidled into his eyes. "Suicide," he scoffed. "How noble."

His words delivered a welcome rush of anger. "I'll do what I have to," she grated, "to keep you from raping me again."

Angered by her defiance, Cellyn bent. He wound his fingers through her long hair, stepping back and dragging her onto her knees. He snapped her head back, forcing her to look up at him.

His once-handsome face was twisted with demonic glee. "More than your body, more than your life," he murmured. "Give me your soul. Worship me as your god and I will let you live."

Dani risked a look into his eyes. The insanity that flashed across his face left no doubt as to his mental stability. Almost out of her mind with fear, she somehow found the strength to refuse him. She shook her head. Her half-naked body was chilled with the sweat of fear. "No," she moaned. "I'll worship no false god."

Cellyn bared his teeth, his canines shifting into long, deadly fangs. "Adore me," he murmured. "Acknowledge me as the one true living god and I will grant you a life you can hardly dare to imagine." His tone grew low, his voice persuasive. "Stand at my side as my queen and I will lay this earth at your feet." His will invaded hers, pressing in from all sides. A single instantaneous impression slammed into her skull. All he needed was one person to say *yes*. The first to fall would seal his power.

Terror swept through her with such force that she couldn't take a breath. *I'm not going to be the one.*

She wondered vaguely what it would feel like to die.

27

Pressing her palms to her face, Dani shook her head, refusing to let him take control again. Her body she could sacrifice. Her life hadn't been guaranteed to last long either. But her soul— her immortal soul. That was something she'd never give up, no matter how much torture he leveled against her body, and her mind.

Not for the first time, she realized just how delusional Cellyn really was—and how dangerous. Except that he wasn't living out some kind of warped fantasy within the confines of his own brain. Quite the opposite. He was capable of making his perverted fantasy her gruesome reality.

Knowing her last moments were trickling down to mere seconds, Dani made her final decision. Centering her thoughts, she quickly murmured the words of a spell. She had to tell Casedren good-bye, that she would soon be leaving this earthly plane for another.

Obey my words of command, watcher at the gate, unbar the guarded door, send this message to my mate. She opened her mind completely, pouring all her energy, strength and determination into the enchantment. An intense pressure built behind her eyes, knocking at the walls of her skull like a wrecking ball slamming into concrete. In a last, final effort, she sent her silent plea winging upward, forcing it out of her head and into infinity. *I love you,* she thought through a wave of nausea and dizziness. *I wish you were here.*

Feeling more alone than she'd ever felt in her life, Dani resisted the urge to cry. Her tears would be wasted on such a pitiless creature. Of all the things Cellyn could have done to her, being separated from Casedren was the worst. The idea that she would never see him again slashed an agonizing path straight to her heart. Without him, she had no sense of purpose.

Cellyn's cold fingers curled around her throat. He dragged her to her feet with the ease of a child lifting a doll. "Oh, how sweet," he hissed. "Too bad Casedren is not here to rescue his lady love."

Their gazes locked in hostility. Revulsion swamped her. "What would you know about something you've never had," she spat back.

Cellyn's grip tightened on her throat. "I could squeeze the life right out of you."

Enduring his grip, Dani swallowed down the rise of bitter acid. Fighting the pressure threatening to drive her into unconsciousness, she glared back. "Do it now." Her voice shook with inner anxiety. Her pulse raged behind her temples like an avalanche of blinding white snow down the side of a mountain.

Oh God. She didn't relish having the breath squeezed out of her. That would be a miserably slow way to die, knowing every second before she slipped into oblivion that she could do nothing to stop him. "And do it quickly."

Her defiance infuriated him.

Cellyn tossed her across the lobby like trash. "Your wish is not my command. I am not finished with you yet."

Dani landed face first, skidding into one of the fallen bank guards. A wash of cold, slippery blood coated her skin as she slammed into the man's inert body. Panic threatened, and she tried desperately to separate her mind from what was happening to her. She couldn't. She was too weak, too human.

It was then she saw her sole chance to walk away alive. Though powerful, Cellyn was by no means immortal.

She had a chance. A fighting chance.

Adrenaline pumped her heart into overdrive, giving her a burst of renewed strength. Her survival instincts kicked into motion. She didn't need magick to fight him.

She just needed one lucky shot.

Slamming her mind shut so he couldn't sense her intention, Dani quickly rolled onto her side, throwing her body over the pistol holstered on the man's hip. Hand sneaking under her body, she reached for the weapon. Her fingers circled around its grip. She eased it out of its holder, thanking her lucky stars her brother was a cop. A cop who had taught her to use a gun.

Thumbing off the safety, she flipped over and took aim. Her heart hammered wildly in her chest, but she ignored it. She aimed down the barrel of the gun. Forefinger curling around the trigger, she slammed down on it.

Blam. Blam. Blam.

A series of explosions tore through the air. Bullets plowed straight toward her target. Three shots. Aimed right through the center of his abdomen. There was no way she could miss. A fleeting sense of satisfaction flashed through her.

And vanished like a puff of smoke.

Cellyn didn't fall. He didn't even stagger. Her aim was true, but the bullets didn't strike their target. They didn't get anywhere near him. Instead they took a detour, riddling the walls around him.

Hardly believing her eyes, Dani lowered her weapon. Shock rippled through her. She hadn't even come close to hitting him. Having the power of a god and the will of a psychopath, Cellyn appeared to be an unstoppable force. Despair pressed down. Her attempt felt leaden, useless. Her disappointment was so intense she could barely draw a breath. Bitter acid welled up from her gut. She choked.

An amused smile curled the corners of Cellyn's mouth. "The only thing you accomplished was to piss me off." His grip tightened on his blade. "Good try, but not good enough."

Finger poised over the trigger, Dani scowled at him. Not so fast, buster. She slammed her finger down in rapid succession, determined to use every last bullet.

Nothing.

Her despair darkened. The trigger clicked uselessly.

Hand shaking uncontrollably, Dani swore under her breath. *Mother-killing son of a bitch.* She cursed fate for being so cruel. Nothing she could throw against him was effective. Not even a speeding bullet. That sucked. Really sucked. "Damn."

Cellyn grinned wickedly, relishing the moment of twisted pleasure her fear gave him. "Your weapons are no defense against my kind."

The gun slipped out of her grip. She'd taken her best shot. And lost.

Consequences would soon follow.

Darkness suddenly flowed around the edges of the lobby, the black mist twisting with a vaguely human-shaped figure. For an instant the thick fog thinned and Dani saw a wisp, a shadow step out of its cloak.

Recognition sparked like a flint striking stone, sending a flood of relief straight to her brain.

Casedren. Armed and ready to fight.

Dani stared, speechless and shocked to the bone. She shook her head, as if trying wake herself from a dream. Her first fleeting thought was that she was seeing an apparition conjured by her desperate mind. There wasn't a single spark to indicate any communication between them.

Catching her confusion, Casedren shook his head, silently warning her. *Do not betray me.* Positioned behind his twin, he'd have only a single shot to make his plan work. Blow it, and he wouldn't have a chance against Cellyn.

Mistaking her move as a plea for mercy, Cellyn strode her way. His heels clicked smartly on the faux marble as he walked toward her. The hairs prickled at the nape of her neck when he tapped her chin with the flat side of his blade.

Cellyn regarded her through narrow eyes. "I had thought to spare your life," he said coyly. "But I changed my mind. I'd much rather take your life now. Your corpse would make such a nice present to take back to my brother."

Casedren nodded, giving her the signal. It was now or never.

Dani grinned. "Not mine, motherfucker. Yours."

Snarling viciously, she opened the floodgates of her mind, smashing the images inside her skull straight into his. She put every bit of her energy behind the invasion, driving his evil intent right back toward him.

Smacked by her vision, Cellyn cried out. Lips peeling back from his fangs in a furious snarl, he jerked his sword in an upward arc, intending to parry his brother's blow. "You will never be king!"

He was one second too slow.

Advancing with a smooth, silent motion, Casedren ran him through with brutal savagery. The blade grated on bone as it penetrated vulnerable flesh. "That is for our parents," he snapped viciously.

Lanced like an insect on a pin, Cellyn stared down in disbelief at the blade protruding from his gut. Enraged, his features morphed into something far from human. "Impossible," he gurgled. A thin line of blood trickled from his mouth.

Casedren's smile was ice cold. The blade slid out with a sticky gurgling sound. "Very possible," he corrected.

Staggering, Cellyn slowly pivoted around to face his twin.

Propelled by fury, he made an effort to lift his weapon, stumbling toward Casedren with the intent to kill. "You can't."

Casedren gave him no chance to follow through. "Oh, yes, I can. By my will and order as king." Steel flashed, the sword whistling through the air with lethal intent. He didn't miss.

Cellyn's head dropped. And rolled. Crumpling in a heap, his lifeless corpse immediately set to shimmying, intense shafts of light tearing through skin and clothing alike, consuming him like a wildfire taking off across dry prairie grass.

A blur, a howl, a scream of dark despair. The light consuming him grew brighter, as hot as the surface of the sun. The energy behind it hit like an atom bomb.

Unable to look at him, Dani threw up her hand, screaming as his soul passed through her on its way straight to a blistering eternity.

And then there was silence. Nothing.

Dani lowered her hand in time to see the last remnants of Cellyn's body disintegrating into ash.

Her gaze searched for, and found, Casedren. He stood swaying, staring at his brother's remains in dazed horror. His hand dropped, and his weapon slipped from his numb fingers. The heavy sword clattered at his feet. "Cellyn is dead," he said, looking at her through grief-dulled eyes.

Dani breathed a sigh, closing her eyes in relief. "Thank God," she murmured.

Casedren walked to her slumped form. There was blood all over her. Dropping to his knees, he dragged her close. She wrapped her arms around him, hanging on tight. His lips brushed her forehead. "It is over," he murmured against her hair. "We did it. He is defeated, never to rise again."

She stared up at him, an angelic presence snatching her from the jaws of hell. She reached up, cupping his cheeks in her palms. "I thought I would never see you again," she breathed. A single tear slid down her cheek. "How did you find me?"

His compelling blue gaze settled into hers. "Your spell brought me here."

She blinked. "My spell?" she repeated stupidly.

A slow smile turned up the corners of his beautiful mouth. "Once again, you summoned me and I answered your call. In this case, the magick was all yours, Danicia." He pressed another kiss against her forehead. "I had no way to find you until you sent out the spell, connecting us. It wasn't much, but it was enough to break through Cellyn's hold on both of us."

Dani's chest tightened. "Has his—" she started to ask.

Casedren lightly stroked her face, his thumb swiping at the hateful cut Cellyn had inflicted. "His evil hexes died with him." He shuddered briefly. "Thanks to you, he has no hold over me anymore."

She blinked back the rise of unbidden tears. "You lost so much today. Minister Gareth. Your father." Two innocent bystanders had also died, men cut down in the prime of their lives because they'd been in the wrong place at the wrong time.

He nodded, looking so sad it made her heart ache. "I think my father welcomed the blade," he said slowly. "He knew Cellyn murdered our mother. We all suspected, but how can you prove it among mind-walkers dabbling in the forbidden arts?" Releasing a pent-up breath, he shook his head. "He wanted to be with her again. Somehow I believe his wish has been granted. For that, I shall not mourn. He had a long and honorable rule. I can only hope to accomplish half his achievement as king."

King. It dimly filtered into her mind that Casedren was, indeed, the man who would follow Bastien to the Jadian throne.

She gulped. That made her . . . No, she didn't want to think about that right now. She didn't feel qualified.

She nestled closer to him, drinking in his warmth, his solidity. "You will do fine," she murmured quietly. "I'm sure of it." She tightened her arms around him, vaguely aware she was so weary she might drift into unconsciousness right there on the spot.

"Are you ready to go home?" He meant home, as in that dumpy little apartment in her brother's basement.

No way. As much as she loved her brother, it was time to move on and move out, make her own way in the world.

Dani opened her eyes. Looking at him, her heart ached with breathtaking ferocity. "Only if *home* is in Sedah."

Casedren looked at her stunned. "Do you mean that?"

Dani smiled and curled closer to him. "Not backing out on your proposal now, are you?" She cocked her head, waiting for his answer.

He stared down at her gravely. A smile quickly blossomed across his face. "Never, my lady." Gently untangling himself from her hold, he climbed to his feet. He reached down, pulling her to her feet before sweeping her up into his arms. "I will never let you out of my sight again."

Arms circling his neck, Dani shivered. "Promise?"

He leaned toward her, lips brushing her bruised temple. "I promise."

She rested her head on his strong shoulder. "Then let's go."

"Home," Casedren murmured. He spoke a few strangely familiar words. The mists of the spellbinder's continuum commenced to churning around them.

To those left behind, there would be no reasonable or logical explanation for the day's events, nor could anyone explain how two bank guards had ended up beheaded. Some would theorize it was a terrorist attack, some branch of radicals got out of hand. Others would call it a conspiracy, the government at work testing new mind-bending weapons on innocent bystanders. Whatever the speculation, few, very few, would ever know the real truth.

Those who did would breathe a temporary sigh of relief. The world was safe. Disaster prevented was not forever averted.

One beast had fallen. Always, always, another was destined to rise. That was the way of the world, a pact between a god in heaven and a demon in hell. The vigilant would watch. And wait. For now, the uneasy peace between the Magus and the Wyr world would stand unbreakable. But nothing was destined to last forever, not even peace.

Dani smiled up at Casedren. It didn't seem strange to think of Sedah as home. His world was where she belonged, a queen standing at the side of her king. Whether they were to be together forever or a day didn't matter. Hers was a destiny fulfilled.

For once, one of her damn spells had worked the way it was supposed to.

Finally.

Turn the page
for Kate Douglas's "Chanku Honor,"
in SEXY BEAST VI!

On sale now!

1

San Francisco, California

"Hey, Jazzy. What's up?"

"Yo, Deacon. Nuttin'. Just enjoying the sunshine." Jazzy Blue stepped over her buddy's long, bony frame, rapped his head with her knuckles and flopped down on the ground. She lay back in the warm grass beside him and flung her arm over her eyes to block the glare—as well as any further conversation. It was better, this way, when all she wanted to do was think about the dreams.

She felt the ripples of arousal between her legs and wished that particular feeling would go away. That and the itchy skin. At least she could scratch her arms. She couldn't very well sit out here in the park and rub her clit. Sex with the johns hadn't done it for her.

It never had, not since she was a little kid and her pimp had her out working the streets, but that wasn't unusual. Not for a kid who whored to stay alive. Sex was work, not pleasure, but damn it all, she really could use some pleasure about now.

Even Deacon was starting to look good.

She lifted her arm and glanced his way. He'd always felt more like a big brother than a potential lover, but beggars couldn't very well be choosers. It was getting worse, that sense that if she didn't have an orgasm *right now* she'd explode.

The odd thing was, the sexy feelings and all the weirdness seemed to be tied into the strange dreams she'd been having.

Really weird stuff about wolves and tall trees and the sound of animals huffing and growling beside and behind her. She'd been waking up scared half to death, waiting for something wild to pounce.

Of course, camping under a bush on the fringes of Golden Gate Park wasn't necessarily conducive to a good night's sleep, but it was the only place she had after trying to kill the man who'd kept her all these years. The corner of Jazzy's mouth curved up in a grin. It had definitely been one powerful moment, when she'd finally cut loose and attacked the bastard.

Of course, that had been the end of a roof over her head. One does not try to gut one's pimp with a serrated kitchen knife. Made for bad working relations. Crap. She was well rid of him.

All she knew about him was that he'd bought her from a slaver when she was about six and set her to whoring right away. No actual intercourse until she was ten or so, but the pedophiles who wanted to play out their sick fantasies would always disgust her. She'd rather not think about her not so pleasant childhood . . . as if she'd ever had a chance to be a kid. Thank goodness she'd always had an active fantasy life. It had given her a way out, even if it was just in her mind.

Jazzy stretched her arms over her head and closed her eyes against the glare. Red flashed through her eyelids and she flopped her arm across her face once more. Images from the dream she'd had last night slipped uninvited into her mind. She felt again the bunch and stretch in her muscles as she'd leapt over a woodland creek in a futile attempt to run down a rabbit.

On four legs. She'd had big paws, a long, bushy tail and she'd awakened exhausted, as if it had all been true. She wished she could ask the rest of the guys about their dreams, whether they ever had nights like hers, but they'd probably think she was nuts.

Amend that. More nuts than usual. Of course, that's what friends were for, wasn't it? To tell you when you were headed over the edge?

Either that or hold your hand and take the leap with you. Sanity's overrated, anyhow. Jazzy heard footsteps and the rustle of clothing. She lifted her elbow from her eyes enough to see who all was wandering by. Matt flopped down on the grass next to Nicky and Beth. It looked like the rest of the guys were hanging out as usual, down here at the memorial garden instead of their old turf over on Stanyan.

The crowd there was just too edgy, always looking for trouble. She used to fit in with them. Not anymore. Now she preferred hanging with the pack—Deacon, Matt, Nicky and Beth.

And Logan. She couldn't forget Logan.

They fit together, almost like family. Like a pack. Logan was the one who started it when he called them a mangy pack of wolves, said they had a feral kind of connection. Jazzy liked that. She could handle being called mangy as long as she got the feeling of being connected to someone.

It was a long time coming.

Maybe that's why she'd been dreaming of wolves and sex. Face it, anything that had to do with Logan was enough to make her horny.

She sat up and yawned, leaned over and picked a long strand of the grayish green grass that grew in clumps around the memorial garden. She ran it between her fingers and popped the thick stalk between her teeth. It was such a beautiful day. Perfect for hanging with her buds, nibbling on sweet grass and watching the jet trails in the clear, blue sky.

She slanted another look toward Logan. He leaned against one of the slabs of granite that made up the heart of the memorial garden. With his face and all its sharp angles and planes lifted to the warming rays of the sun, he almost looked like a part of the stone. Damn, she could watch him all day. That long, lean body of his moved with a rhythm all its own. He gave her a hot, liquid tingle deep in her gut. Logan was way special.

He was tough, too. And really strong. Older than the rest of them. Kind of scary, sometimes, with his head shaved half way and all the tats. His body was a veritable canvas, covered in some absolutely rad artwork.

Nicky'd said even Logan's cock was covered in tattoos. Now that was something she'd like to see.

Sometime.

Of course, Matt had whispered to her one day that Nicky had studs in his dick, something he called a Jacob's Ladder. Little barbells running from the tip to his balls. She couldn't care less about Nicky's dick, but she couldn't help but wonder about the tats on Logan's.

Was he hard when the guy did it? How much did it hurt? She had a little tat of a flower on her ankle and it hurt like hell to get that one. She couldn't imagine sitting still while some guy stuck needles and dye *there!*

What was it with guys and their parts?

Jazzy turned away from Logan, flopped back down in the grass and closed her eyes. She scratched at her itchy arms and wished she could just eat Logan up—after she got a look at his dick, of course. That wasn't going to happen. He didn't like it when anyone tried to get close, and checking out those tats would mean she'd gotten way too up close and personal.

"Jazzy? You got any of that cream?"

She blinked and there was Nicky, kneeling so close he blocked out her sunlight. "Your skin itching again?" She sat up and dug into her jeans pocket for the tube of skin cream she'd gotten a couple days ago.

"Feels like I'm ready to crawl right out of it. Just pop myself free of this bod and turn into . . ." He bared his teeth and growled. ". . . a wolf!" He laughed and took the tube, squeezed a little lotion into his palm. "Sounds good in theory."

Nicky was such a sweetheart. Tall and slim, yet so gentle and quiet with dark eyes and olive skin. She wondered if he might be Indian, or maybe even Middle Eastern. His skin was almost as dark as hers, but right now his arms were covered with red streaks where he'd scratched himself raw.

Just like hers.

Nicky sighed as he slapped the lotion over his long arms. "I feel like a dork using your girly stuff."

Beth flopped down on the grass next to Jazzy and laughed. "That's because you are a dork." She swung her dark hair back over her shoulder and tilted her chin. Nicky snorted and jabbed her with his shoulder. She bumped him back, and took the tube from Nicky's outstretched hand. "I need it too."

Jazzy noticed Beth didn't really look Nicky in the eye. If she did, he'd know for sure how much she loved him. Jazzy knew, but only because she'd guessed. Beth never said a word about her feelings. She was afraid to, Jazzy was sure of that. Beth was really shy, not anything like Jazzy. She kept her chin tucked close to her chest and squeezed a thick spurt of white cream into her hand. Then she handed the tube back to Jazzy. "I wonder if we're allergic to something around here? Your arms are all red, too."

Jazzy chewed at the stalk of grass. She shrugged her shoulders. "Nothing here but grass and trees."

"Hey."

Jazzy swung around at the sound of Logan's deep voice. "Holy shit. Check this out."

When she looked in the direction he nodded, Jazzy felt her skin go cold. Beside her, Nicky went very still but he radiated an almost palpable tension. Jazzy grabbed his forearm. He shrugged her away. She turned him loose and watched the drama unfold.

Montana was nice, but it really felt good to be back in the city. Tala picked up her pace as she headed down Stanyan to Haight where she planned to cut through the park to check on Keisha's memorial garden. She'd promised, after all.

As if she'd had a choice?

That thought alone was enough to make her smile.

Are the plants doing okay? Is the rock work still in place? Please, don't let there be graffiti . . . like that's all Keisha had to worry about. Still, she had won a national prize and the chance to design the garden, and it was lovely. Planted entirely with grasses native to the Himalayan steppe . . . amazing, the varieties she'd chosen.

The same mix of grasses the Chanku needed to shift.

Only Keisha hadn't yet known of her Chanku heritage. That alone had made her choices special.

Tala reached the corner of Haight and Stanyan. The usual group of homeless youth whistled and made lewd comments. No big deal. She smiled and waved when she walked past the half dozen young men lounging around the street corner.

At another time, she might have been terrified by the suggestive leers and off-color comments, given her small stature and feminine gender. Since she'd become Chanku, it took an awful lot to frighten her.

Still, it never hurt to be cautious. She held her head up and kept walking. The sun passed behind a small wisp of fog. Tala shivered. Moments later, as she drew near Keisha's garden, she caught the sound of footsteps behind her. Memories of the recent attack here in the park were way too fresh to ignore. Luc, the leader of the San Francisco pack, had assured all of them that the wanted posters were off the Internet and for the moment, at least, no one seemed to be hunting Chanku, but . . .

Tala risked a look back. Two of the young men she'd passed had broken off from the group and now followed her toward the memorial garden. Dressed in black, lips, noses and eyebrows pierced with metal studs, they both had the glittery-eyed look of chronic drug users.

Rather than risk a surprise attack, Tala turned and faced them. She sent out a mental call for help and hoped like hell Mik or AJ heard.

The larger of the two kept coming until he was well within her personal space. He reached out to touch her hair, but Tala twisted away.

She wasn't afraid, but she wasn't stupid, either. Just very, very pissed off. She raised her chin and glared at the jerk. "Keep your hands to yourself."

"Bitch. Think you're too good?"

Tala heard something moving behind her, but who? She'd only noticed these two and her senses rarely failed her. She heard a low growl, sensed Chanku power—a wolven presence.

An unfamiliar wolven presence.

The kid groping her had his eyes glued to her breast. He grabbed her right arm with one hand, her left breast with the other.

Tala let her legs go limp, using her body weight to help her twist free, but his fingers tightened around both her breast and her arm.

Pain twisted through her body. She screamed in anger.

His friend screamed in fear and took off running.

A flash of gray knocked Tala to the ground. Her head hit the pavement, hard. Lights flashed behind briefly closed lids. She opened her eyes to a dark shape, spinning, snarling. Flashes of red, the coppery taint of blood. Nausea welled up with a rolling wave of vertigo when she tried to raise herself on one elbow.

More snarling and growling, a choked scream.

Another scream, behind her. A woman crying out, "Ohmygod, Nicky! Ohmygodohmygod . . ."

Tala blinked. She was too close to focus. Her nostrils twitched with the thick smell of blood. Lots of blood, and bits of gray still spinning, a kaleidoscope of life and death and horrible sounds that seemed to go on forever.

Sounds that ended in a heartbeat, leaving only silence.

Harsh sobs broke the momentary hush, the cries of the dark-skinned woman who knelt beside her. Who put her hand out and touched the shoulder of a slender young man lying naked on the path in front of Tala.

All around them were pools of blood, and the torn, lifeless body of the punk who had grabbed her. One of the guys knelt beside the body and touched the chest, the side of his neck, the pulse point at his wrist. His movements appeared surprisingly competent, as if he'd done similar examinations before. He raised his head and frowned at Tala. "He's bled out already." His deep voice showed no emotion. "Nicky got both his jugular vein and carotid artery. The kid didn't have a chance."

Tala raised up on one elbow. She shook her head and caught her breath . . . waited for her vision to clear. "Who?"

"The wolf or this kid?" He stood up. "I don't know who he is, the one who grabbed you. The wolf was . . . is, Nicky, our friend."

The young woman kneeling beside her looked totally traumatized. She raised her head and stared at Tala. "He just changed," she said. "He joked about it, but I thought he was only kidding. I didn't believe him. Nicky saw that guy grab you, and he ripped off his clothes and changed." She shoved her knuckles into her mouth and closed off a sob.

Another young woman ran up and wrapped her arms around the first girl. Two more young men appeared, both of them dressed in black, lips, noses and eyebrows pierced, arms and hands tattooed, heads shaved in strange patterns. They knelt beside the unconscious youth lying in the trail. The first punk, the one who'd examined the body, stood off to one side, apart from the others, but Tala knew he was one of them.

They'd all come from the direction of Keisha's garden.

The garden where the Tibetan grasses grew.

Suddenly Mik was there, and AJ beside him and Tala's head was still spinning, though not nearly as badly. The three guys pulled back, cautious, obviously intimidated by the two large men.

All but the first young woman who stayed beside her co-matose friend.

"Are you okay? What happened?" Mik touched Tala's shoulder, but his eyes were on the naked young man lying next to her on the ground. He was alive, his chest barely rising and falling with each breath.

"Do you have the car?" Tala glanced up at AJ.

He nodded. "I do."

She held out her hand. AJ grabbed it and helped Tala sit up. She bowed her head a moment against her bent knees while the world spun. Then she looked up at AJ. "We need to take them with us. All of them. Now." Tala touched the shoulder of the young woman kneeling beside her on the path. "I want you and your friends to come with us. We can help you, but not if the police get here first. Mik, can you carry him?"

Mik nodded. The girl nodded as well, but it was nothing more than an automatic response. Her black hair swung like a silken curtain, her eyes still looked glazed.

Her amber eyes.

Mik carefully picked up the unconscious youth and cradled his lanky, naked body gently in his arms. The others watched him, each with a feral gleam in eyes the color of dark amber. All of them shared the same look—the tall, lean bodies, the golden eyes with flecks of green. Tala took the hand of the young woman who'd cried out and gestured to the other girl, who'd walked back toward the garden, still obviously dazed. "Come with us. We'll keep you safe. We'll take care of your friend."

"Why?"

It was the one who'd been playing doctor, a tall, lean man. He appeared to be a bit older than the others, but he wore the same kind of silver studs in his eyebrows, nose and ears. The same heavy, dark clothing. The left side of his head was completely shaved while hair hung in long tangles from the right. His face and hands, all that showed outside his black shirt and pants, and heavy, knee-length coat were covered in tattoos. He stared at Tala a moment longer. "Why do you want to help us?"

"Because your friend helped me," Tala said, slowly rising to her feet. "And because we," she gestured at AJ and Mik, and then herself, "we are just like you."